FOREVER

PATI NAGLE

Evennight

Evennight Books
Cedar Crest, New Mexico, USA

Published by Evennight Books, Cedar Crest, New Mexico, USA, an affiliate of Book View Café Publishing Cooperative

Publication team: Deborah J. Ross, Nancy Jane Moore, Chris Krohn
ISBN: 978-1-61138-415-4

Book View Café Publishing Cooperative
P.O. Box 1624, Cedar Crest, NM 87008-1624
http://bookviewcafe.com

For Eric

Acknowledgments

Heartfelt thanks to Nancy Jane Moore and Deborah J. Ross for editorial feedback, to my esteemed colleagues in Book View Café for advice on everything from the cover to the end notes, and as always to Chris Krohn for proofreading and being the ideal writer's spouse.

= 1 =

Her throat was torn out. I could tell, though she was face-down on the steps to a service door outside Clark Hall. The way her head was lying was ... wrong. Worse, she looked familiar. From one of my classes.

Glasses, broken, a few inches from her head. Blood pooled on the concrete steps, so dark it almost looked black. Coagulated. She'd been there a while.

A lump of something red lay not far from her shoulder—at first I thought it was a rag. Then I realized it was meat.

Oh, god.

I stepped aside and lost my breakfast. Stumbled away from the mess, leaned my hands on my knees and took a few deep breaths. Heart still pounding, I took out my phone and dialed 911.

A bird somewhere nearby sang a cheerful morning song. I glanced back toward the body—Kimberly Darrow, I suspected—and turned my back on the short stairwell, one of three on the west side of the chemistry building. A wall of adobe-colored stucco masked each of them. I'd come to catch up on some lab work before going to my physics class, glimpsed a booted foot as I approached, and gone closer to look.

"911, what is your emergency?"

I inhaled, coughed on bile, and spat. "I just found a body."

"Where are you?"

"UNM campus, outside Clark Hall. West side."

I looked back at the stairwell. Noticed a backpack now: black, with Lobo stickers on it. Couldn't see much of her face, but the short red hair and the thunder thighs made me pretty sure.

"Name?"

"Kimberly Darrow, I think."

"No, *your* name."

1

"Oh. Harrison. Steve Harrison."

"What number are you calling from?"

I gave it to her. "It's a cell phone."

"Are you sure the victim is dead?"

"Pretty sure, yeah. Her throat's ripped up bad—I don't think she could breathe."

"Is she bleeding?"

"There's blood, but it doesn't look fresh."

"Campus police are on their way. Please stay on the line."

"OK."

Feeling pretty shaky, I moved around the corner to the south side of the building and sat with my back against the wall. My mouth tasted like bile. I wanted a drink of water.

So the campus killer was back.

There'd been a series of rape/murders the previous fall. They stopped abruptly after a couple of months, but the killer had never been caught. Some sightings of a creepy guy with long, white hair had been reported. Then a couple more killings in the summer, but the victims were men. The police hadn't said it was the same killer, but it had pretty much the same effect on campus, only now everyone was scared, not just the girls.

I had my own thoughts, based on personal experience. They didn't quite fit with the rapes.

The bird twittered again. I looked up at the nearby trees, trying to spot it. The leaves were just beginning to get a yellow tinge, flickering in the morning light.

I wondered what Kimberly had been doing by Clark Hall. It was across campus from the dorms, where I was pretty sure she lived. The only place I'd seen her was in the 100-level physics class I was student-assisting, and that was also across campus. I'd graded her papers, and talked to her maybe three times about assignments.

"Steve?" said the dispatcher.

"Yeah?"

"Did you see anyone else in the area?"

"No."

"The police should be there soon. They'll want to talk to you."

"OK."

I heard a siren not thirty seconds later. I stood and stepped out into the sunlight, blinking. Not even eight, and the day was heating up. September in Albuquerque was always either roasting or pouring rain. If the state fair was running, more likely the latter, but not today.

A campus police squad came into the parking lot and two cops got out. I stepped forward.

"They're here," I told the operator. "Can I hang up now?"

"Yes."

I put my phone away and waited, keeping my hands in sight. One of the cops had short brown hair and a nice build. The other was beefier, with a blond buzz-cut. He hooked his thumbs in his belt loops and stopped in front of me.

"You Steve Harrison?"

I nodded and gestured. "She's around the corner, there. Second stairwell."

The brown-haired cop headed for the body.

"Watch your step," I called after him. He glanced at my former breakfast and detoured around it.

"Tell me what happened," said Buzz-cut.

I told him what I knew. He listened, nodded occasionally. I could hear the first cop talking on the radio.

"So you know her?" the cop asked when I stopped.

"Not really. She's in one of my classes." Was.

I wondered if I should have tried to revive her. No—not in the condition her neck was in. No chance.

"When's the last time you talked to her?"

I blinked. "I'm not sure. Maybe last week?"

"When was she last in your class?"

"Tuesday."

"You talk to her then?"

"Not this week. There's a hundred students in the class."

He nodded, holding my gaze. Said nothing for a few seconds, then asked, "So where were you last night?"

"At home. My apartment."

"You got a roommate?"

"No."

Another nod. "OK, we'll need you stay here until we can get your fingerprints."

Holy crap! He thought *I* did this? Holy freaking *crap!*

"I have a class at nine," I said, my throat tightening.

"Yeah? Well, you might miss it. Sorry."

He didn't sound sorry. He gave me a long look, then went to join his partner.

I stepped to the building and leaned against the stucco wall. They couldn't seriously think I'd killed Kimberly.

Queasiness settled in my stomach. I told myself to stay calm, but I felt alone, and wanted to alert someone to what was happening.

Who, though? I wasn't dating anyone. My advisor probably couldn't help.

Amanda Richards. She'd get it. She'd been through some tough stuff over the summer, and I'd helped her out a little. Stuff involving a woman with long white hair.

I sent her a quick text:

> FOUND BODY @ CHEM LAB - MIGHT NEED
> HELP.

Her answer came a minute later:

> OMW. HANG TIGHT.

I put away my phone and felt better.

Paramedics arrived, bringing cases of equipment. I stayed out of the way. They hustled toward the stairwell, then returned at a walk for more gear, with body language that told me there wasn't any urgency going on.

More police came. A lot more. The parking lot looked like Christmas.

Some of them went into the building, and I heard the commotion of the place being locked down; standard procedure in case of violence on campus. Clark Hall was full of dangerous chemicals, some of which could be used as weapons. People began coming out of the building. So much for chemistry classes today.

Other police showed up to work the crime scene. One of them, a nice female cop who actually smiled at me, took my fingerprints. "It's just so we can eliminate you," she said.

Yeah, I'd heard that on TV, in a million crime shows.

"Did you try to revive her?" she asked.

"No. Didn't seem like there was any hope."

She gave me a sympathetic nod, handed me a couple of packaged wet wipes, then went away with the card of my prints. I took out a wipe and cleaned the ink off my hands. It was sticky, took some work, and both the wipes.

The cop came back with a long cotton swab. "Need you to open your mouth, please."

DNA test. Well, that should exonerate me. I complied, and she left again.

I took out my phone: 8:57. Looking like I'd miss my class, unless they were done with me.

Buzz-cut came back, carrying a clipboard. He made me tell him again what I'd seen, when I'd arrived, name, address, phone, all that. Wrote while I was talking, asked me several of the questions a third time, then handed me the clipboard.

"Sign here."

I read his notes, which were reasonably accurate. I signed my name.

"OK, you can go."

I watched him walk away. Initial confusion gave way to relief. Maybe they didn't suspect me after all.

I took out my phone. Twenty past nine, and it would take me at least five minutes to walk to the Physics and Astronomy building. Probably not worth it.

"Steve!"

I looked up and saw Amanda hurrying toward me from the parking lot, accompanied by a guy whose face I would never forget. My heart started pounding harder than it had when I'd found the body.

He was slim, with high cheekbones, green eyes, and long russet hair pulled back in a pony-tail. My looks put me in the pretty guy category, but his put him at the top of that class. He moved with captivating grace. European, I had thought when I first met him over the summer, partly because of the name.

Lomen.

His gaze locked with mine and he slowed. My body's reaction was immediate and intense. I forgot about everything else but the desire to touch this incredibly beautiful man.

Amanda ran up and caught me in a hug. She smelled like cocoa-butter lotion. "You OK?"

"Yeah. Thanks for coming."

Lomen's gaze shifted to the crime scene, and a slight frown creased his brow. I glanced that way and saw yellow tape around the stairwell. I hadn't noticed them putting it up.

I looked at Amanda. "They said I could go, so I called you out for nothing. Sorry."

"Not for nothing," Amanda said. "Jeez! It must have been awful."

"Yeah, well."

"You need a ride somewhere?"

"Actually, if you don't mind, I'd really like a cup of coffee. Kind of jangled."

"Sure."

We walked down the street to her car, which gave me plenty of time to feel guilty. I was jangled, it was true, but more than that I wanted time in Lomen's company.

I'd first met him while rescuing Amanda from a white-haired, female attacker who had stalked her into the women's restroom at Zimmerman Library. Well, if you can call it meeting: Lomen immediately took off after the attacker while I worked on stopping Amanda's neck from bleeding.

It was later, at the hospital, that Lomen and I had been in Amanda's room for a while. We didn't talk much then, either.

I didn't need to talk. I knew.

I've been told I'm too picky. Maybe so, but I refuse to settle. I want more than just sex. More than a night or a weekend. That makes me unlike most guys my age who are gay. It also guarantees that I'm alone more often than not. I don't care.

"Frontier OK, or you want to get farther from campus?" Amanda asked as she unlocked her car, a well-traveled Camry.

"How about The Range?"

Another twinge of guilt. The Frontier was right across Central Avenue; The Range would take a few minutes to drive to. A few more minutes in Lomen's space.

It wasn't unreasonable. I could have picked someplace a lot farther away.

Lomen insisted that I get in the front seat beside Amanda. My back prickled with awareness of him behind me.

I wondered why Amanda had brought him—not that I was complaining. He was part of Len Whiting's set, and Len was Amanda's best friend. I hadn't seen much of them since that day last summer. I'd run into Amanda a couple of times on campus, and seen Len and her boyfriend Caeran—who looked so much like Lomen that I'd wondered more than once if they were brothers—one time in the library. I hadn't seen Lomen at all since the day Amanda was attacked.

I had thought about him a lot, though.

Besides being gorgeous, he seemed like someone I could care about. He'd defended Amanda against an attacker armed with a knife. For a brief moment of dismay, I wondered if he and Amanda were a couple, but no. The way he had looked at me...

I wanted to know him better. And I'd be delighted to explore any kind of knowing he might be interested in.

As we headed north, my gaze fell on the Sandia Mountains rising above Albuquerque to the east, a mass of stone jutting into the sky, higher but less rugged than the mountains I'd grown up with further south. The trees up there would be turning soon.

In a few minutes we were pulling into the parking lot at The Range. The smell of coffee and cinnamon rolls hit as soon we I walked in. My stomach grumbled, but I wasn't ready to face food yet.

I felt kind of disconnected, walking into the restaurant as if it was a normal day, as if I hadn't just found a dead body. The décor, done by a local artist, was all turquoise, pink, and purple, with blue coyotes hanging from hot air balloons. It made the morning seem even more surreal.

We sat in a booth and a waitress brought us menus and asked what we wanted to drink. Amanda and I ordered coffee and I asked for a glass of water, too. Lomen opted for hot tea. I glanced at him, but he was reading the menu.

Beside him, Amanda leaned toward me, eyes wide behind her glasses. "What happened? Do you feel like talking about it?"

"I was heading for the lab to do some work before class, and she was just lying there."

"Do you know who it was?"

"Pretty sure it was Kimberly Darrow."

Amanda frowned. "Don't think I know her."

"Neither do I. She's in the physics class I'm assisting."

"Physics, not chemistry?"

"Right."

"Then what was she doing by Clark Hall?"

"I've been wondering that myself."

I glanced at Lomen again. He was still gazing at the menu, but I had the feeling he was listening.

"And you're sure she was dead?"

"Her throat was torn out. I think her neck was broken, too."

Lomen's gaze shifted to me. "Torn?"

I looked back into those green eyes, wanting to drown in them. "Yeah," I said in a low voice. "Ripped. Not just a knife."

Amanda's attacker had used a knife. One small, clean cut. Of course, I had interrupted her, and Lomen had come in right after me, at which point she abandoned her prey.

"Did they ever catch that woman?" I asked, still gazing at Lomen.

He blinked, then looked back at the menu. I turned to

Amanda. "The one who was after you?"

"She was caught," Amanda said in a small voice.

I hadn't heard anything about it on the news.

Our drinks arrived in colorful mock-Fiesta-ware mugs. We were silent while the waitress set them before us.

"So, have you decided?" she said with a cheery smile.

"You hungry?" Amanda asked me.

I had a mouthful of water already. I shook my head. Amanda handed the menus to the waitress.

"Just the drinks for now. Thanks."

Deprived of the menu, Lomen stared at the table top. Avoiding my gaze?

Crap.

I drank some more water, grateful for the clean, cold taste of it. I swished it around, trying not to make a production of rinsing my mouth. When I felt fresher I sipped my coffee. Too strong. I added some cream, stirred, sipped again.

"Did you see anyone?" Amanda's voice was low.

I shook my head. "It looked like she'd been there a while."

Amanda traded a glance with Lomen. "Seen anything else...weird...lately?"

"Compared with a corpse? No."

Amanda picked up her orange mug and took a long pull. I got the impression she had something more to say, so I waited.

"Well." Amanda cleared her throat. "I'm sorry that happened to you, and I hope it all works out all right, but I'm actually glad you texted me. I've been meaning to get in touch with you."

That caught me off guard. We weren't friends, really. More like acquaintances. Amanda worked at the library, and I occasionally bugged her for books that other people were late in returning. Other than that one day when she was attacked in the library restroom, we hadn't done much more than exchange passing hellos.

I waited. She took another swig of coffee.

"Would you maybe be interested in a part-time job?"

I thought about the lab, and my assistant-teaching, and my

double major. "I'm a little booked up."

"This is a start-up. It's pure research. Not lucrative, but interesting."

I remembered the conversation she was referring to, in her hospital room last summer, about career possibilities. The smart path for me was into some lucrative science, like pharmaceuticals, but I was drawn more toward innovation. Hence the double major in physics and chemistry. I was still trying to make up my mind.

"I'm listening," I said.

"Medical research. Might involve DNA analysis."

"A bit outside my focus," I said.

"I bet you could pick it up."

I shrugged. "There are plenty of places that do DNA analysis these days."

"This is a private effort. We have to do our own."

I met her gaze. "Why?"

She looked at her mug, and swirled it a couple of times. "Privacy. It's a specific project to combat a disease that affects a small minority. The treatment will have no lucrative potential, I'm afraid, but we'll pay you."

"Human interest?"

"Not enough to generate any clout."

"Who taught you to talk so politically?"

She gave me an ironic look. "You're the one that recommended I study business."

"And did you?"

"I signed up for a couple of classes. Not sure if I'll stick with it. Don't change the subject."

"What *is* the subject? What disease is this? Not AIDS."

"Oh, hell no. This is obscure. You've never heard of it."

"Try me."

"Steve, it doesn't even have a scientific name. That's how obscure it is."

"No one's written about it at all? How do you expect to get any funding?"

"We have a private backer."

"Better have pretty deep pockets."

A small sound—just an exhalation, a hint of a laugh—drew my attention to Lomen. Our gazes met briefly, just enough to waken a response in my groin, then he looked away again.

If Lomen was part of this, I might be more interested. I wondered if the deep pockets were his. Not likely; he wasn't much older than me or Amanda. Unless maybe he was a trust-fund kid, but he didn't have that polished look.

"The pay is good," Amanda said. "Could help cut down your student loans."

"How good?"

"Twenty-five bucks an hour."

That was good. Way more than I was getting for grading papers.

"How many hours a week?" I asked.

"It's flexible. We'll work around your schedule."

Tempting. Sounded too good to be true. I would much rather do research than teach, but if I gave up my student-assisting gig for this job and the deep pockets ran dry, I might be sorry.

"Let me think about it."

"OK."

Amanda drank the last of her coffee and looked around for the waitress. Lomen looked up from the table top, right at me.

"Please consider accepting. We need your help."

His voice was quiet, his eyes were earnest, and I felt like I'd been kicked in the chest. I wanted to do whatever he asked of me. Anything.

I was the one who looked away. Down at my coffee, which was now cold. I swallowed.

I was not thinking rationally. The day had started badly, and I was still off-balance. My feelings were getting in the way, and I knew I should just step back and calm down before making any decisions.

He was still watching me; I could feel his gaze. I looked up again into those emerald eyes.

"I'll do it."

= 2 =

Amanda turned to me, looking startled. "You will? Great!"

She grinned and held out her hand. I shook it. She glanced at Lomen, who had gone silent again.

"We'll need to meet with Caeran and Len," Amanda said. "Maybe tonight, if you're not busy?"

"I'm open."

"Good, good! We'll talk about scheduling. It's early in the project—we still don't have a work space."

"Fine."

I should give the Physics 102 prof some warning anyway. She wouldn't be pleased to have me quit. Or maybe I wouldn't have to; if this startup hadn't quite started up yet, I might have until the end of the semester.

Secretly, I hoped I wouldn't. The minute I'd said yes, I'd been filled with excitement. The student-assisting job was dead boring and I'd be happy to drop it immediately. I already knew I didn't want to teach.

I looked at Lomen. He was staring at the table top again, frowning slightly.

Amanda flagged down the waitress and paid our tab, insisting on buying my coffee. We headed out to her car. The sun was hot enough to make me wish I'd worn a hat.

"Where should we drop you?" she asked.

I checked the time; 10:15. My next class was at 1:00. I didn't feel like returning to campus; I wanted some down time.

"My place, I guess."

I gave her directions to my apartment in the student ghetto. It was a decent place, an easy walk from campus. I had a bike, but I'd left it at home that morning.

"Thanks," I said as she pulled up to the curb. "And thanks for answering my distress call."

"No problem." She smiled softly. "I owe you."

I got out. She rolled down the window.

"I'll text you about tonight."

"OK."

I looked toward the back seat, where Lomen was maintaining his Zen detachment. He made no move to switch to the front. Not even a glance at me as the car pulled away.

Well, hell.

I went inside and opened the refrigerator. I should have been hungry, but the thought of food did not appeal. I poured myself a glass of water and sat on my sofa, thinking over the conversation.

I still didn't know whether Lomen was interested in me. When he looked at me I felt like he was, but he didn't look at me much. In fact I had the impression he was trying not to.

What was that about?

I had an afternoon class: Calculus. Ordinarily I liked math, but I felt no enthusiasm. Since the alternative was driving myself crazy trying to second-guess Lomen, though, I dug out my text and went over the assignment I'd already completed.

The phone rang. I looked at the number—local, but I didn't recognize it. I let it go to voicemail, then listened. Turned out to be a reporter, wanting to interview me about finding Kimberly.

No, thanks.

I studied, heated up some soup for lunch, studied some more until it was time to head to class, then stuffed the text, notebook, and my assignment into my pack. I hauled out my bike and put on a gimme cap—Isotopes freebie I'd picked up over the summer—and rode back to campus.

Amanda's text came in partway through the class. I glanced at it, but the prof hated phones and had been known to confiscate them from inattentive students, so I shoved mine back in my pocket. After class I stood outside the building under a tree and read Amanda's message.

MEET 7 PM – PICK YOU UP 10 TIL, OK?

I sent back "OK," then put on my cap, climbed on my bike. I'd avoided Clark Hall on my way to Calculus, but it was just a couple of buildings away and I was curious. I cruised past on my way home. There were still cops and yellow tape, and a few looky-loos. Building no longer locked down, apparently. The body was gone.

What had brought Kimberly to this part of campus?

Her killer, maybe.

There was no reason for her to go there that I knew of. Certainly not at night; and since I'd found her in the morning I assumed she'd died overnight. The student union building and the theatre complex were a bit of a walk, kind of far for nighttime wandering. Kids looking for fun were more likely to head straight for the Nob Hill district from the dorms, not this far west.

I took a deep breath. Not my problem.

I headed home and spent an hour or so surfing and looking at UNM's course offerings in medical science. DNA sequencing would require ten or fifteen hours of course work before you got to the good stuff. That was a big time commitment, if that's what they'd want me to do.

On the other hand, more fun than grading papers. And definitely a marketable skill. It was early enough in the semester I could probably pick up the first class and catch up fairly easily.

I made myself eat a peanut butter sandwich, though my stomach was still kind of knotted. Went back to surfing, trying to keep my mind off of Lomen. Was only partly successful.

Amanda knocked on my door at eleven minutes til seven. Lomen was not with her, much to my disappointment. The sun was still up, but heading for the horizon. I followed Amanda to her car, wondering if Lomen would be at this meeting.

"Where are we headed?" I asked.

"Len and Caeran's. It's not far."

Turned out to be less than a mile, south and east of my place, closer to Nob Hill in an area that was gradually improving. Old houses, many being remodeled or expanded. Mature trees shading the street and nicely landscaped front yards. Beautiful, big back yards.

Len and Caeran's place was a single-story house, stuccoed in white with yellow trim. The front yard was xeriscaped and yet completely lush, with drought-tolerant plants framing a winding flagstone path to the front door. We walked up this, and butterflies rose from nearby bushes to dance around us before settling again. A windchime somewhere nearby sang in the breeze.

Len came to the door and welcomed us with smiles. Her hair —kind of mousy brown—was longer than I remembered, and she wore loose, light, cotton clothes and looked generally more feminine than when we'd first met. In the past I'd mostly seen her at the library where she worked with Amanda, but she'd switched to pre-med in the spring semester.

The event that had drawn us all together was the attack on Amanda in the summer. Since then, even though we hadn't spend much time together, we'd shared a silent connection. I wanted to understand that better; I had never heard what became of Amanda's attacker, though I assumed she'd been apprehended. The "campus killer" murders had stopped after that—until now.

"Hey, Steve!" Len opened the door wide. "Good to see you. Come on in."

The living room had a couch, coffee table, a couple of comfy chairs, and lots of plants. The back of the room formed a small dining area with a beautiful wooden table—looked handmade. Crystals in the window at the back of the room glinted rainbows now and then, though a pergola outside kept the afternoon light from blasting full in through the window.

No sign of Lomen. Dammit.

"Make yourself comfortable," Len said. "Want something to drink? Fuzzy water?"

Fuzzy, not fizzy? OK.

"Sure," I said.

I sat on one end of the couch. Amanda and Len went into the kitchen and came back with three glasses of sparkling water over ice. Len handed me one, then settled in one of the chairs while Amanda joined me on the couch.

"Caeran will be out in a minute. I understand you had an exciting morning."

"Yeah." I sipped, not really wanting to talk about it.

"Did you see anyone in the area?"

"Not until the cops showed up."

Len nodded, then let it drop. "I'm glad you're willing to join our project. Right now I'm the only one on the research team, which makes us pretty lame."

"Adding me won't improve that by much."

"Sure it will. You're a genius, Steve. Don't deny it. And you've got courage."

I wondered why courage was needed for a research project, but let it pass. "I don't have the training for DNA analysis. I was looking at it online, and it takes a bachelor's and a master's, with a whole lot of forensics."

"You wouldn't need the forensics," Len said.

"May I ask a possibly-dumb question? Why don't you just have a lab do whatever analysis you need?"

She sipped her water. "We want to protect the privacy of the subjects."

"Any reputable lab will guarantee that."

"Not good enough. This is non-negotiable. We have to do it ourselves."

I frowned. "It could take years for you and me to develop the skills we'd need. Seems really inefficient."

"That's OK. This is a long-term project."

I leaned back, watching her, waiting for the pitch about getting in on the ground floor of a really big thing. From what I'd heard so far, making money wasn't the objective. In fact, keeping it quiet seemed to be worth spending a lot more money, and time, than necessary. I wondered if whatever they were doing was somehow illegal.

Caeran came in from the back of the house. He had his hair down over his shoulders, and looked so much like Lomen that my pulse quickened. They could so easily be brothers. I didn't quite have the nerve to ask if they were. My impression of Caeran based on the few times we'd met was that he was more serious than Lomen, but today he smiled as he sat in the other chair.

"Thank you for coming, Steve. Amanda tells us you're interested in joining our research team."

I wanted to say I was interested in hearing more about it, but I'd kind of already agreed, so I just nodded.

"We're just getting started, so right now we don't have anything for you to work on. Until we do, we can pay you a retainer for each semester you take six hours or more of courses that will help build your skills for the project."

"Wow. That's generous."

"In return, we ask that you sign a confidentiality agreement."

Amanda produced a single page and a pen and laid them in front of me on the coffee table. I read through the agreement, which specified a retainer of a thousand dollars per semester. Just for taking classes I was probably already taking.

It also specified that I not discuss the project with anyone outside of Ebonwatch, LLC. At all, ever.

"Ebonwatch is your company?"

Caeran nodded, and gestured to the girls. "It's us, Lomen, several of my cousins, and Len's mentor, Miguel de Madera."

"He's a curandero," Amanda added.

Folk medicine? Interesting. Not willing to trust a mainstream lab, but willing to accept input from an alternative practitioner who could be legit, or could be as bonkers as the UFO crowd.

"Can you tell me a bit more about your objectives?" I asked.

Caeran leaned forward, resting his elbows on his knees, fingers laced loosely. He met my gaze. "We want to find a cure for an obscure disease. It affects only a small population with a specific genetic profile, or so we believe. That's one of the points we want to confirm."

"And what attracted you to this problem?"

He took a deep breath. "Some of my kin are afflicted with the disease."

I blinked. "So it's personal."

"You could say that."

"Do *you* have it?"

"No. That is, I haven't manifested it. I was exposed to it last year."

Len leaned over and touched his arm. They traded a glance and he gave her a reassuring smile.

"I think, after the time that's passed, I'm unlikely to develop the—disease. But a cousin of mine is less fortunate."

"Lomen?" I was instantly sorry I'd opened my mouth. I took a swig of my water.

"No," Caeran said. "Lomen is probably safe."

"Probably?"

Len spoke up. "We're not exactly sure how the disease is transmitted. We suspect it takes an exchange of bodily fluids."

I looked from her to Caeran. "So you could be in danger, too."

"No." She gave Caeran a long look, then turned back to me. "I can't get it. Neither can you, so that's not an issue."

"How do you know?"

"We're not in the genetic group that's vulnerable," she said. "You know how sickle cell anemia mostly affects African Americans?"

"Not exclusively, though."

"True. In this case we're pretty certain it's exclusive."

"Why?"

"Because the disease has never manifested in a—person outside our genetic group," Caeran said.

I looked from him to Len. There was something they weren't telling me.

"Never?"

"Never," Caeran said.

"In how long?"

"Many centuries. Millennia."

"It's been around that long? Why doesn't it have a name?"

Len cleared her throat. "It doesn't have a scientific name. It's known as the curse."

I had to laugh. "OK. Maybe a scientific name is in order. 'Cause, you know, otherwise it sounds kind of like the *Twilight*

Zone."

"You're right," Caeran said. "Maybe you and Len can decide on a name."

Len nodded. "We'll talk about it. Do you have other questions, Steve?"

"Yeah," I said slowly. "I gather you have a backer."

"Several of us have pledged resources to the project," Caeran said.

"Forgive me, but it sounds like it could get expensive. Are your resources going to cover the cost?"

"We expect they will."

"It's all in the business plan," Amanda said. She gave Caeran an inquiring look. He nodded.

"I can show you that, if you're interested," she added, pulling out a tablet.

I watched her stroke the screen. Amanda the organizer. Not interested in science, but she was good with planning and decent with numbers, as far as I knew. I'd pointed her toward economics, but she'd be good in any branch of business. Looked like she was handling the administration for Ebonwatch.

"Yeah, I'd like to see it. You said it was a long-term project, Len. How long?"

"Our plan covers thirty years," Len said. "We hope that's a high estimate, but it could possibly take longer to find the cure."

"And you've got the budget for thirty years?"

"Uh-huh," said Amanda. She handed me the tablet.

I glanced at the numbers. They looked realistic based on what little I knew. The bottom line, thirty-year budget, including establishing and equipping a private laboratory, was over two hundred million dollars.

I swallowed.

I'd known Caeran was well off. He'd bought Len a Lexus, after all. But this budget went beyond well off into ridiculously wealthy. Even if there were several—what, five, ten?—people in on it, that meant an average of at least twenty million per investor.

I handed back the tablet. "You're really serious about this."

"Yes," Caeran said.

I looked at Len. "Thirty years is a long time."

"It's going to be my life's work," she said. "Well, unless we're successful a lot faster than we expect. Then I could go on to something else. But we're not asking you to make that commitment, Steve. We do realize you've got your own life to live. Since we're asking you to steer your college plans in a direction that will help us, we're willing to compensate you for that."

"What if I decide I want out after a couple of years?"

"Then you're free to go," Caeran said. "That's one of the reasons we're asking you to sign the confidentiality agreement."

I leaned back against the couch. "Worried about competitors?"

"No. Just concerned about our privacy."

I looked at the agreement. If I signed it, and something went sideways with the project, I wouldn't be able to ask for help.

"Everything we're doing with this project is legal and legitimate," Caeran said.

I looked up at him sharply. Had my thoughts been that obvious?

He gazed back at me patiently, and again I thought of Lomen. What was his role in all this, I wondered? Why wasn't he at this meeting?

"You know, I'd like to think about it some more if you don't mind," I said.

"Sure," Len said. "It's a big decision. There's no rush."

She stood and collected our empty glasses, then looked at me with a smile. "Want to see the back yard?"

Caeran headed down the hall while Amanda and I followed Len into the kitchen. She opened the back door and we stepped onto a patio shaded by the pergola, which looked fairly new. It was built of wood and the posts were carved in knotwork patterns. Vines had been planted by each post, and were being trained to climb them. Pots of flowers sat along the edge of the patio. Eventually the pergola would be a shady bower.

The yard itself was lush, with a thick lawn, bushes around the sides, and shade trees, mostly cottonwoods. A tall fence provided privacy, and a vegetable garden against it on one side looked well-tended. Here and there, rose bushes were covered in flowers.

The sound of water trickling made me look around until I spotted a small fountain mounted on the wall of the house. I wandered over to it, musing as I watched the water splash into the basin.

Amanda joined me. "Nice, eh? I come over here a lot to hang out in the garden. Len and Caeran are really nice about having visitors."

I nodded, and turned to walk out to the lawn. Amanda followed and stood beside me. The sun had set, and while it was still warm, the temperature had already dropped to a more comfortable level. A few wispy clouds picked up sunset colors, gold and peach and ruddy red.

"So what are they not telling me?" I said.

She didn't answer immediately. That told me a lot right there.

She squatted down and ran a hand through the grass, picked up a yellow leaf and twirled it. "You know how you mentioned the *Twilight Zone*?"

"Yeah."

"That's a factor."

I sat on the grass so I could see her face. "Meaning what?"

"Meaning there's some stuff you'll find hard to believe. I'm not the one who should explain."

"Who, then?"

"Caeran or one of his kin. And once they tell you, they will feel obligated to protect you, just so you know."

"Protect me from what?"

Amanda blinked a couple of times, staring at the grass. "Remember when you came in the bathroom and saved my butt?"

"Yeah."

"And Lomen was there too, and took off after—the attacker?"

I nodded.

"Well, he was protecting me."

I took a minute to digest this. "So you mean Caeran and his family—"

"The clan."

"—OK, the clan—would protect me from the campus killer?"

"Well, yeah."

"But what does the campus killer have to do with finding a cure for this disease?"

Amanda bit her lip. "I think I should let someone else explain."

I watched her, trying to make sense of the clues she'd dropped. One of them didn't work.

"The woman who attacked you wasn't the campus killer," I said.

"Yeah, she was."

"But the first victims were raped."

Amanda took a deep breath and let it out in a sigh. "There's been more than one campus killer."

"Oh?"

"The one you saw was the second. Looks like now there's a third. The clan thinks so—they think the body you found was killed by a new one."

Three murderers with the same hairstyle? What was it, a cult?

"How do you know it's not the same one who attacked you?"

"Because she's dead."

I took a careful breath. "And how do you know that?"

"I was there."

This had not been on the news. I tried to remember everything I'd heard about the campus killer. The sightings of a white-haired guy last fall, and the white-haired woman who had attacked Amanda. Victims both male and female. I hadn't heard whether the males had been raped.

And now Kimberly. Too close for comfort.

And Amanda was there when her attacker died? Or was

killed?

The whole thing made my stomach turn. How were these murders connected to Caeran's search for a cure for some obscure disease?

I was pretty sure I didn't want to find out.

A cricket started chirping nearby. Dusk was falling, dimming the shapes of the trees at the back of the yard. I heard a car engine shut off out in the street. I stood, gave myself a cursory dust-off, and started toward the house, trying to compose a polite refusal of Caeran's generous offer.

"She was trying to kill me at the time, by the way."

I stopped and looked back at Amanda.

"She'd been trying to kill me all summer. You saw the ... second attempt, I think."

"Did you tell the police?"

"That time, yeah."

"I mean about the last time."

She shook her head. "They wouldn't have believed me."

I took a step toward her. "Amanda, that's illegal. You have to tell the cops if you witness a murder, or you're guilty of conspiracy."

"It wasn't a murder. It was self-defense. She was trying to kill us."

Us?

Voices from the house intruded on my attempt to understand. Someone had arrived, and the tone of one of the voices made my pulse race.

I started toward the house again. I could hear Amanda following me.

Len glanced up at me, in the act of putting something in the oven. I kept going through to the living room, then paused.

Lomen stood by the couch. He looked at me, raising all the hopes that threatened to shut off my brain, then away.

Beside him stood another guy from the same family: russet hair, slender but well-toned body, green eyes—a little darker than Caeran's and Lomen's. These guys had strong genetic traits, that was for sure.

He and Caeran were talking in a language I didn't recognize: fluid, with soft consonants. The conversation stopped as I came in. The new guy looked at me warily, then his attention shifted to Amanda, who walked up and plastered herself to him. He bent his head to whisper something to her, still watching me.

Lomen turned and greeted me with a civil nod. My gut clenched with conflicting emotions: pleasure at seeing him, frustration at his distant attitude, irrational fear that I'd done something to annoy him.

Caeran spoke up. "Steve, this is Savhoran, another of my kin. He is vital to the research we'll be doing."

I looked at the new guy again. He had on a loose-woven cotton shirt and pants, the fabric similar to what Len was wearing. Amanda loosed her hold on him and he took a step toward me, then made a quaint little bow.

"I am glad to meet you," he said.

His hair was braided back, but as he moved, the light caught streaks of white amid the brown.

= 3 =

White hair. Caeran's kin.

"You've got the disease," I blurted.

And so did the campus killers.

Savhoran straightened and a swallow moved his throat. His eyes had gone cold, but he nodded. Amanda slid her arm around him again.

"Savhoran will give us whatever samples are needed to study his DNA," Caeran said. "We hope that comparing it to that of a healthy—relative—myself or Lomen, will help in identifying the cause."

"It might not be genetic," I said, though my mind was racing.

"Possibly not, but we are prepared to try every avenue of research."

"Is it just coincidence, or does this disease make people into homicidal maniacs?"

Caeran glanced toward Savhoran, but he was staring at the floor. "That's not quite it. May I suggest we all sit down?"

Caeran gestured toward the couch, then moved to the chair he'd taken before. Savhoran took the other chair and Amanda sat on the arm, still clinging to him. That left the couch for me and Lomen. I sat on the end near Caeran, leaving plenty of room. I didn't look at Lomen, but a rush went through me as he sat and his weight moved the couch.

Caeran laced his fingers and leaned back, hands to his chin, thinking. After a moment he straightened up and looked at me.

"What I am going to tell you will sound fantastic, like something out of fiction. I ask that you bear with me, and set aside the myths this will conjure for you."

"OK."

"The disease does not make people homicidal, exactly. It makes them crave blood."

My jaw dropped. "Vampirism?"

"The basis of that myth, yes. But the myth carries misconceptions."

"I'm listening."

"This disease cannot affect you or Amanda or Len, or any other human. Only my kindred and I are vulnerable to it."

I frowned. "You're implying that you and your kindred aren't human."

"That is correct."

Silence. I stared at Caeran, who gazed back calmly.

I bit back several sarcastic comments, and finally managed to just say, "Then what are you?"

He took a slow breath. "This, also, will bring myths to mind."

"OK."

"We are ælven."

Long pause. Part of me wanted to laugh, but no one else seemed to think it was funny. I glanced at Amanda, who gave a tiny nod and a crooked smile.

Len came in from the kitchen. She shot me a sympathetic look, then went to sit on the floor by Caeran's chair.

Caeran was watching me. Waiting for me to accept or protest.

"So...only elves can be vampires?" I said, my voice quavering. The impulse to laugh was part disbelief, part panic.

"Only ælven can be afflicted with the curse, yes," Caeran said. "And only ælven blood, or human blood, will satisfy the hunger that it brings. The killings that have occurred on campus here in the past year were done by alben."

"Wait, what?"

"Alben is the name we give to those of our kind who are afflicted and turn away from our creed," Caeran said. "The campus killers are alben."

"But Savhoran isn't," Amanda said.

Caeran nodded. "Savhoran upolds the creed, therefore he remains ælven."

I closed my eyes. "OK, I'm getting overloaded."

"This is a great deal of new information," Caeran said. "Take your time. There is no hurry."

I looked at him, then around the room. They were all watching me, including Lomen. His face showed concern, and for some reason that sent me over the edge.

I stood up. Had to get out. My hindbrain, reminding me that I had no vehicle there, sent me toward the back door instead of the front.

I strode to the middle of the yard and stood taking deep breaths. Venus was glowing in the last strip of fading blue that remained on the western horizon. I stared at that planet as if I could anchor myself to it.

I heard footsteps behind me in the grass. Turned to see Lomen had followed me.

Everything in my brain shifted sideways. Elves, vampires, research jobs—I didn't care. I stared at Lomen, then swallowed the dryness in my throat.

"Just tell me," I said, my voice rough. "If you're not interested I won't bother you."

"Steven..."

I could just make out his face in the growing dusk. The concern was still there, but at least he was looking at me instead of avoiding my gaze.

"Do not base your decision about joining Ebonwatch on me."

I blinked. Ebonwatch couldn't have been farther from my thoughts.

"I understand your feelings." His voice was just above a whisper. "And yes, I am open to sharing with you, but I do not wish you to be hurt. It might be best to avoid promises."

"Are you saying you're up for a fling but no more? That's not what I want."

My gonads screamed at me that it was enough for now. I ignored them.

"I've had it with short-term," I said. "I want forever."

He stood still, and I heard him exhale.

"Forever is a long time."

I knew I was being an idiot. I wanted him, so much that I was actually willing to take whatever terms he laid down, but I'd been there before, had my heart crushed before, and I was sick of it. If I couldn't have stability, I'd stay alone.

These were demands I'd had no intention of making. They came out of left field, a reaction to my confusion and too much emotion. I stood frozen, dreading and expecting his refusal.

He put a hand on my shoulder and leaned close, his cheek brushing mine and setting off sparks in my brain. I caught a whiff of scent: evergreen and spice.

I will be here.

I gasped, stunned by his voice in my head and by the sensation that accompanied it, of his soul touching mine.

Regardless of what you decide for Ebonwatch, I will be here. Set me aside while you make that choice. We will have time.

He backed away, releasing my shoulder and slipping out of my mind as suddenly as he had come in. I staggered, disoriented.

He walked back to the house, leaving me alone with the biggest hard-on I'd had in months.

I went to the nearest tree and leaned my head against it, bark pressing into my forehead. What had just happened?

Breathe.

I sucked deep breaths of the cool night air and tried to sort out my thoughts. I'd been half-sure that they were all putting me on about the elf and vampire stuff, but Lomen's voice in my head had changed that.

Telepathy. Vampire elves.

And they wanted me to commit to a career trying to find this cure. For vampirism.

Not human. That's why they didn't want to use a lab for DNA analysis. They were a different freaking species, and that would show up in the DNA. Holy crap!

The prospect of studying a humanoid species that human science didn't know about was tantalizing. Jeez, if not for the non-disclosure agreement, it could lead to a Pulitzer!

I hadn't signed that agreement.

For a moment I saw an alternative. If I walked out now, I

could pursue the study of this new species—scratch that; this probably very old species—on my own. Claim that Pulitzer, and whatever other prizes came with it. My ticket to fame and fortune.

All I had to do was betray Lomen and his friends.

I closed my eyes. I couldn't do that.

In the brief moment of our contact, I'd had a glimpse of Lomen's heart, and it was glorious. I wanted to know him, to love him. Forever.

If I was ready to devote my life to Lomen, why not spend it fighting the disease that threatened him and his family?

He'd said to leave him out of the equation, but I didn't see how I could. Impossible to separate him from the choice. If I agreed to help, I'd see him frequently. He was part of the project. If I chose to stay out of it, but got involved with Lomen, I'd be constantly reminded of what they were trying to achieve, and that I'd refused to help.

If I walked away from both the project and Lomen...

I couldn't.

I straightened up. Took a couple of deep gulps of air. A leaf drifted down past my head, fluttering like a butterfly on its way to the ground, flashing golden as it caught the light from the house.

I headed back inside. Soft murmur of conversation from living room, and as I reached the door I smelled fresh-baked cookies.

I went in, and through to the living room. They all stopped talking and looked up at me. This time it was I who avoided Lomen's gaze; no distractions. I walked to the couch, sat down, signed my name to the non-disclosure agreement, then carefully laid the pen down on the coffee table. The click it made on the wood filled the silence.

"I'm in."

Most of them started talking at once. I glanced at Lomen. He smiled slightly; that was all. It was enough.

For now.

Len offered me a plate of cookies. I took one, though my stomach was pretty knotted. Bit off a small taste. Buttery, not too sweet, with piñon nuts. I chewed it slowly.

"Thank you, Steve," Caeran said. "We'll make it worth your while."

"I'm going to buy some books, if that's OK," I said. "I'll check the library first, but they may not have everything I want."

Caeran nodded. "Just give your receipts to Amanda. She'll reimburse you."

I turned to Len. "Have you looked at rare forms of anemia? Could be related."

"I'm just taking basic pre-med courses right now."

"Let's compare schedules. No need for us to overlap." I looked at Amanda. "You in on the research?"

She shook her head. "Not my forte. I'm handling the business end."

"Ah. Yes, you'll be good at it."

I realized the ... ælven ... had stopped talking and were all listening to me. I glanced around at them.

"Any of you scientifically inclined?"

"Lomen is something of a dabbler," Caeran said. "He is also taking courses at the university."

I met Lomen's gaze and swallowed. "I'd like to see your schedule too, then."

He nodded. "We could meet tomorrow."

"Yes," Len said. "Why don't you all come for dinner? We can talk about getting the lab up and running, too."

"Great idea!" Amanda said. "I'll bring the wine." She glanced sidelong at me and grinned. "Len's a great cook, and Caeran isn't bad either. Wait 'til you taste his homemade bread!"

This seemed to be the signal for the gathering to break up. Everyone stood. Len picked up the cookie plate and strolled to the kitchen, and Caeran followed her. Amanda and Savhoran went out the front door.

I stood by the couch, feeling foolish with half a cookie in my hand. Amanda was my ride; had she forgotten?

I supposed I could walk home. It wasn't that far.

"Not at night," Lomen said softly.

I faced him, stunned and momentarily angry. He'd read my mind.

"Sorry," he said. "We'll need to teach you to shield your thoughts."

"You can hear everything I'm thinking?"

He bit his lip, laughter lighting his eyes. "Only if we're listening."

I looked away, swallowing. I could feel my face starting to burn.

"Steven. Don't worry. I generally make it a point not to listen."

I spotted a wastebasket by the front door. Walked over and dropped the cookie into it.

"Actually, we tend to tune out human thoughts most of the time," Lomen said. "Otherwise they're too distracting."

I turned to face him. "You knew all along, then."

He came over to me, stopping a couple of steps away. "That you were attracted to me? Only because I have felt the same."

"You sure hid it well."

A tiny frown creased his brow, making me regret my bitter tone. "I didn't want to interfere with you. For your sake."

I was so confused and frustrated, I just said, "What?"

Lomen glanced toward the kitchen, where Caeran and Len were talking in low voices. "This is not the time or place to discuss this. I have a class tomorrow morning, but I'm free in the afternoon."

"I'll be done by two."

He nodded. "Where shall we meet?"

My place, I thought, but maybe he didn't want to be that private yet. "The duck pond."

"At two o'clock. I'll be there." He took a step closer and lowered his voice. "I have been drawn to you since the day we both assisted Amanda."

I looked up into his eyes. So green.

"Same here."

His gaze shifted toward the front door. He turned and picked up an empty glass from the coffee table, then headed for the kitchen. For the second time that night, I was left with an enormous hard-on.

A moment later, Amanda came in. I shoved my hand in my pocket and shifted my stance to make my condition less obvious.

"Did you think we'd forgotten you?" Amanda said. "Sorry— we just needed to talk a minute."

"It's OK."

She picked up the pen and the agreement I'd signed. "Ready to go?"

Len and Caeran came in from the kitchen, with Lomen following. Len smiled at me.

"See you tomorrow night. Come hungry!"

We exchanged good-nights, then I followed Amanda out. Lomen stayed behind.

It was dark, now. A light on the front porch glowed golden. A breeze kicked up as we walked to the street, raising the scent of bark mulch.

Savhoran was waiting by Amanda's car. He got in the back seat without a word, leaving me the shotgun seat.

"Really glad you joined Ebonwatch," Amanda said as she started toward my apartment. "I think you won't regret it."

"Where'd the name come from?" I asked. "It's pretty poetic for a research firm."

"It's the name of Savhoran's clan. Actually a very old clan that's just been revived. It's made up of ælven who've got the disease, but who still live by the ælven creed."

"Meaning what, exactly?"

"The creed is our code of honor," Savhoran said, his voice low and quiet. "Among other things, we are bound to protect beings lesser than ourselves."

The "lesser" made me bristle, but I kept my mouth shut.

"When we hunt, we give thanks for the sustenance we receive, and offer atonement for the harm we have done to our prey."

"Atonement?" For murdering humans? My throat went dry.

"We in Ebonwatch do not take the lives of our prey," he said, his voice almost a whisper. "It is not necessary. We take only what we need."

I was going to have to learn that thought-shielding thing.

"Sounds kind of like what the Navajo do," I said, trying to make up for my cynical thoughts.

"Yeah, kind of," Amanda said. "The ælven are very aware of the impact of their actions. They have a pretty holistic worldview."

"Too bad humans haven't managed that."

Neither of them had anything to say to that.

"What kind of atonement do you do?" I asked for the sake of conversation.

"Usually we offer a small gift," Savhoran said. "Something we have made ourselves, put our thought and energy into."

"That's nice. How do people react to that?"

"We do not usually see their reactions."

Why was that? I decided I didn't want to know the answer. The whole subject gave me the creeps, actually.

A virtuous vampire. Hard to wrap my brain around that. Myths getting in the way, I figured. Caeran was right, they distorted my understanding.

We reached my place, and Amanda shut off the engine. "I'll walk you in. Be right back," she said over her shoulder to Savhoran.

She accompanied me to my door. I took out my keys.

"Savhoran's having a hard time," she said quietly. "He's still adjusting to living with this thing. It's only been a few months since he manifested, so please, cut him some slack, OK?"

"Sorry," I said. "I didn't mean to make him feel bad."

She sighed. I could see the worry in her face. "He's thought about suicide."

Oh. Crap.

"It's a major danger for them—all of the ælven. More so if they're unlucky enough to get hit with the curse."

Why? I could understand if they got the disease, but why would a healthy ælven consider suicide?

"See you tomorrow." Amanda said. "Want a ride? I could pick you up."

"Thanks, but it isn't far. I'll probably ride my bike."

"Then I'll drive you home after."

"That's not necessary."

"Yes it is. Either that, or one of them will escort you. Caeran doesn't want any of us going out alone after dark, not while there's an alben active in the area."

"Isn't that kind of extreme?"

"After you've been attacked a few times, you'll feel differently."

I blinked. "How many times have you been attacked?"

"Oh—four or five. It was kind of a vendetta, though. She fixated on me as a way to get back at the clan."

Great. What the hell had I gotten myself into?

= 4 =

My dreams that night were restless. Lomen was chasing me and I kept running away, even though I didn't want to. Then I started chasing Savhoran. He ran into a barn and I followed, but it was dark and I tripped and fell into a pile of hay and couldn't get up. I woke up frustrated and still tired. My brain was mush.

The classes I had that day were Organic Chemistry Lab followed by its accompanying lecture class, both in Clark Hall. I'd never made it in to work on the lab assignment.

I resisted the temptation to enter the building from the parking lot and thereby avoid the spot where I'd found Kimberly. I decided that looking at it without a dead body there would give me some closure, so I walked around to the west side of the building.

The yellow tape was gone, and a line of glass votive candles sat atop the wall that masked the stairwell. A heap of store-wrapped bouquets sat at the foot of the steps, with a couple of bigger, nicer arrangements and one stuffed bear with pierced nipples. I stopped and stared, then slowly went over to look. The candle flames flickered in the shade of the building.

More candles on each of the steps, some sitting on top of notes written on scraps of paper. More flowers on the little landing at the top. There were a few greeting cards, and a photo of Kimberly that had been printed on a color inkjet and then gotten wet and smeared. It was still recognizable, barely.

A lot of people had liked her, I guess. I'd barely known her; I had lumped her and her classmates together and labeled them annoying in my mind. I felt a little bad about that.

As I stood there, a girl came up and propped a bouquet wrapped in cellophane against the half-wall. She shot me a glance and I recognized her from the Physics 102 class. One of Kimberly's classmates.

I gave her a nod. She ducked her head and hurried away.

I'd see her later. Should I say something to that class? Did they know I had found Kimberly?

I went into the building, trying to shake off the discomfort of seeing the impromptu shrine. People did that a lot these days.

There were a few other students in the lab, already working. The assistant—a grad student—glanced up at me, then went back to whatever she was reading.

It was a relief to sit at a counter and pull out my lab work. Quiet, time to think, and be normal in a classroom. I needed that. I was a little distracted, but got through my assignment before it was time to head to class.

As I walked down the hall, passing other students, I had the feeling that everyone was looking at me. That was a feeling I was familiar with, and it had never boded well for me. My shoulder muscles tensed despite my reminding myself that it was just curiosity because of the dead body.

I had chosen UNM to get away from the anti-gay attitude in my home town. It was present in Albuquerque, too, but less so. Bigger city, without the heavy southern influence of Cruces. More liberal.

I turned in my homework, then took a seat in the front row and immediately opened my text to start reading. Kept my nose in the book until the prof started his lecture.

I failed to take useful notes, despite good intentions. Couldn't keep my mind from wandering. Eventually I became aware that everyone around me was standing up. It was 12:20; class was over. I hadn't absorbed a single concept.

I put my notebook in my pack and joined the throng shuffling out the door. Professor Baker, a thirtyish guy with Scandanavian looks—likeable, though married—stepped up and caught my eye.

"Heard you had a rough day yesterday."

I blinked. Took a minute for me to realize he meant Kimberly.

"Oh. Yeah."

"I half-expected you not to be here today."

The crowd parted around us like a stream around boulders, heading for the exit. A couple of the students gave me knowing looks.

"Well, I kind of wasn't," I said. "Sorry—I had trouble concentrating."

"I figured." He handed me an index card with some page numbers written on it. "Go over that section in the text again. Should help."

"Thanks." I stared down at the card, touched and embarrassed.

"Call or stop by my office if you have any questions."

"OK." I slid the card into my pack, then met his gaze and managed a smile. "Thank you."

"Sure thing."

He turned to go, following the last few students filing out. I went out, too, and stood in the hall, blinking.

Afraid to move.

What if Lomen didn't come? What if he'd changed his mind?

I took a deep breath, and forced my frozen feet to move. It would be ironic if, after all my fretting, *I* was the one who didn't show up.

I chickened out and left the building by the east door. I didn't need to see the shrine again. Outside, the sun was blinding. I paused to let my eyes adjust, then strode toward the duck pond west of Zimmerman library.

Amanda wasn't working at the library this semester. I'd been disappointed to learn that, but now I wondered if it was because Ebonwatch had made her a better offer.

I swallowed. Don't think about Ebonwatch. This is about Lomen and me.

I slowed as I reached the pond. All I saw were a couple of girls sitting on the grass and one chubby guy sacked out in the sunshine on the far side of the pond. My throat tightened as I scanned the people farther away, walking by on their way to and from classes, then I noticed someone sitting on a bench in the shade of some trees on the library side.

Crazy, the relief that went through me. I took a steadying breath and walked toward the trees.

Lomen was tearing pieces off a bread roll and tossing them to the ducks. Now and then a crumb would fall between his feet, and a little bird would hop out of the nearby bushes, snatch it up, and fly away.

As I stepped into the shade, he looked up and smiled at me. His clothes were rustic cotton, vaguely hippie-looking, like what Savhoran and Len had worn. His hair spilled loose over his shoulders. I caught my breath at the sight, wanting to run my fingers through that hair.

He tore the bread in half and offered a piece to me, but I shook my head. He went back to feeding it to the ducks, bit by bit.

I joined him on the bench. The ducks flinched away from me, but only for a second. The temptation of the bread overwhelmed their natural caution.

I took deep breaths, trying to slow my racing pulse. Watched Lomen's hands: long fingers, every movement graceful. Thought about those hands on my body, about my hands exploring his.

When the last of the bread was gone, he laced his fingers and was still. Gradually the ducks gave up hoping for more and drifted away.

I looked up to find him watching me. Clear, green eyes, steady and calm. My heart gave a hard thump.

"So," I said, then couldn't find more words.

"I apologize for seeming cold yesterday," he said. "I wanted to give you the chance to walk away."

I gave a soft laugh. "Why would I want to do that?"

He lifted one shoulder slightly. "Relationships between humans and ælven can be ... painful."

"Any relationship can be painful. That's one of the risks in life."

He tilted his head and a tiny line of concern creased his brow. "There are added complications."

I stared back at him. Obviously, I had missed something.

He turned to face me on the bench. "You understand that we are immortal?"

Immortal. I gaped at him. Yeah, I'd missed that.

"You're never going to die?"

He shifted and glanced toward the pond. "I could die. We're not indestructible. Accident or illness, or attacks, can kill us. But we do not age."

I swallowed. "How old are you?"

"Not quite two—"

Holy crap.

"—thousand years."

Holy *crap!*

"I'm rather young, actually."

I had trouble taking a breath. My voice came out a hoarse whisper. "Why do you even bother with us?"

"Usually we avoid you—not because we dislike you, but for our own safety." He sighed. "But we are easily tempted. Look at Caeran, and Savhoran."

"I don't understand why you'd be interested in us at all."

He looked at me and broke into a smile. "You fascinate us. You live with such urgency—such fire! And you are amazingly inventive."

These words almost turned off my brain. I took a deep breath, trying to stay on track. "Can I ask a question?"

"Of course."

"If you're immortal, how come you aren't the dominant species on the planet?"

His smile faded and his gaze dropped. A shadow of grief came into his face.

"You breed far more easily than we. For us, conceiving a child is rare. Many ælven never achieve it."

I felt an odd sorrow, though I'd never been interested in kids myself. "Can you have kids with humans? Is that any easier?"

"Yes, in some cases. But the offspring are mortal."

His voice was soft with sadness. I wondered if he had watched children of his own grow old and die.

There was another way that aelven could die. Amanda had told me about it: suicide.

"Yes," he said. "Grief drives many of us to seek death. The memories of a long life can become too heavy to bear." He leaned forward, staring at the water lapping the edge of the pond. "And there are so few of us now—eventually, we will pass from this world altogether."

My throat tightened and my eyes began to sting. It wasn't fair! They were so amazing, and they might go extinct? No!

"This is one of the reasons the Ebonwatch project is so important to us," Lomen said. "If we can cure those of us who have been stricken..."

"I'll help however I can," I said, meaning it. "Don't know how much that will be. If a cure was possible, I'd have thought you'd have found it by now."

"We've only just started looking."

I blinked. "You're not serious."

His mouth curved into a lopsided grin. "Most of us are not very scientifically inclined, I fear. We tend to leave the innovations to you."

"You mean Ebonwatch is the first attempt to cure this—this— jeez, you've got to give it a name!"

"The curse. Yes, it was Len's idea to use human technology to seek a cure. Quite brilliant; you're right that we should have thought of it."

A weight of responsibility settled on me, much to my dismay. I knew I wasn't equipped for the job.

"There is time," Lomen said gently. "And this is not what we came here to talk about."

I closed my eyes, completely boggled and confused. "I don't want to fail you," I whispered.

"You can't, because I ask nothing of you."

And somehow, that lack of demand was the straw that broke me. I put my face in my hands, overwhelmed by the grace and tragedy of the ælven, by my hopes and now fears for Lomen.

"Steven."

I was struggling just to breathe without melting down. I heard him shift on the bench, then felt his hand on my shoulder. So warm.

We have told you too much, too quickly. Forgive us.

And he was there, right before me. A pool—no, an ocean—and I could dive in and lose myself in bliss. All it would take was to let go of who I was.

But who was I, anyway? The last twenty-four hours had changed me so much I didn't even know any more.

You will not lose yourself. I promise you that.

Maybe I already have.

I felt him smile, a warmth that rippled through me. No. I see you.

He wasn't talking about normal vision. I held still, breathing easier now, just trying to understand the situation. I could feel that he was waiting, patiently. In no hurry.

Waiting for what, I wasn't quite sure.

This was so messed up. I'd come looking for a relationship, I hoped—one that would last a while—but I couldn't shake the whole Ebonwatch thing, and it had me confused. And now, overlying it all was a sense of inevitable doom. They would die out, this amazing, breathtaking race of non-humans. It broke my heart.

His hand squeezed my shoulder, bringing me back to an awareness of my body. I inhaled, catching a hint of sandalwood and pine.

My flesh, reminded of why I'd come here, responded. I was sure he could tell.

My body had no doubts or hesitations. It didn't care that we were sitting on a bench in the middle of campus, with people all around.

I swallowed. Desire was welling up so strongly that it overrode my confusion. I would have given into it right then if not for the thread of caution that I had learned early on never to let go of.

I couldn't help the memories that flashed through my

thoughts, and I knew that Lomen was aware of them.

Sitting on the bleachers at a football game, knowing something was going on beneath them. I could hear the muffled thumps of a beating, the savage voices muttering, "Faggot!" A glimpse between the seats and I knew who it was: a boy I'd admired. A boy who didn't show up to class the next day, or the next week.

I had made no move to help.

I had known that to do so would only focus their rage on me as well. But it still wasn't right.

Lomen's hand slid from my shoulder. I sensed something briefly—dismay? It was gone the next instant.

Your first instinct was best. We should have met at your home.

I took a ragged breath. Sat up and blinked.

Go there now. If you want me to follow, I will.

I turned my head to look at him. His gaze was soft, and made my heart rise in my chest.

If you prefer some time alone, I will understand. The choice is yours.

I stared at him a long time. It would probably be wise to do as he suggested. Take some time to calm down, get my thoughts in order.

No. I'm tired of being alone.

Then you need not be.

He stood and shouldered a pack. It was like any other student's backpack, heavy with books. Didn't go with his clothes at all.

A memory flashed into my thoughts—a black backpack with Lobo stickers, one corner steeping in a puddle of blood.

I gave my head a shake and collected my own pack. Lomen stepped away from the bench, motioning to me to lead.

We didn't talk, in any way. I was too wound up to trust myself to discuss all the potentials before us out in public, and way too tense for chatting about the weather. I could feel Lomen's presence, like a sphere of warmth radiating from him. I wanted to stay close to that, to bask in it.

We strolled across campus, passing other students, teachers, staff. I kept noticing couples; mostly boy-girl, but there was one flamboyant pair of girls marching defiantly arm in arm along campus.

Good for them.

By the time we crossed Central Avenue and headed into the student ghetto, my feelings had settled down a lot. I was still on edge, and hyper-aware of Lomen, but I was no longer on the verge of meltdown from emotional overload.

We walked past the first couple of blocks of restaurants and stores, and into the residential area shaded by old elm trees. I led him to my apartment, unlocked the door, and invited him in with a gesture. He gave a small nod and a smile, and went in, looking around the front room.

A tiny kitchen and a bathroom separated this from my bedroom. It was nothing fancy, but it was in an older building, single-story, with hardwood floors, which I liked. I had dreams of setting it up with classy, streamlined, modern furnishings, but for now the décor was student yard-sale.

"Want something to drink?" I offered. "Glass of water?"

"Yes, thank you."

"Have a seat."

I waved him toward the furniture—a futon couch and a couple of weather-beaten armchairs—and went to the kitchen. My hands shook a little as I put ice into two glasses for us. I filled them with filtered water, reminding myself to breathe slowly.

Lomen had chosen one of the chairs. He was sitting in it cross-legged, gazing over his shoulder out the front window. The trees outside cast dappled light over the little rectangle of lawn shared by all the apartments in the unit.

I set the glasses down on the coffee table, moved my laptop to the table I used for a desk, and sat on the futon. Lomen picked up his glass and drank deeply. I watched his throat move as he swallowed, then closed my eyes. If we were going to talk, I had to avoid getting distracted by his body.

"Yes, we should talk," he said.

I reached for my own glass and took a swig, then kept it in

my hands. The ice chill kept me focused.

"I have a question," Lomen added. "I understand the memory of fear that you showed me, but is such hatred common among humans?"

I looked at him. "Don't you watch the news?"

"On TV? No. I am not very up to date, I fear."

"I thought you were fascinated by humans."

He gave me a sidelong grin that shot straight to my groin. I took another swig of ice water.

"I am," he said, "but until this past year I have not had much to do with humans for several centuries."

Jeez.

"Um, yeah. It's a big issue for us right now—gay rights. One of the major things our culture is debating. There's a lot of hate."

"I see. Then I understand your caution."

"My turn." I took a deep breath. "Are you gay?"

He met my gaze. "That description is...limiting, I believe."

"You're bi?"

He leaned back in his chair, gazing into the distance with a soft smile. "In the course of a long life, one has many opportunities to experiment. There are not many that I have declined."

Oh.

"My general inclination is to have one partner at a time, if that makes a difference."

I nodded. One at a time was good for me.

We fell silent. I stared at my glass. Was I really hoping for a relationship with this...alien being? More and more, I was realizing that's what he was.

I felt his gaze. He was waiting for me to make a move.

That was nice. My looks often attracted the alpha type. Not that I objected to alphas, except that I hadn't had much luck with them. They never seemed to want what I wanted.

On the other hand, I couldn't really call Lomen a beta. He was neither. Or both. He defied classification.

I glanced at him. He was watching me, a slight smile of

amusement on his lips.

"Don't think too much, Steven."

I looked away, feeling my cheeks start to burn.

He stood, pulled the curtains on the front window closed, and came to me in two steps. Reached a hand out for my glass. I gave it to him, and he set it down, then sat beside me. I moved over to make room for him.

"Let me show you something," he said, holding out his hand.

I wiped my clammy hand on my jeans and put it in his. Immediately I sensed him. Had to close my eyes.

It's hard to describe how it feels. Like lying in bed next to someone, but it's your souls, not your bodies. We were close, just touching. My hand tingled; his felt hot.

This is how you shield. Follow me.

Our contact deepened. I was aware of his breathing—slower than mine. Then a brightness above my/his head. Light poured down, and he welcomed it. It came in through the top of our skull and spread through our body, out to the tip of each digit. Then it seemed to congeal in the middle of our chest, and flow out again, this time surrounding us.

For a while we were still. Just basking, enjoying the light. Gradually he drew away, enough for me to become aware of my body as separate from his. The feeling of the light was still there.

That was all? White light?

It takes practice. You might do it each morning when you wake, and at night before going to sleep. And any time you expect to be in company with ælven.

I sighed. This would take some getting used to.

His hand slid from beneath mine. I caught it and opened my eyes.

My body had not forgotten. I stared into his eyes, noticing flecks of gold in the green. The lids drooped slightly as he smiled, then leaned toward me.

His lips brushed my cheek and I caught a whiff of sandalwood. Did ælven wear cologne?

It's soap. Madóran makes it.

Who?

One of our investors. You will meet him eventually.

His lips closed on the corner of my mouth and I took a sharp breath. Then a real kiss, and I was lost.

To kiss with body and soul at once is indescribably wonderful. My whole being rose up to accept his welcome. The taste and smell of him were intertwined with emotions that I knew weren't just mine. The relief was mine; from him came a quiet joy that blew away all my anxiety.

My phone rang.

Crap. Ignore it.

Are you sure?

For answer I wrapped my arms around his neck and kissed him harder. He responded with enthusiasm and silent laughter that echoed through my heart.

A buzz goosed me: the phone again, signaling a text.

I could have screamed in frustration. Lomen released me and nudged my hand toward my pocket. I took out the phone, blinking as I tried to read the text through a haze of mixed sensations.

CAERAN WANTS 2 MEET EARLY - OMW 2 GET
U

I turned the phone to show it to Lomen, though he'd already seen it through my eyes. He took it from my hand and set it on the coffee table.

There is little time, then.

He moved to the floor and reached for my fly.

"Wha—what are you—"

You need release.

He slid my jeans down my hips in one swift movement. I felt his hands on me, then his mouth, and then I stopped thinking.

He was very good.

He teased me, bringing me to the brink of climax and then commanding, *Wait.*

I held as still as I could, trembling, the echo of my own flesh in my mouth. He waited what seemed like forever, then slowly began again.

Twice more he told me to wait. The third time I couldn't hold it. He let me feel everything he could feel: the taste of myself, the pounding of my heart, the rough carpet under his knees and his arms tight around my hips.

Sensory overload.

Gradually, as I lay with the throbbing ebbing away, I became aware of myself as separate again. Lomen gently pulled back, with both body and mind, but he kept a light touch in my thoughts. Unlike every other encounter I'd had, there was no sense of loss, no let-down, because he was still with me.

I felt him stand, heard the rattle of ice in his glass and his footsteps going toward the kitchen. Tasted an echo of ice water. Swallowed.

I couldn't sit up yet. I just wanted to lie there, glowing, but I knew Amanda could show up any minute.

Lomen came back and sat on the futon beside me. I opened my eyes. He held out a damp cloth.

"Thank you," I said as I took it. It was warm.

"What about you?" I asked.

He smiled. *I can be patient.*

Outside, a car pulled up and its engine turned off. Lomen went to the window while I frantically cleaned myself up.

It's Amanda.

OK.

He took the cloth from me the moment I was finished with it, and headed back to the bathroom. I pulled my clothes together, then pushed myself to my feet just as the broken doorbell clanked.

Lomen returned, glanced at me, then opened the door. Amanda came in, all bluster.

"Sorry, guys, but Caeren wants everyone there as soon as possible." She sounded out of breath.

"What's happened?" Lomen asked.

"You haven't heard? Jeez, it's all over the news!"

"What?" I said.

"There's been another killing."

Lomen and I both started talking at once, and Amanda held up her hands. "I'll tell you about it in the car. Let's go."

Lomen grabbed his pack, and I picked mine up, too. We followed her to her car. Lomen climbed in the back and I got in next to Amanda.

"It happened last night," she said as she drove east. "Near the business school, which has got me freaked out."

My throat was dry, and I was having trouble concentrating. "Same M.O.?"

"No, but Caeran went by the scene and he said there was alben khi there."

"Wait, what?"

"Energy," Lomen said. *I'll explain later.* "There's another alben in the area, then."

"Couldn't it be the same one?" I asked.

"No. The first one would not be hungry again so soon."

"Yeah, and this time the victim's a guy," Amanda said.

I'm not following this.

Alben often hunt the opposite sex, because they can use sexual allure to bring their prey closer.

I thought about that. *That doesn't mean it has to be boy-girl.*

True, but the majority of humans are heterosexual. Alben tend to hunt accordingly.

Amanda pulled up in front of Len and Caeran's house. We hurried up the path and Amanda went straight in without knocking or ringing.

Caeran was sitting in the living room, dressed in black jeans and a green caftan-looking shirt. A savory smell wafting from the kitchen made my stomach growl. I had sort of forgotten about lunch.

"I've called Madóran," Caeran said, looking at Lomen. "Bironan and Faranin are on their way. They should be here tomorrow."

"Does Savhoran know?" Lomen asked.

"I called him," Amanda said.

"He will join us after dark, and will try to bring Pirian," Caeran said.

Feeling cross, I glanced at Lomen. *Who are all these people?*

Members of the clan. Pirian is in Clan Ebonwatch with Savhoran. Guarding against alben is their traditional duty.

Will they bring more people from Ebonwatch?

At the moment, they are all of Ebonwatch.

Great. Clan Ebonwatch consisted of two guys? This was the start-up's mighty namesake?

It is an expression of hope.

The others had fallen silent. Amanda was messing with her phone. Caeran was watching us, and I had the feeling he knew we were talking.

I did a little white-light shield thing, feeling silly. Better late than never.

Caeran stood and went to a cabinet by the fireplace. He opened it, revealing a flatscreen TV. He turned this on, changed the channel, then muted it, bringing the control with him back to his chair.

Earliest news was at 4:30, unless they did a breaking news flash. I wondered what time it was. I'd forgotten my phone.

It wasn't like me to be so scattered—but then, I'd just had my brain rearranged by psychic sex. And Lomen was on the couch just a couple of feet away, and we had very unfinished business.

"Amanda said you'd been to the scene of last night's killing," Lomen said.

Caeran nodded. "The body was gone, but there were still traces of khi. It was a ... vicious killing."

"You are certain it was done by an alben?"

"Oh, yes. One who likes knives, apparently."

"Oh, great!" said Amanda. Her hand went to her neck, taking me back to the summer day when I'd pressed a handful of paper towels to the bleeding slash there.

"Most alben use knives in their hunting," Lomen said.

"This one used it more than necessary." Caeran glanced at Amanda, then looked back at Lomen. "There was a crowd of onlookers at the scene, so I was able to stay and pick up a little from the thoughts of the police. The killer took her time."

"How do you know it was a woman?" I asked.

He looked at me. "I'm not certain the killer was female, but it is a reasonable assumption, given that the victim was male. It is not common for alben to torment their prey, but in this case she did so, using her knife. The police were horrified."

I took a slow breath. "Um, forgive me for asking what may be a stupid question," I said. "I'm sorry to hear about another killing, but why does it necessitate this meeting?"

Caeran turned to face me. "For our own safety and that of our clan. We are in the process of establishing a territory, if you will. When an alben begins to hunt here, we take action to discourage them."

"How?"

"The first step is to find them," Lomen said.

"Yes," Caeran said. "Savhoran and Pirian patrol the city, but it is a large area. Until these alben are located, they will need help."

He went to the kitchen and returned with a tray of glasses and a pitcher of tea. I accepted a glass and chugged half of it. Caeran refilled it without commenting.

The cold hit my belly hard enough to make me shiver. I set the glass on the coffee table and leaned back.

"So," I said, "if I understand correctly, this is the third time in a year that alben have started hunting here. What's attracting them to Albuquerque? And to UNM in particular?"

Caeran and Lomen exchanged a glance before Caeran answered. "A university campus is an ideal hunting ground, a concentrated population of young and healthy adults who are enjoying an independence that is new to them."

"Less likely to be cautious than older humans," Lomen added.

"As to what brings the alben to this city," Caeran said, "they tend to travel. Too many attacks in one area arouse the attention of police. It may be that the interchange of two interstates makes it more likely for them to pass through the city."

Lomen shifted on the couch, and I saw his brow tighten in a frown.

"But the first two alben who came here were looking for Madóran," Caeran added.

"Madóran?" Lomen had mentioned that name earlier.

"A friend of ours. We came here seeking him ourselves."

I glanced at Lomen. "Popular guy. You think these new alben are looking for him, too?"

"We have no way of knowing."

Caeran's attention shifted to the TV, which had just flashed a "breaking news" slide. He turned on the volume.

Video of yellow tape, on campus, surprised me. My gut tightened. There was nothing to see—a few police standing around—and apparently not much to tell. The voiceover gave the brief details I'd already heard from Amanda and Caeran, without mentioning the knife work.

The news shifted to another story. Caeran muted the TV.

I shook my head. "I don't see how we're going to find them. There are almost a million people in Albuquerque."

"A million humans," Caeran said.

"So? Except for the white hair, an alben looks a lot like a human, and the hair can be changed."

"But their khi marks them as different."

Khi again. Energy, Lomen had said.

"You mean chi?" I asked, avoiding the hissing consonant of the ælven word.

"The concept of chi is based on khi, yes," Caeran said. "Ælven khi is distinct from that of humans, and alben khi differs from ælven."

"What are you going to do? Walk around campus looking at everyone's khi?"

A brief look of impatience crossed Caeran's face. "The alben will not return to the campus until they hunger again. Meanwhile we will search the places where they are likely to seek shelter. Unless they are unusually integrated with human culture, they will be limited by lack of identification. They are unlikely to have funds other than cash. This narrows our field."

"Well, I'll help however I can, but it sounds like more than a handful of us can do."

Everyone was silent. I had said something wrong.

"You cannot help us, Steven," Lomen said quietly.

"Sure I can."

"No," Amanda said. Her voice sounded choked.

Caeran turned to me. "I am sorry, Steven. You are too vulnerable to assist us in this—search, and far too valuable to be risked. We must ask you to remain here."

"Look, I'm no prize fighter but I'm not a wimp either."

"It is not a question of your strength," Caeran said.

"No human can resist an alben," Amanda said flatly.

I turned to her, surprised. "What are they, supermen?"

"Compared to us, yeah. They can control us with a thought." She drew her knees up and hugged them. "The freeze. You don't even have time to yell for help, usually. There's no way for us to fight it. They're too powerful. They can even control ælven, sometimes."

"That depends on the relative strength of the individuals," Caeran said.

I looked at Lomen.

"Yes," he said, looking unhappy. "They use khi to control their human prey. It is against the ælven creed to do so, but most alben do not honor the creed."

I remembered Kimberly, lying in her own blood. No sign of

struggle, except the broken glasses, but that could have happened when she hit the ground.

A door in the south wall opened and Len came in, carrying car keys and her pack. Caeran got up to greet her, then turned to me. "This has reminded me that we should allow Steven to bring some clothing and whatever else he needs to the house. It's best to go get these things before dark. I can drive you now," he said.

"Uh...I'm OK at my place, really."

Caeran shook his head. "I am sorry, but until we locate the alben you will be safer here. Amanda, you will stay as well."

"Yeah, I brought a bag over."

"Excellent." Caeran looked at Len, who handed him her keys.

I was thinking about refusing. These people had turned my life upside-down already; now they wanted me to move in with them?

Please go with Caeran, Steven. He wants to talk to you.

I looked at Lomen. His face didn't show much, but his eyes were pinched with concern. I would do pretty much anything to wipe away that anxiety.

I got up and followed Caeran through the door Len had come in, which led to a garage. We got into a Lexus sedan and the garage door rolled up. Caeran seemed at ease, and I wondered how long he'd been driving.

Strange, because he looked so similar to Lomen that they could pass for twins, but I wasn't attracted to Caeran at all. I wasn't repulsed by him either, mind. Ælven are easy on the eyes. But sitting in a car with Caeran just made me miss Lomen.

The sun was still up but it was definitely slanting. The breeze had grown stronger, tossing stray leaves around in the gutters.

"You may be wondering who elected me president," Caeran said as he drove toward my apartment. His voice was a little lower and throatier than Lomen's, I noticed. "I was the one who chose to act, is all. When we first arrived here, one of our clan was ill. I knew that Madóran, who is a healer, might be living north of this city. Indeed, we decided to come to New Mexico because Madóran had done so, centuries earlier."

Centuries. They tossed that word around pretty casually.

"So I went to the library at UNM to look for information that would help us find him."

"And met Len."

Caeran nodded, and a smile softened his face. He was silent as he concentrated on turning right onto a busy one-way street.

"She helped us find Madóran. He lives well to the north, past Mora. Do you know where that is?"

"Not really. I'm a Cruces kid."

He accepted that without comment, and I wondered if he knew what it meant. My home town, Las Cruces, is in southern New Mexico.

"Sadly, we were not the only ones seeking Madóran," he continued. "A former lover of his, one who had become alben, also came here looking for him."

"The first campus killer?"

"Yes."

"The one who attacked Len."

Caeran inhaled deeply. "Yes. And others, including Madóran."

"What happened to her?"

"Him." Caeran pulled up to the curb outside my apartment, turned off the engine, then turned to face me. "We killed him."

Holy crap.

"We do not kill lightly. The burden of taking an ælven life, or a human life, weighs heavily on us. Gehmanin left us no choice."

"What about the second one?" I asked, my voice rough.

"Kanna. She followed Gehmanin here. Their relationshp was...complicated. Kanna fixed upon Amanda shortly after she arrived." He ran a hand over his face. "That was our doing, I fear. Len and I convinced Amanda to join us in donating blood. Kanna spotted her as she was leaving the donation center. The scent of fresh blood was on her, and Kanna was hunting."

"Bad timing," I said. "Not your fault."

He shook his head. "It began that way, but Kanna soon learned that we were involved in Gehmanin's death. She decided to kill Amanda in order to hurt us."

"So you killed her, too?"

"Savhoran killed her. She was hunting him and Amanda. It was self-defense."

A gust of wind buffeted the car. "What about these new ones? Are they looking for Mad—Mad—"

"Madóran. I hope not. We won't know until we learn who they are."

"Are you going to kill them?"

He hesitated, but didn't deny it. "Only if we have no other choice. We will first try to convince them to hunt elsewhere."

Hunt elsewhere? Where? How far away was far enough? Santa Fe? Denver? They would still be killing humans.

"But before we can do that we must find them." Caeran looked at his hands, lying in his lap. "I know it is annoying for you to be asked to leave your home. I promise you it will be temporary. Your safety is our main concern."

"Honestly, I don't see how your house is safer than mine. You'll be out hunting these alben."

"No. I will stay to watch over you and Len and Amanda while the others hunt."

My first thought was why couldn't Lomen stay, but that was selfish. Len and Caeren were an established couple. And it was their house.

"We should go in," Caeran said. "If you have more questions, I will answer them while you pack."

I opened my door and got out, looking around for any lurking homicidal alben. The wind was getting stronger, and the sky had clouded over. The air smelled like rain—life-giving rain, always welcome in the desert. I sucked a deep breath, then led Caeran up to my door.

My neighbor, a freshman with freckles and a Marilyn Monroe figure, came up the path at the same time. She welcomed me with a big "I like you" smile, then stopped in her tracks when she saw Caeran, eyes wide and her mouth making that classic "O" shape that drives straight guys crazy. I gave her a non-committal wave and unlocked the door.

Inside, I stood looking around for a minute, wondering what to take. I picked up my phone from the coffee table. The futon's cushions were rumpled, reminding me of what had happened there earlier. I clamped a white light lid on that memory and headed for my bedroom.

Caeran followed me and watched while I pulled a gym bag out of my closet and stuffed some random clothes into it. Clean underwear, socks, t-shirts. Extra pair of jeans.

How do you pack for going into a bomb shelter?

I fetched a plastic grocery bag from the kitchen and filled it with toiletries. No telling when I'd be back so I took shampoo and shaving stuff. Added that to the gym bag and pulled a pillow out of my bed.

Entertainment. I carried the bag and pillow out to the living room and collected my laptop. "You have wireless?" I asked Caeran.

He nodded. So books and movies would be available. I went to the shelf that held my textbooks.

"We'll fall behind in classes."

"No, you can keep going to class. Alben shelter during the day. It is only at night that you are vulnerable."

I met Caeran's gaze. "So that part of the myth is true? Sunlight kills them?"

His mouth twisted. "It hurts them. I think they'd have to be restrained and exposed for a long while to suffer fatal damage."

He looked as though the idea bothered him. For a killer, he didn't seem so ruthless.

I piled my textbooks next to the laptop and stared at the heap, wondering what I was forgetting.

"You might check your refrigerator for food that could spoil," Caeran said gently.

I went into the kitchen, annoyed that he'd read my thoughts. I practiced white-lighting while I filled another grocery bag with fruit, salad stuff, yogurt, and a quart jug of milk that was mostly full. I brought this out to the living room and added it to the pile.

"I'd like to take my bike. Your place is farther from campus."

Caeran glanced toward the window. "We'll come back for it, if that's all right."

The darkness outside was mostly from the gathering storm, but it made me nervous and obviously bothered Caeran as well. Those alben probably loved stormy weather.

Caeran helped me carry my stuff to the Lexus. We piled it all in the back seat, went back to lock the door of my apartment, then ducked into the car just as the rain broke. Caeran drove back to his house with the wipers on high. I was grateful that the house had a garage that wasn't full of junk, and therefore actually had room for the car.

The smell of dinner set my mouth to watering the minute I stepped in the house. Lomen met me with a smile and took my laptop and pillow from my arms.

"I'll show you where you'll be sleeping."

He led me down the hall and into a bedroom. At first I thought it was a guest room, then I noticed some personal touches on the nightstand: a small deer carved out of wood, a candle in a pottery holder, a deck of playing cards.

"This is my room," Lomen said.

A tingle went down my arms. "Shouldn't I let Amanda have it?"

"I offered it to her first. It was her room when she lived here, but she insists she prefers the couch."

Caeran brought in my textbooks and put them on a small desk in one corner of the room. Lomen set my laptop beside them.

"Dinner's ready," Caeran said.

I left my bag and pillow on the bed and followed them to the little dining nook off the living room. The table there had been set with five places, a cozy fit for a table more suited for four. Caeran and Len brought out dishes of food and put them on the sideboard. The heavenly smell was coming from a roast chicken. There were roasted potatoes and carrots, fresh green beans, and a big bowl of salad.

At Len's invitation I grabbed a plate—stoneware, looked hand-made—and filled it, then took one of two chairs sharing a side of the table. Lomen took the other. No one said anything. Not so much as a raised eyebrow.

"Savhoran called," Amanda said. "He's heading out to find Pirian."

Caeran frowned. "The sun hasn't set."

"He said it's worth the risk." She didn't sound happy about it.

"We saw the weather forecast while you were gone," Len said. "This is a big storm and it's moving slowly. He should be all right."

"Is he on the bike?" Caeran asked.

Amanda stabbed a carrot. "Yeah."

Motorcycle, I assumed. Dangerous on wet pavement.

I didn't comment. I was too busy eating. Everything was fantastic, and not just because I was hungry.

I chewed a mouthful of green beans with butter and almond slivers, thinking. All these people had just been acquaintances of mine two days ago. Now here I was, committed to a business contract and spending the night in one of their homes. How had it happened so fast?

I had followed my instinct. I'd learned to trust it years ago. Lomen was a big part of why I'd agreed, but if there had been any warning bells, I'd have walked.

I poured more lemony gravy over my chicken and poured some white light through my brain, then asked myself if vampires with a taste for knives did not constitute a warning bell.

Apparently not.

I would spend some time sorting out my feelings later, I decided. For now, I was reveling in the sensory pleasures of a really good meal that I hadn't had to cook or pay for, and the tantalizing buzz of sitting next to Lomen. Now and then I caught a tiny hint of his sandalwood soap.

"Can you tell me about Madóran?" I said to the table in general.

Caeran looked at me. "He is a very old soul. Older than any of us."

"You said he was a healer."

"He's an *amazing* healer," Amanda said. "A curandero, too. Len's studying with him."

"I'm learning ælven healing techniques more than herbalism, but yeah. He's phenomenal at both." Len smiled at me. "You'll meet him in a couple of weeks. He's coming down for Evennight."

"Unless we haven't found the alben by then," Caeran said. "He should not come near the city while they are here."

"You're pretty protective of him," I said.

"He has had grief enough in the past year."

"They're protective of the whole clan," Amanda said. "You'll get used to it."

I was still stuck on Evennight. It sounded familiar but I couldn't dredge up a reference.

We talked about safe subjects until we'd all eaten our fill. I wanted to go back for seconds, but my stomach said no.

Caeran got up and started taking leftover food to the kitchen. I stood and collected Lomen's and my plates while Amanda took the rest. When we'd cleared the table I started organizing the sink.

"You don't have to do that," Len said.

"Least I can do. That was a great meal."

"Caeran cooked it. He's good with roasting."

I was good with a can opener, but couldn't claim much more. "These are beautiful dishes," I remarked, pausing to admire the leaves twining along the edge of a plate.

"Thanks," Len said. "Madóran made them. Now, shoo. I'll make coffee."

I wandered into the living room. Caeran was in what I gathered was his chair. Lomen was on the couch. I joined him.

"You mentioned a couple of others were coming," I said to Caeran.

He nodded. "Bironan and Faranin."

"They here in town?"

"No, they live on Madóran's land. They will not arrive until tomorrow, most likely."

I looked at Lomen. I didn't like the idea of him going out alone tonight, looking for these alben.

Savhoran will be hunting them as well. And probably Pirian.

Dammit. Do I have to constantly do the white-light thing?

You'll get used to it.

The mental contact increased my physical awareness of him. I took a deep breath and thought through the steps of shielding again.

Good.

But it didn't work. You can still hear me.

While I maintain contact, yes. You are shielded from Caeran, though.

Caeran picked up the remote and turned on the TV, then muted it and started changing channels.

How can you tell?

You have shifted your khi.

Oh, yeah?

A smile curved Lomen's lips, though his gaze was on the TV.

You are learning very quickly. I look forward to teaching you more.

My throat went dry. Feeling paranoid, I shielded yet again.

Tonight?

I doubt it. I will probably be out all night.

Do you have classes tomorrow?

One.

When are you going to sleep?

His lips twitched again. Looked like he was trying not to laugh. I realized I was staring at him and shifted my gaze to the TV. Kids in bright-colored clothes; a commercial for some kind of snack food.

We do not sleep, Steven. We rest—rather like your meditation—but we don't need to sleep.

Damn. Why couldn't I have been born one of you?

I felt an echo of sadness, then it was gone like a stray scent.

OK, I wouldn't think things like that. Shouldn't remind him of my mortality. Or remind me, for that matter.

There was pain out ahead. Inevitable pain. Far away right now, but it would arrive someday.

Len came in from the kitchen, carrying her cell phone. She sat between me and the end of the couch near Caeran, unceremoniously pushing me aside. I shifted closer to Lomen.

"You wanted to compare class schedules," she said to me.

"Oh. Right."

Took me a minute to remember why. My head was so not in the space of Ebonwatch's project.

I got out my phone and pulled up my schedule. Amanda and Lomen did the same.

We compared schedules and found no crossover with Amanda, who was taking business classes plus one humanities course (French lit, bleh). Len and I were both heavy on science, though her emphasis was pre-med. Lomen had two classes in common with Len. Mine were all over the map, since I had been trying to figure out which direction to go.

"OK, I don't need the pharma," I said. "I could maybe drop chemistry."

"Won't we need pharma to look for treatments?" Len asked.

"Not until later, if at all. But you're right, I'll keep it. Maybe add microbiology and drop the physics major."

I stifled a sigh. I liked physics, but it probably wouldn't be needed for the project. I'd definitely be quitting my job, then. Professor Warner would not be pleased.

I surfed to UNM's website and pulled up the course catalog. While I was looking up biomedical, I heard an engine pull up outside and shut off.

Caeran looked up. "Savhoran."

"Alone?" Len asked.

"No."

The room was suddenly tense. I shielded again, as if that would protect me.

The door opened and Savhoran came in, rain dripping from his black leathers. He had a motorcycle helmet in one hand, and held the door open for his companion.

My gut clenched as I saw the white hair, soaked with rain, and the coal-black eyes. Campus killer. I'd only glimpsed Amanda's attacker and she'd been female, but this guy rang the same bell.

It was more than just appearance. He felt *deadly*.

= 6 =

"Pirian," Caeran said, standing. "Thank you for coming."

This was Pirian, the other half of Ebonwatch? A virtuous vampire?

He didn't look virtuous. He looked scary as hell. My hindbrain was screaming at me to flee.

Len got up. "Something hot to drink? There's coffee and tea."

Savhoran smiled at her and set his helmet on a rug by the door. "Tea would be welcome, thank you."

"There's some salad, too, if you'd like."

Savhoran shook his head, unzipping his leather jacket. Len turned to Pirian, who gazed flatly back at her. She went into the kitchen.

Caeran hung up Savhoran's jacket and the long, black coat that Pirian peeled off. Underneath he wore a loose cotton shirt and what looked like suede pants. He was slim, almost gaunt. If he were human I'd have suspected bulimia.

He glanced at me and I couldn't help looking away. I focused on my phone, trying to remember my place in the maze of course descriptions.

Savhoran joined Amanda, sitting on the arm of her chair. Caeran pulled a chair from the dining nook and placed it on the other side of Amanda's chair for the alben.

Not an alben, I told myself, but in his presence it sounded like a philosophical distinction and possibly wishful thinking. This guy drank human blood to stay alive. I felt extremely rabbit-like.

"Savhoran has told you of our concerns?" Caeran asked.

I didn't look, but got the impression that Pirian nodded. "I can tell you that at least one of them came from the east, traveling by car." His voice was low and a bit gravelly.

"How do you know?" Caran asked.

"I felt their khi. I often watch the traffic in the canyon."

I wondered why. Shopping for dinner?

He meant Tijeras Canyon, the pass through the mountains that I-40 ran through east of Albuquerque.

"When was this?" Caeran said.

Pirian hesitated. I glanced sidelong at him. He was staring at the ceiling, thinking.

"Three nights ago."

"Then they began to hunt right away," said Lomen. "Two killings in two nights."

Len brought out a tray with a bunch of mugs and a teapot, and set it on the coffee table. She poured a mug and handed it to Savhoran. "Anyone else want tea?"

Caeran was already pouring for himself. No one else spoke. Len went back in the kitchen. I thought wistfully about joining her there, then did a fresh white-light shield.

"If they came from the east into the city, they might have camped in the bosque," Lomen said.

"They might not be together," Caeran said.

"True, but the bosque is still a good place to begin the search," said Savhoran, who'd been pretty silent. "There are a limited number of bridges crossing the river. If they passed over one, we might find traces of their khi."

"Kanna camped in the bosque," Lomen added.

"Briefly," Caeran said.

Len returned with another tray, this time bearing a coffee pot, sugar, cream, and some spoons. She started pouring and handing around the coffee.

I was stuffed, but it smelled good, and the mug warmed my hands while I sipped. It was beautiful: hand-made pottery, glazed in a soft, pale green and lighter weight than it looked, similar to the dishes we'd eaten from.

"It is natural for our kind to be drawn to a forest," Lomen said. "I propose we begin searching there."

Savhoran gave a nod, then looked at Pirian. Everyone else looked at him too.

Pirian shrugged one shoulder. "As you wish."

"You disagree?" Caeran asked.

Pirian's gaze shifted to him. "I think it likely to be a waste of time. They have fed; they have probably already found shelter. They will rest for a few days."

Len brought another chair from the dining nook and set it next to Caeran's. She sat and picked up her coffee mug.

"Where did you shelter when you first came here?" Caeran asked Pirian.

"I didn't stop here. I continued north."

Amanda shifted in her chair. Savhoran put a hand on her thigh.

"And now?" Caeran's voice was quiet, but I thought I heard a hint of challenge.

Pirian's eyes narrowed. "I prefer the mountains to the bottomland."

Caeran nodded and sipped his tea.

"If we are to search, we had best begin," said Savhoran. He drained his mug and set it on the coffee table. "Thank you for the tea, Len."

She smiled. "Any time."

Savhoran stood. Amanda handed him her car keys. He squeezed Amanda's hand, then went to the door and picked up his helmet.

Caeran followed and fetched coats. Pirian stood, leisurely, and turned his head to look straight at me.

So Caeran and his friends have a new pet.

I flinched, unable to help physically recoiling from the unpleasant contact. His soul did not feel beautiful. There was definitely something wrong.

He dropped the contact, much to my relief. I sat frozen, watching him put on his coat, which still looked wet. He didn't seem to notice, or maybe he didn't care.

Steven?

I almost cried out with relief. I flung myself into Lomen's mental embrace.

What happened?

He spoke to me.

Lomen glared at Pirian. *What did he say?*

Nothing important. An insult.

Lomen stood, and for a moment I feared he'd start a fight. Caeran was helping Savhoran into his coat.

"Success to you," Caeran said.

Savhoran smiled as he and Pirian went out, and I couldn't help wondering if he would become like Pirian. He seemed nice enough, now, and Amanda liked him. What would the disease do to him, long-term?

Don't let Pirian bother you. You probably won't see much of him.

OK.

I didn't want to argue; not then. Lomen was leaving, going out with them. I had a hard time thinking about him in Pirian's company. I hoped he wouldn't do anything rash. I shielded again, then looked at him.

Be careful.

He smiled. *Don't worry. I know better than to respond to Pirian's taunts. He is angry at his fate.*

He felt wrong. He felt bad.

It's the curse.

Lomen went to the closet and pulled out a heavy suede coat, slung it over his shoulders, and went out. Caeran gently closed the front door behind him, then returned to his chair.

Awkward silence. I glanced down at my phone, still in my hands. It had gone dark.

"There's dessert," Caeran said.

My throat tightened. I shook my head and stood. "Will you guys excuse me? I've got homework."

Silence followed me down the hall, along with the feeling that they'd be discussing me the minute I closed the door of Lomen's room. I didn't care. I needed to be alone.

I sat on the bed and poked my phone to wake it up, stared at it until I realized I wasn't registering the words. Set it aside and rubbed my eyes.

What was I doing here?

I felt exhausted, terrified, confused.

Hopeful.

I lay back and threw an arm over my eyes. Thought over the past couple of days, everything that had happened.

It had started with finding a body.

No. It had started when I texted Amanda. That message had set all this in motion.

And when I sent the text I'd wondered—hoped—it would lead to my seeing Lomen.

So face it, he was the reason I was here. Was he worth it?

Oh, hell yes.

We were just at the start of something. I was thrilled, and terrified that I would screw it up. And be alone again.

I took a deep breath and sat up. Realized I hadn't turned the light on when I came in, but a soft glow warmed the room from the candle on the nightstand. Lomen must have lit it.

I looked around the room again, this time taking in small details. The walls weren't white, but a pale green, maybe sage. The candle cast a golden tint on it.

Opposite the bed stood a matching bookcase and dresser, hand-carved from pine. The bookcase held textbooks, a few small nicknacks, and two very old, leather-bound books. Their titles had once been gilded but were now so worn they were almost illegible. I didn't want to turn on the light to try to make them out, and I was afraid to handle the books in case they were fragile.

I looked at the nicknacks. There was a brass compass no bigger than a half-dollar. It looked very old, so I didn't touch it. Next to it was a metal cup decorated with grape vines, and behind that was a small portrait in a silver frame.

I carefully picked up the picture and carried it to the candle. It was a painting of a woman. An ælven; the shape of her eyes— green—and the expression on her face made me sure of it. She was dressed like something out of Shakespeare, a lot of pearls sewn onto her sleeves and a hat hiding her hair. She seemed wryly amused.

The frame looked old, now that I had it in the light. It was slightly tarnished but well cared for. There was a nick on the right side, result of some misadventure.

Had she been Lomen's lover?

I swallowed, trying to clamp a lid on the anxiety this thought raised. No sense in being jealous of her. Was she even still alive?

I put the portrait back in the shelf and went to the little desk, intending to follow through on my homework. The desk looked like the same handiwork as the bookcase and dresser, and come to think of it, the style was familiar. I'd seen something else made by the same artist. The sideboard in the dining nook?

Focus. Homework.

What day was it?

Took me a minute to remember. It was Thursday.

So, Friday. Two classes: Computational Physics and the Physics 102 class I was student-assisting. I'd be dropping them both.

I looked up the course catalog again, searching through the upper-level classes. Molecular Biology caught my eye. The biomedical track led straight into genomics, and that sounded exciting to me—right on target for the Ebonwatch project. So I'd drop both the physics class and the student-assisting job, then add Molecular Biology and the corequisite Genetics.

I hadn't put this much intense thought into my college education before, not even when I first enrolled. Despite Len's assurances that we had time, I felt an underlying urgency to get as much of the necessary science under my belt as soon as possible.

My brain was fried. I put away the laptop, got out my bag of bathroom stuff and got ready for bed. The bathroom was across the hall from Lomen's room. Someone had cleared a shelf in the medicine cabinet, so I put my toothbrush and all there, wondering how long this would be my home.

Thunder rumbled in the distance. I glanced westward. Lomen was out there somewhere, driving around in the rain. If they were searching the bosque they'd have to get out of the car. I wouldn't want to be there in a storm—those old cottonwoods dropped limbs when it got windy.

I ran through the white-light shield, then on impulse I pictured Lomen with white light around him. Figured he could use all the protection he could get.

I went back across the hall, blew out the candle, and got into bed. The sheets were the softest I'd ever felt, and the pillow smelled like Lomen.

My loins immediately started to ache, and after taking the precaution of shielding I allowed myself to remember our encounter earlier in the day. Probably stupid to think about it, because it made me horny as hell, but I couldn't help myself. I was ready for more, ready to give Lomen as much of a thrill as he'd given me, or at least to try.

I fell asleep thinking about him, and dreamed of sex. Some of it was weird vampire sex, which was disturbing.

I woke up alone.

At first I didn't remember where I was. I looked around for a clock, but there wasn't one.

I had classes. Tempting to skip them, since I'd be dropping them anyway, but I didn't want to be rude to the Prof.

I dragged my ass out of bed, saw my bag on the dresser where I'd left it. Went to get out some clothes and found a note on top of the dresser.

> *Steven -*
> *Your face in sleep is like a child's – very beautiful. I did not wish to wake you.*
> *I will meet you on campus midday, at the pond unless I hear otherwise from you. I have put my number into your phone.*
>
> *Lomen*

Ridiculous, how relieved I was by that note. I pulled on my jeans, then folded the note and shoved it deep in my pocket.

Didn't want any chance of it slipping out.

I found some more clothes and stumbled to the bathroom. Smelled coffee in the hallway, which made my stomach growl. Got myself presentable and went to the kitchen.

No one there, but the coffee pot was on the warmer and breakfast was lined up on the counter: granola, bowls, spoons, a pottery pitcher of cold milk, and a bowl of sliced fresh peaches. I helped myself, grabbed one of my yogurts from the fridge, and went out the back door.

The garden smelled rain-washed, cool and wet, but the sun was shining and it would soon be hot. Amanda was sitting under the pergola, nursing a mug of coffee.

"Morning," she said.

I nodded to her, dragged a side table in front of a chair, and didn't say anything until I'd eaten half my breakfast.

"Where are Len and Caeran?" I asked as I opened the yogurt.

"He drove her to class. He'll be back."

The coffee pot clock had said 7:45. "I have to be on campus at nine."

"Me too," Amanda said. "I'll drive you."

"Did they find anything?"

"Don't know, but we probably would have heard if they had."

I leaned back to look at the garden. The pergola's ornate carved columns caught my eye—that's where I'd seen the carving before. Whoever had done these had also made the furniture in Lomen's room.

"Who carved these?" I asked, gesturing with my spoon.

Amanda glanced at a column, then smiled. "Madóran."

"Multitalented guy."

"Oh, yes. Wait 'til you see his place—he built it himself."

"He lives up north, right?"

"Mm-hm. Guadalupita."

I'd never heard of it. Probably one of those tiny towns where the post office was in the general store.

I finished eating and took my dishes back to the kitchen, topping off my coffee before heading to my room to collect my pack.

My room. I'd settled into that fast.

Amanda was waiting for me in the living room. We headed out to her car, which was parked at the curb. The gutter was full of yellow leaves that the storm had brought down.

"So you didn't see Savhoran."

She shook her head. "I tried to wait up for him, but I fell asleep. I usually do, but I still try."

"Do you see him every day?"

"Every night, you mean?" She started the car and headed toward campus. "Not always, but most nights. In the winter when it's dark by dinner time he tries to see me every evening. It's harder in daylight savings time."

"I was under the impression you two lived together."

"Sort of. He's at our apartment about half the time. The other half he finds someplace to hole up for the day. He spends a lot of time in the bosque."

"So he would notice if some alben moved in."

"Well, it's a big forest. Since he got the bike he's able to patrol the whole length of the city every night, pretty much, but that's not a thorough search."

"So he's been patrolling there before now? Even when there weren't any alben in town?"

She paused to get across a busy intersection. "He considers it his beat, I guess you could say. He likes making sure the bosque's safe for everyone who uses it. He keeps tabs on the homeless who live there, too—and if one of them needs help, or accidentally sets a fire, he calls in a tip to the cops. He's called in four bosque fires this year. He's pretty proud of that."

"If he calls in too many tips, the cops will start suspecting him of starting the fires."

She laughed. "Yeah, we talked about that. He uses a pay phone unless it's a serious emergency."

"Is it hard for you? Being with Savhoran?"

She gave a wry smile which turned into a grin. "It's worth it."

She dropped me at the Astronomy and Physics building. I

wasn't early enough to ask for a private word with the prof, so I resigned myself to visiting his office later. Not a conversation I looked forward to.

I listened to the lecture and made random notes in my notebook, stray thoughts about Project Ebonwatch. All my powerful feelings about the effort had shifted since I'd met Pirian. Ultimately, he was the one I'd be fighting to cure. Was he worth it? Would he even be grateful?

Class let out, and I crossed Lomas and headed for the duck pond. It was warming up, and I'd forgotten to bring a hat. I stuck to the shade of trees wherever I could, hopping from pool to pool of shadow. The last stretch was across open ground. I made a beeline for the trees where I'd met Lomen the day before.

He wasn't there.

= 7 =

One hard, self-pitying swallow, then I took a grip on myself. It wasn't yet noon. Maybe Lomen was still in class, or running an errand. Don't panic.

The thought of errands reminded me there was a book on biochemistry that I wanted to check for in the library. Zimmerman was right next to the pond, so I walked over and hit the catalog. Located the book, ran up to get it, and took it to the front desk to check out.

"Hi, Steve!" said a sharp-boned girl in a black baby-doll dress that gave glimpses of bits of her tattoos: purple and green curlicues peeking out of the neckline. Her hair was black and cropped with a knife-edge cut that ran right along her jaw, then dipped to long points in front.

"Hi, Poppy. How's it going?"

"Ah, sucks since Len and Manda quit." She looked over her shoulder, then leaned toward me across the desk. "The boss is a fucking A-hole."

"I've heard that."

She pushed the book toward me. "Due in three weeks."

"Thanks."

I carried the book back to the pond. Still no Lomen.

I sat on the bench. A trio of ducks swam up, looking hopeful, then drifted away again when I failed to produce any snacks.

I took out my phone to check for a message from Lomen, and discovered my inbox was full. Mostly messages from various reporters, but one was from campus police. I returned the call, got put on hold briefly, and ended up talking to Detective Buzz-cut, whose actual name was Renniger.

"Mr. Harrison, we've been trying to reach you."

"Yeah, sorry. I just now checked messages."

"We need to talk to you. We went by your apartment but you

were out."

"I spent the evening at some friends' house."

"Could you come into the station and answer a couple of questions?"

"Um—after my next class? Gets out at three."

"OK. Where did you say you were last night?"

I closed my eyes. The second killing.

"At home. Alone."

"You didn't see anyone?"

"I was with friends earlier. One of them gave me a ride home."

"What time?"

I thought back. "Around nine."

"Can you give me his number?"

"Hers. Amanda Richards." I gave him Manda's number and made plans to apologize to her later.

"Thanks," he said. "See you at three."

"Right."

I hung up, then continued emptying my voicemail. The reporters had each called at least twice, then tapered off. Hunting leads on the second killing by now.

I became aware that I wasn't alone. Felt an instant of panic, then recognized Lomen's spice-pine scent. I looked up to see him standing beside me, holding a white take-out bag.

"Stealthy," I said, smiling.

"I didn't mean to startle you."

"It's OK." I gestured with the phone, inviting him to sit. He joined me, his thigh brushing against mine, making me want to pull his clothes off right there.

"Um. I've been catching up on messages. If you left me one I haven't gotten to it yet."

"I didn't. Are you hungry?"

"Now that you mention it."

He opened the bag. A familiar greasy aroma arose.

"Golden Fried. Haven't been there in a while." I reached in and pulled out a piece of fried chicken.

"It was convenient."

"Somehow I never imagined ælven eating fried chicken."

He laughed. "Variety is a blessing."

I loved fried chicken. We each had a couple of pieces, then tore up the biscuits and fed them to the ducks. I watched Lomen, drinking in his presence, reveling in the physical contact. A slight frown lingered on his forehead.

"Did you find anything last night?"

He sighed. "No. We checked all the bridges, and searched the central part of the bosque, but found no trace of alben khi."

"Maybe they didn't get that far. Maybe they're closer to campus."

"I fear you may be right."

I tossed my last crumb to the ducks, who arrowed in on it, beaks worrying the water.

"You tired?" I asked Lomen.

"I'll rest this afternoon. I wanted to hear your recommendations for classes. The deadline for dropping is today."

"Is it? Damn. I'd better put in my changes."

He nodded. "We can go to administration together if you have time."

"If we go now. I have a class at one."

We got up, abandoning the bench and the tantalizing near-intimacy. Packed up the chicken bag and ditched it in a trash can on the way to admin. I was horny; I would rather have gone back to my apartment for some privacy.

"I missed you," I said when no one was nearby. "Thanks for the note."

"I missed you as well."

His voice, lowered to almost a whisper, hit me straight in the loins. I kept walking, trying to keep my mind on my class schedule. I told him my thoughts about what we each should take.

"Is there not a way I could test out of some basic classes? I have studied mathematics before."

"Sure, worth asking."

We reached the admin building, which was busy with a lot of other students on the same mission. While we stood in line we discussed options, so that by the time we reached an administrator we knew what to ask for.

I put in my changes—drop physics and the SA job, and add Molecular and Cell Biology and Genetics—then waited while Lomen arranged to test out of three basic math courses, prereqs for chemistry. He had a form to fill out for each one.

"I've got ten minutes to get to my class," I said. "Meet you later?"

"Shall I come to the building?"

"Well..."

Is there a problem?

I blinked, rocked by the sudden awareness of him. It doubled my desire.

I have to go to the campus police building after class. More questions.

He frowned slightly as he wrote his address. *Should I come along?*

No. Meet at my place afterward?

All right. Be safe, Steven.

I left, smiling. So good not to be alone.

The feeling of being contact with him gradually faded, either because I was moving away or because he was gently releasing it. My instinct was to hang on but I had to trust him and let it go. He'd been doing this forever; he must know what was best.

Forever.

I shivered, remembering throwing that word at him, demanding it, early on. What had he thought of my naivete?

We had something. I wasn't sure what or how long it would last. A long time, I hoped. I didn't dare call it forever.

I reached the Physics 102 classroom and stopped in the doorway as a wall of emotion slammed into me. Maybe I was more attuned than usual, maybe talking with Lomen had somehow sensitized me, but the grief in that room hit me like a solid thing.

Heads turned. Many eyes watched me walk from the door to the front of the room, where Professor Warner was looking through a stack of papers I had graded earlier in the week. She shot me one glance over her wire-framed glasses, pushed a wisp of black hair behind her ear, then handed me the stack to pass back to the students.

I swallowed as I turned to face them. I was The One who had found her, their classmate, dead in a pool of her own coagulated blood. They didn't all know her, I was sure of that. But they had all heard.

Some of them avoided my gaze. Others stared at me, mutely seeking answers I couldn't give. A few gave me angry or accusative looks. I said nothing. To the one girl who looked up and thanked me in a whisper, her eyes filled with tears, I could only nod.

It was one of the worst gauntlets I'd ever run, and it erased any regret I had about dropping the job. When I returned to the front of the room with a half-dozen papers of kids who were absent, Professor Warner stood up.

"I'm sure you've all heard about the unfortunate demise of Miss Darrow. To those of you who knew her personally, I offer my condolences. I've been informed that there will be a memorial service in the Alumni Chapel tomorrow morning at ten."

Memorial. Good to know. I wouldn't be there.

She glanced at me again, then instructed the class to turn to the text for the lecture and was off teaching. I retreated to my usual seat in the front corner of the room and kept my gaze fixed on her.

When should I tell her? She'd get the drop notice by Monday morning, probably. I ought to say goodbye, nothing personal, thanks and all.

She'd be in her office after class. I decided to stop there on my way to the campus police building. One more errand I didn't really want to do, but maybe after today I'd be through with them.

Her lecture slid over me without registering. I knew all this stuff anyway. When I'd taken the job I had thought it would be a good review, but I'd been impatient with it almost immediately. I would be glad to leave it behind.

I tried not to keep looking at the clock on the wall. Its hands seemed to creep along. Finally, at ten 'til the hour, Professor Warner checked her watch and reminded the class of their next assignment. Everyone stood up, inhaling relief. The room emptied fast.

I took my time, and was one of the last ones out. Received a couple more looks, without animosity, from the last of the students.

I went straight to Warner's office and knocked on the frame of the open door. She'd arrived ahead of me and looked up from her desk, her face framed by wisps of hair that had escaped her ponytail.

"Steve. Come in."

I stepped in, but didn't take a chair. "I'll only be a minute. I just wanted to let you know I'm resigning the SA job. I've already dropped the class."

She pushed aside the stack of papers she'd been working on and shifted in her chair, facing me. "This is sudden. I hope it's not because of yesterday—that must have been traumatic."

"No, it isn't that. I've decided to go with biochemistry, so I'm dropping the physics major."

She sighed. "I'm sorry to hear it. You've got a lot of promise."

I'd expected her to ask me to stay. So much for me being invaluable.

"Thanks," I said.

"Well, you'll be brilliant wherever you land, no doubt." She stood and offered her hand. "Good luck, Steve."

"Thank you."

I shook hands and left. In the hall I passed two kids from the class, waiting to talk to the Prof. I nodded to them and left the building, heading northwest across campus to the police administration building.

Buzz-cut was waiting, none too patiently, in the lobby. He didn't pause for any chit-chat, but beckoned with a sharp gesture when he saw me.

"This way."

I followed him down a hallway to a room crammed with a mix of office furniture and laboratory equipment. The nice female cop I remembered was there, peering at a computer monitor on a desk piled with stacks of files. She got up, smiling, and went to an equipment shelf. I took note of the name on her badge: Ulibarri.

"Hi! Thanks for coming in. This'll just take a minute."

"Hold out your hands," said Buzz-cut.

I didn't like his tone much. I checked to see that he didn't have a pair of cuffs in his hands, then held my arms out in front of me. Officer Ulibarri shone a hand-held UV light on them, running it up my arms to my elbows.

"Turn 'em over."

I did, realizing what they were looking for.

Blood. The UV would light it up if there'd been any, even if I'd scrubbed myself. I gave Buzz-cut a narrow look.

"You're clean," said Officer Ulibarri. "Thanks."

She put the UV light away and went back to the desk.

"Can I go?" I asked, careful to keep my tone polite.

"We called your friend," said Buzz-cut. "She alibied you for Wednesday night up until 9:05 p.m., when she dropped you at your place."

So they were looking at me for the second murder.

I nodded, trying to keep calm. "I stayed in the rest of the night."

He didn't like that. "You own any knives?"

What kind of question was that?

"Sure," I said. "Kitchen knives."

"Pocket knife?"

"No."

Officer Ulibarri shot him a glance. He took a step back, making me realize he'd been crowding me.

"Just stay available in case we have more questions," he said.

"OK." I turned to go.

"And don't leave town."

I gave him a level look. "Not planning to. I have classes."

He didn't like that either, but he didn't say anything. I had the impression he just didn't like me in general. It was a chord I sometimes struck with macho types, apparently merely by existing.

I glanced at Officer Ulibarri, who gave me a wry smile. I smiled back, then headed out.

It was almost four, and the afternoon heat rose from the pavement as I walked home. I stuck to shade as much as I could, glad to leave campus behind and head into the relative quiet of the student ghetto. About three blocks from home I noticed a subtle shift in the air and turned.

Lomen was following me, several paces back. I hadn't heard his footsteps.

He grinned and joined me. "Very good."

"What did you do?"

"I stopped masking my khi."

"You can do that? Mask your khi?"

"Yes."

"How long have you been following me?"

"Since you went to the police building. I wanted to be sure you were all right."

I wished I'd known he was there, but then if Buzz-cut had seen me talking to Lomen, his opinion of me would probably have plummeted.

"I was all right," I said, starting toward home again. "Thanks for caring."

We walked together, passing through pools of shade cast by old elms and intermittent blinding sun. I felt unsettled—not annoyed, exactly, but not happy—about Lomen's tailing me. After a while I figured out that it was his sneaking up on me that bothered me the most. The fact that he'd done it so easily. Made me feel vulnerable; made me think about Kimberly and the other victim. Had they even seen it coming?

I've displeased you. I'm sorry.

No, I—it's all right.

The contact was a relief. When I could feel him, I knew things were OK. When I couldn't, my paranoid brain made up all kinds of problems.

We reached the apartment and I pulled out my keys. As I unlocked the door I wondered if the neighbors were watching, if the police had asked them about me.

I held the door for Lomen to go in, then closed it behind us. The front room was untidy from my hasty departure. I straightened a couple of books I'd left on the desk. Physics, as it happened.

I couldn't help feeling awkward. He came to me and took my pack, set it on the desk. I took a deep breath.

Would you like to see my room?

Yes.

I led him down the hall, anticipation driving away the weariness of the long, somewhat stressful day. I went in and turned on the lamp on my dresser. Didn't want the overhead light.

I watched him take in my room. The furniture was sparse; my taste runs toward austerity, I suppose. I didn't have any mementos, other than a few favorite books: *Lord of the Rings, Darkover, Sandman.*

I had cut a lot of ties when I left home. Quite intentionally. My family didn't like who I'd grown into, and I didn't like them trying to keep me from being myself. So, high school diploma in hand, I'd said goodbye and come north, hoping to find more tolerance, and maybe even some good company.

It's a nice room. Restful.

Thanks. The walls are kind of thin.

Then we'll be quiet.

A tingle ran through me. I stepped toward Lomen and he turned to me, welcoming. I brushed his hair with my fingers, something I'd been longing to do. It was silky soft.

He waited, letting me take the lead. A kiss, then another, less hesitant. I tasted his neck where it met his shoulder. Hint of salt, and a whisper of sandalwood. I drew him down to the bed.

Your turn.

I echoed what he'd done for me—undid his jeans and found him ready, which made me unbearably hot. He tasted wonderful.

It wasn't long before he pulled off his shirt and pulled me up onto the bed with him. My clothes faded away and our minds blended together along with our bodies.

Words fail to convey how amazing telepathic sex is. Those two words sound flat and technical, when the sensation is ... beyond elation. I can't do it justice.

I don't know how many times we came to the brink and he said *wait* and we both held still, aching to come. The last three times were in quick succession, I remember that. And then complete loss of control. And collapse. And glowing exhaustion.

I became aware of myself with the sensation of his hand gently stroking my back. I raised my head to look at him, found him smiling lazily. I shifted so I could kiss him. He responded with languid enthusiasm.

We should get to Caeran's soon. They will be expecting us.

I looked around him at the clock. Almost six.

OK.

I sat up, feeling a little groggy. We were still deeply connected, which meant our senses overlapped and I had two views of the bedroom, overlaid. I felt him draw back a little.

I wondered if we'd made much noise. Not that it mattered, because omigod. I'd do it again in a hot second.

He chuckled. I gave him a dirty look.

Reading my mind again.

I make no apologies. And by the way, I agree.

You're going out hunting alben again tonight?

Every night, until we find them.

Damn.

I picked up a shirt. It was Lomen's. I handed it over and looked for more clothes among the rumpled bedding.

So rest well. We have no classes tomorrow.

Boy, howdy.

We got dressed. I got out my bike, which I wanted to take to Caeran's so I'd have it for getting around.

"I can walk it," I said, collecting my pack.

No need.

We left, and I locked up. Noticed movement in the neighbor's window; the curtain fell back into place as I looked.

The day was heading toward sunset, light just getting a golden tinge and the shadows slanting long. I walked the bike to the street, got on, then glanced at Lomen.

Go ahead. I'll keep up.

I rode down the street to the corner and turned east. Lomen jogged along beside me. I didn't try to race him—we were going uphill so I wasn't going that fast—but I wasn't crawling along either. He kept pace with me, even though I was working hard by the time we were halfway to Len and Caeran's.

I glanced at him a couple of times. When we stopped for a traffic light I was breathing hard. He hadn't even broken a sweat.

Damn. You're superman.

He laughed softly. *Hardly.*

Compared to me you are.

He didn't answer that. Too close to uncomfortable truths, maybe.

I didn't apologize. Turned away from regret. Kept going.

The porch light was on at Len and Caeran's. I parked my bike by the front door and hesitated, wondering if I should knock. Lomen answered that by opening the door and walking in.

I heard the clink of plates and saw Amanda setting the table in the dining nook. Caeran was in the living room, on his feet. He turned to look at us—Lomen, then me, then Lomen again. His eyebrows went up a bit.

"Dinner's ready."

I went down the hall to the bathroom to wash my face and hands. Cold water cooled me down and gave me the chance to shield. When I came back the sideboard was full of food and Amanda and Lomen were already helping themselves.

It was lasagne, with salad and garlic bread on the side. I was hungry, and forgave myself for loading my plate. I'd had a vigorous ride up, after all.

Len poured red wine all around and raised her glass. "To Ebonwatch's success."

I drank the toast, reflecting on all the things it could mean.

"So," she said, "how was today?"

"Good," Amanda said. "I figured out how to set up the business so the seed money isn't taxable."

She rattled on a while. I listened with half an ear while I dug into my dinner. Len talked about her own classes—she liked them—and Lomen mentioned changing his schedule.

I wasn't hot to talk about my day. Not all of it had been fun, and the most fun part wasn't appropriate for dinner conversation.

"I changed my schedule, too," I said. "Dropped physics and the student-assisting job. Added molecular biology."

"Be sure and let me know about any fees," Amanda said. "And your texts. We'll pick up the cost."

Texts! I'd forgotten to check about texts for the biology and genetics classes. I'd do it after dinner.

"I talked to Madóran today," Caeran said. "We've decided that the Evennight celebration will be at his place."

Len looked unhappy. "Aw, I had it all planned!"

"I'm sorry. It is better this way—with alben in Albuquerque, we dare not risk..."

"No, you're right, of course." Len put on a smile. "We'll host Midwinter."

"If the situation here is resolved by then."

Lomen picked up his glass. "Here's to that."

We all drank. This time I noticed the wine: fruity but not sweet, dry on the finish. I reached for the bottle to read the label. Montepulciano, Italy.

"You a connoisseur?" Amanda asked.

"Hardly. Just trying to educate myself."

"Caeran picked it," Len said. "He knows a lot about wine. He's educating all of us."

I glanced at Caeran, who tossed it off with a shrug. "Madóran knows more. He actually makes wine."

"And carves furniture, and makes pottery. And soap," I said. "What else does he do?"

Amanda chortled. "Name it. He's a great cook, too."

"He's a healer," Len said, her tone suddenly serious.

"Yeah," Amanda said. "That's his main thing."

"We all have cause to be grateful for his skill at healing," Caeran said.

All their faces went sober. Amanda and Len both nodded. I met Lomen's gaze, and he gave me a tiny nod as well.

I did a quick shield, wanting to keep my reflections to myself. The conversation moved on while I thought about why they might all have needed healing. I told myself that it was in the past, that those alben were gone. But there were the new alben to deal with. The clan wouldn't be trying to track them down unless they considered them a threat.

Depressing. I tried to pay attention to what the others were saying, but I couldn't quite reconnect. By the time we'd finished eating and clearing away the leftovers, the sun was down and Lomen was on the phone with Savhoran. I sat next to him on the couch, and picked up Amanda's tablet from the coffee table.

"Can I use this?" I whispered.

She nodded. I looked up the texts for my new classes on the UNM Bookstore's website. There were ebook versions available. I'd download them later.

With a pang of envy, I handed the tablet back to Amanda, mouthing my thanks. I'd been scrimping, hoping to eventually get one, but the good ones weren't cheap.

Lomen hung up the phone and looked at Amanda. "I'm to take your car and meet them, if you don't mind."

"Sure," she said, and dug the keys out of her pocket.

He stood and took them. "See you later."

I watched him head for the door. He looked back and caught my eye, smiled a little, then went out.

"I didn't know he could drive," I said into the silence.

"He can handle an automatic," Amanda said. "Barely. What the hell, it's second-hand."

Len laughed. "Manda's teasing you," she told me. "They all learn fast. Caeran got his license a month after he started."

I looked at Caeran. "Is it strange for you? Driving a car?"

He shrugged. "Easier than driving a wagon. Horses are unpredictable."

Horses. Jeez.

"If the hunting looks to continue much longer, we'll get Lomen a car. You should not have to sacrifice yours, Manda."

"Eh, I'm not going anywhere at night anyway," she said. "I'm getting itchy for a poker tournament, though."

"Aren't there some during the day?" Len asked.

"Yeah. Hey, let's play now! You know how to play poker, right Steve?"

"Uh...I know the basics."

"Ever play Texas Hold'em?"

"No."

"It's easy. Come on!"

She got up and pulled two decks of cards out of a cupboard, then went to the dining table. The rest of us followed.

"I'd prefer to play bridge," Caeran said as he took a chair. "There are four of us."

Amanda frowned. "That takes too long to learn. Do you know bridge, Steve?"

I shook my head.

"He's a math whiz," Len said. "He'd pick it up fast."

"Poker first," said Amanda.

I glanced at Caeran, sitting across from me, and hid a smile. We shared a guy moment.

Amanda pulled the cards out of their boxes and handed one deck to Len to shuffle. She launched into an explanation and started dealing.

At first I thought the game stupidly simple. Each player had only two cards, with five more shared on the board in a version of seven-card stud. It seemed mostly a game of chance, but as we played I realized a lot depended on the players' choices. By the end of an hour I was intrigued.

Len went out first, yielding most of her chips to Amanda. I was still figuring out the odds, which were different from those of regular poker. A couple of miscalculations cost me most of my stack, and a last-ditch attempt to recoup failed when none of the cards that would give me either a straight or a flush—outs, Amanda called them—came through.

"Heads up," Amanda said, looking at Caeran as she handed the made deck to Len. "Don't let me win."

"I would not dream of insulting you so," Caeran said.

Len pushed the cards from the previous deal toward me. "Steve, would you shuffle?"

"Sure."

I couldn't do the fancy riffle Amanda did. I could barely keep up with shuffling each deck a few times and handing it over as it was needed.

Amanda had the majority of chips, but with a win now and then Caeran made steady gains. I found myself wondering if he was reading Amanda's thoughts. He gave me a sharp glance and I focused on the shuffling for a while, cheeks burning. The girls didn't notice.

I quietly shielded, then ventured a glance at Caeran. He gave me a cool look. I was oddly reminded of the old tradition of duelling, where one gentleman could call another out to fight with pistols or swords over an insult such as the accusation of cheating at cards.

It wasn't quite so formal in the old west. The pistols were right handy and the shooting could happen at the table.

I wondered if I would ever get used to being around these ælven. It was sure training me to watch what I thought about.

The chips evened up, then Caeran edged ahead. Amanda's betting got even more risky. She bet heavily on a flop of ace, jack, ten, mixed suits. Caeran called her. She continued to bet hard and Caeran kept calling, for a turn card of seven diamonds and a river of nine clubs. She showed two pair, aces and tens, and Caeran laid down queen-eight.

"Straight," Len said, pushing the pot to Caeran.

"You should have taken me all in," Amanda said grumpily.

"You might have had the higher straight," said Caeran.

He now had about two thirds of the chips. Amanda pulled back and won a couple of small pots, but Caeran kept the lead. It took about half an hour more for him to get the rest of her chips. Finally she went all in on three fives, but Caeran had a flush.

She sighed. "You win."

Caeran smiled. "Good game."

Amanda returned a wry smile and collected the cards, stuffing them back into their boxes. I checked the time and was surprised to see it was almost ten.

"Who wants dessert?" Len said. "It's tiramisu."

We all opted in for that. Caeran offered to make coffee. I ducked away to my room to download my textbooks before I forgot. When I got back, they had the TV on and were watching the news.

Caeran served up the tiramisu and steaming mugs of coffee. Amanda was in her chair, Len on the couch near Caeran's chair. I sat cross-legged on the other end of the couch and balanced my coffee on the arm.

As we watched the news, I realized I was bracing for a story about another killing. Everything the clan had told me about the alben, though, indicated that there would be about a week between killings. They didn't need to feed more often than that.

A week here, trapped indoors after dark. I had a feeling cards would get old.

We got to the weather without anything worse than a domestic violence incident. By the end of the forecast I had finished my dessert. I glanced at the others, whose plates were also clean.

"Great dessert, Caeran," I said, standing up. "Thanks."

"There's more."

"Oh, no. I'm stuffed."

I collected the others' plates and took them to the kitchen.

Caeran followed me in and poured himself more coffee. I caught his eye.

"Sorry," I said softly as I rinsed the dishes. "I knew you wouldn't do that."

He didn't quite smile, but his face softened. "No, I wouldn't. I do value your trust. And the Creed bids us to honor the privacy of others."

"I'm just paranoid, I guess."

"You have good reason. I sometimes forget to ignore unshielded thoughts."

I took a dishtowel off its hook and dried my hands. "I'm still learning."

"Yes. You're doing fine." He added a dollop of cream to his coffee. "I put your bike in the garage. Things have disappeared off of porches in this neighborhood from time to time."

"Thanks."

He smiled briefly, then went back in the living room. I headed for the bathroom; after my bike ride, I needed a shower. By the time I was done, Len and Caeran had gone to bed.

Amanda was sitting in the living room, watching a late night talk show with the sound off. I went in to say goodnight.

"Finally," she said, glaring at me. "I've been waiting to brush my teeth."

"I'm sorry. I should have asked if you needed the bathroom."

"Yeah." She got up and started down the hall.

"Amanda?"

She turned, arms crossed. I didn't want to leave things on that note, so I followed her and lowered my voice so as not to disturb the others.

"I'm sorry," I said again. "I know I've made it uncomfortable for you here. Would you rather sleep in the bedroom? I don't mind switching."

Her frown faded and she sighed. "No, you don't have to do that. Sorry, I'm just cranky. Guess I'm a sore loser."

"Is that it? Want to play a few hands with me? I'm sure you'll skunk me."

She laughed. "No, thanks. I'll beat Caeran next time, maybe. We'll have plenty of chances for a rematch."

"Yeah, I was thinking about that. I'm not used to this routine yet."

"I'm not either. I hate it."

That surprised me. It must have showed in my face, because she went on.

"This is how Savhoran got infected. Hunting alben. I hate thinking about him out there. Not that he can get any more infected."

I didn't know what to say to that. The thought that Lomen was in danger that way made my gut sink.

I went to bed, expecting to like awake fretting, but the day had been long and stressful and I fell asleep almost immediately. If I dreamed, I didn't remember.

I woke up feeling warm. Gradually I realized it wasn't a physical warmth.

I opened my eyes. Lomen was in the room.

He was sitting on the floor with his back against the dresser, eyes closed, hands on his knees. Looked like he was meditating. I figured I shouldn't disturb him.

Going back to sleep was not going to be possible, so I lay on my side and watched him for a while. Just gazed at his face, memorizing its lines. The morning sun seeping in around the edges of the curtains cast a soft light on his features.

At rest, he looked peaceful, Buddha-like, except for the tiny crease that never seemed to leave his brow. I wondered if it was etched there. Ælven might not age, but stress could do things to a person's face.

He didn't seem stressed now. His body was relaxed. His hair was loose and spilled down his shoulders over his chest. I loved that it was long.

Now that I knew both of them better, I didn't think he looked at all like Caeran. That puzzled me, because I knew that they were extremely alike physically. It was themselves showing through the physical that made them feel so different.

Caeran was more formal, more serious. When I looked at him I did not have the same gut reaction that I got from looking at Lomen. He was different, plain and simple. Not to mention, he was taken.

I liked Len. I'd never want to hurt her. She'd always been helpful when she worked in the library and I needed some obscure book. Amanda, too, but it was Len I had first made friends with.

And now, because of that friendship, I was here in her house, gazing at my new lover who was just breathtaking. In the last few days I had seriously changed the course of my college education, and possibly my future career. I'd quit the job I had counted on to offset my already-frightening student loan balance.

I was either a brilliant risk-taker, or a stupid ass.

A knock on the door startled me.

"Waffles," Amanda called from the hallway.

"OK," I said thickly.

I looked back at Lomen, who had opened his eyes. "You hungry?" I whispered.

He nodded, and the sharpness in his eyes told me hungry was an understatement. I threw off the covers and got up, stepping around Lomen to rummage in my bag for fresh jeans. There were none; I found a pair of shorts and pulled them on.

A hand on my thigh made me gasp. He was still on the floor, looking up at me, touching me with a different kind of hunger in his gaze.

I knelt beside him. He touched my face, then closed his eyes as he leaned his forehead against mine.

I really must eat something.

OK.

His weariness surprised me, worried me a little. I felt him smile.

Don't fret. I've been neglecting to rest, is all. The last few days have been...eventful.

No kidding. Did you find anything?

No. We searched the area around the university, but there was no new sign of them.

I kissed his cheek, then pulled back.

Let's get you some waffles.

I stood and adjusted my shorts, wishing again for jeans. Maybe I'd ride home after breakfast and collect some more clothing.

Lomen got up, rolling his shoulders as if they were stiff. I wanted to offer to rub them, but that would delay his breakfast.

Later, I will take you up on it.

He was still wearing yesterday's clothes. I pulled on a t-shirt and we went out.

The hallway smelled of hot bread and coffee. Amanda was in the kitchen scooping batter out of a mixing bowl into a waffle-maker. There was a bowl of sliced strawberries on the counter and another of whipped cream, plus a carafe of hot maple syrup.

There was tea, too—there was always tea—and I took some of that, not wanting coffee that moment. Lomen filled a mug with tea and chugged half of it, then refilled it.

"They're keeping warm in the oven," Amanda said, leaning against the counter with both hands around a mug. Beside her, the waffle-maker gently steamed.

Lomen was still focused on his tea. I grabbed a plate and opened the oven, took two off a stack of Belgian waffles, and put one of them on a plate for Lomen. I added berries and some syrup to mine, pretending to be virtuous by skipping the whipped cream. Lomen slathered his waffle with butter, berries, cream and then syrup.

Ælven probably had great metabolisms, too. I'd only met a handful, but none of them were fat.

We shuffled out to the dining nook, where Len and Caeran were sitting.

"Morning," Len said, cutting a bite of waffle. "Sleep well?"

"Uh-huh."

I'm not much for conversation in the morning. I took a swig of tea and started in on my breakfast. It was wonderful, just like every other meal I'd had in that house. I watched Lomen wolf down his waffle and get up to get another. He looked a little better.

Caeran's gaze followed him, and I realized he was waiting for a report.

Well, not my place to give it to him. I wiped up syrup with the last bite of my waffle and sat sipping my tea.

Lomen returned with a slightly less heaped plate. I got up to fetch more tea for both of us. I could hear Caeran's voice, low and questioning, not in English, from the other room.

I took Lomen his tea. He and Caeran stopped talking, and I decided I was a third wheel, so I took my own tea out to the back porch. The air was cool out there, enough to raise goosebumps on my bare legs. I sat in a lounge chair and huddled with my mug.

I heard the screen door open and glanced up at Len as she joined me.

"There are more waffles," she said.

"No, thanks. One was perfect."

She sat in a chair and gazed out at the yard. "Less than two weeks to Evennight."

"What is that?" I asked.

"It's the equinox. The ælven celebrate the equinoxes and solstices—those are their big traditional holidays."

"Oh, I see." Even-night. And I'd even taken Latin in high school. Duh.

"It'll be good to see Madóran. We haven't been up there in a while. You're invited, of course."

"Thanks."

"There's a little ceremony but it's mostly a party. A clan gathering."

"I see."

"You can skip the ceremony if you want, or just watch. It would be nice if you came, though—Amanda and Savhoran are going to cup-bond."

"And what's that?"

"It's a committed relationship. It lasts for a year, and then you can renew. Caeran and I are cup-bonded."

"So, sort of a practice marriage?"

She tilted her head. "Practice isn't quite the right word. It's a genuine commitment, it's just short-term. The only other form of formal commitment the ælven have is a handfasting, and that's for life, so it's rare."

"Divorce is a dirty word?"

"It's a non-existent word, for them. If you don't keep a pledge you're in violation of the creed."

"They take this creed pretty seriously, I gather."

"Very seriously."

"Is it written down anywhere?"

"I have a copy I made from one of Madóran's books, but it's in ælven."

I turned my head to stare at her. "You speak ælven?"

"I'm learning. Manda is, too, a little. It's not an easy language, though some of our words are borrowed from it."

A hummingbird came up to a feeder hanging from the pergola. We watched it take tentative sips, hovering and keeping an eye on us, then finally settle onto a perch and start chugging the nectar.

"So do you understand the creed?" I asked. "I'd like to know more about it."

"I understand most of it, I think. You know, I ought to try doing a translation. It would be a good exercise."

"I'd like to read that."

"Maybe I'll start on it today. It's kind of long."

A second hummingbird flew up, had a sharp discussion with the first one, then they both settled down to drink.

"So, the ælven don't get married? I mean like we do."

"They marry humans, sometimes. Caeran was married a couple of centuries ago."

I looked at her, surprised. "Caeran?"

She nodded. "It's a sad story. She couldn't handle his immortality. Couldn't handle getting older while he stayed the same. After she died he kept track of their kids, and their grandkids, but after a couple of generations he stopped. They had no connection to him, so it was just a painful reminder."

"Does it bother you, knowing that?"

"You mean am I jealous? She died over two hundred years ago." She finished her tea and set her mug down. "If I started worrying about his past loves I'd drive myself nuts. I don't think he even knows how many he's had."

I took a swallow of tea. I should probably emulate her attitude.

"He entered her culture for her sake," Len said. "I don't think she really understood what a gift that was. I'm going to make sure I don't take him for granted in any way."

"They're amazing," I said softly.

"Uh-huh."

"We have to save them."

She met my gaze. "Yes."

That was probably the moment when I fully committed myself, heart and soul, to the Ebonwatch project. We made a silent pact, Len and I. We'd give our lives to this.

The screen door banged open. The hummingbirds flew away. Amanda came out, coffee mug in hand, and sat on the other side of Len.

"They still talking?" Len asked.

Nose in her mug, Amanda nodded.

"Something must have happened."

"I don't think so," I said. "Lomen told me they didn't find anything last night."

"They searched all night," Amanda said. "They didn't get back until almost dawn. Savhoran's still got my car; he didn't have time to drop it off."

Len gave her a concerned look. "Well, if you need to go out there's our car."

Amanda shrugged.

I wondered how I could help her break out of her bad mood, then decided it was probably something she needed to work her way through. I finished my tea and got up.

"Think I'll ride down to my place. Looks like I'm going to

need some more clothes."

"We have a washer and dryer," Len said.

"Thanks, but washing the same ten garments every three days will get old, I think. Besides, I could use the exercise." I paused by Amanda's chair. "Anything I can get for you while I'm out?"

"No, thanks."

I went in the house, rinsed my mug, then rinsed the other stuff in the sink and put it all in the dishwasher. Caeran came in as I was finishing.

"Thank you," he said.

"Least I can do."

Lomen brought in his empty plate and mug. I rinsed them and loaded them in the machine, then started it washing.

"I'm going to ride home and get some more clothes."

"I'll come with you."

"I thought you needed to rest."

I caught Caeran's eye. He was frowning a little.

"It's broad daylight," I said to Lomen. "It's just a few blocks. I'll be fine."

Lomen looked at me, eyes tense at the corners, then suddenly he relaxed. "You are right. I'll rest until you're back."

I followed him down the hall to get my wallet from his room. I stuffed that and my phone into my pockets, pulled the remaining t-shirts and socks out of my bag and stacked them on top of the dresser, then sat on the bed to put on my shoes.

Lomen sat beside me and sighed. His arm slid around my waist.

"You really are exhausted."

I'm getting better.

I looked at him, wondering if he was familiar with Monty Python.

Who?

Comedy troupe. Doesn't matter.

I finished tying my shoes and leaned over to kiss him.

Rest up. I'll be back soon.

You'd better. You owe me a backrub.

Yes, sir!

I grabbed my shades and put them on, gave Lomen a quick hug, then picked up my bag and went out. On my way down the hall I shielded.

I let myself into the garage, took note of the laundry room at the back of it, and opened the garage door. My bike was against the far wall. I wheeled it out onto the driveway, left it there while I dashed back and hit the button to close the door, then ducked out. Strapped my empty bag on the back, put on my helmet, and mounted.

The day was already warming up. The ride was an easy downhill in this direction. Traffic was busy on a beautiful September Saturday. I kept an eye out for inattentive drivers and got to my place without incident.

As I wheeled my bike up the sidewalk I noticed a piece of paper taped to my door. Just a sheet of copy paper, with "FAGGOT" written on it in black marker.

= 8 =

I stood fuming, my gut twisting. I leaned the bike against the wall and pulled off the sign. I was about to crumple it, then changed my mind.

I could hear music playing faintly from the neighbor's apartment. I stepped over to her door and knocked.

She answered in leggings and a Lobo football jersey, hair pinned up in a tousled mop. I smelled a hint of window cleaner. I put on my best manners.

"Sorry to bother you," I said. "Did you happen to see who put this on my door?"

I showed her the sign. Her surprise seemed genuine.

"No," she said. "God, who would do that?"

"OK, thanks," I said, folding the sign in half. I started back to my place.

"Hey—"

I turned back, waiting. She took a couple of steps closer, leaving her door open.

"The police were here a couple of days ago, asking about you."

"Yeah. I found a body on campus Wednesday."

"That was *you*? Oh, how awful!"

"If they come around again, you can tell them I'm staying with friends. They have my phone number."

"OK. Gee, I'm really sorry!"

"Thanks."

I was about to turn away again, then decided some public relations work was in order. I tried to dredge up her name from when we'd first met.

"Say—Mary, right?"

"Carrie."

"Carrie, sorry. Listen, if you don't mind, I have a plant that

101

needs watering. Could I bring it over for you to take care of for a while? I may be away for couple weeks."

"Sure!"

"Thanks. I'll be back in a minute."

I let myself in my place, brought the bike in, threw the sign on the floor, and fetched a neglected spider-plant from the window. It had been a gift from a guy I'd dated briefly the previous year.

I brought the plant, including the pie plate that sat underneath the pot, over to Carrie's place and knocked. The door wasn't latched; it creaked open a little. She came back and opened it, smiling as she reached for the plant.

"Oh, how cute! How often should I water it?"

"Twice a week. Thanks, I owe you."

She blushed and smiled, confirming a suspicion I'd had. I gave her a polite smile as I stepped back.

"Take care."

"You too."

I went back to my apartment, carefully closed the door, and took off my helmet. Then I picked up the sign and methodically tore it into sixty-four pieces, which I threw in the kitchen trash. That was smelly, so I took it out to the dumpster and put a fresh bag in the can.

So Carrie hadn't put up the sign, unless she was a really good actress. The apartment on the other side was vacant last I knew, but it was the start of the semester. Maybe an anti-gay student had moved in.

I stood in the middle of my front room, still fuming. I'd always considered this place my retreat. I was paying more for it than I probably should, but it had been a haven for me. Now it no longer felt safe.

I looked around the room, deciding whether anything there was so important I'd regret losing it. The furniture was unremarkable. I had one framed art poster that I really liked, an Amado Peña. I took that down, then realized I couldn't carry it on the bike and hung it back up.

Breathe.

I made a conscious effort to calm down. Ran through the white-light shield and felt better.

I grabbed my bag and took it to my bedroom. The bed was still mussed from my play with Lomen. That memory gave me a hard-on; I ignored it and tidied the bed, then stuffed all my jeans and a couple more shirts in my bag. Added a sweatshirt, just in case.

I got an old backpack out of the closet and filled it with socks and the picture of my sister from my dresser. I left the one of my parents. Who knew, could have been them who put up the sign.

Finally I went to the kitchen and looked through the drawers for anything I'd regret losing. I stuffed a really good corkscrew into my pack, then remembered I had a couple of bottles of wine in a cupboard. I put these in the center of my bag, padding them with jeans, and strapped it back on the bike.

I wondered if I should leave a light on, then decided that a light that stayed on 24-7 was probably worse than no lights at all.

I was leaving my home. It hadn't quite hit me before. I swallowed, telling myself it was temporary. Once the damn alben had been found and persuaded to move on, I could come back.

With Lomen?

That was too complicated to think about right then. I made sure all the windows were closed and latched, then wheeled out the bike and locked up.

With the added weight of my bag and the backpack, the ride up to Len and Caeran's was slow going. I got off the bike to wait for a traffic light and walked it the next couple of blocks.

The day was heating up. Some clouds were puffing up, too— might mean more rain later.

By the time I reached the house I'd worked up a pretty good sweat. Amanda was on the couch, engrossed in her tablet. Len's car was gone; they must have gone out on some errand. I tiptoed down the hall to Lomen's room where I paused to listen at the door.

Come in.

Sorry, I should have shielded.

I went in and set my bag and backpack down by the dresser. Lomen was lying on the bed, eyes closed.

I cleared out two drawers for you.

Oh, thanks!

There is also room in the closet.

I didn't bring anything fancy.

I didn't own much that was fancy, anyway. Certainly living the way we were, I wouldn't need to dress up, although come to think of it I should probably bring up my suit, in case there was some kind of business meeting.

I put the backpack in the closet and turned to look at Lomen. He seemed less tired—*felt*—less tired. I guessed that was his khi I was sensing.

I'm going to shower.

I'll join you.

My groin tightened at that.

Amanda's here—won't she mind?

We'll be quiet.

I stifled a chuckle, remembering how well that had worked the day before.

I kicked off my shoes, got out some clean clothes, and headed for the bathroom. Lomen stayed where he was. If he needed more rest, that was fine.

I padded down the hall to the living room. "You need the bathroom? I'd like to shower."

Amanda shook her head without looking up. "No, thanks."

I took possession of the bathroom and stripped down. I could smell my own stink; maybe that was why Lomen had hung back. I hopped in the shower, turned the water on hot, and lathered up.

The shower was big. There had once been a bathtub, if I judged the neighborhood right, but it had been removed and replaced with a spacious shower with stone tile on the walls and floor. A stained glass window of water lilies shed blue-green light.

I had shampoo all over and my eyes squeezed shut when I felt the air in the room change. Heard the door quietly close. Knew an instant's panic, then recognized Lomen's khi.

Recognized it. Wow.

May I come in?

Please do.

By the time I rinsed the soap out of my eyes, he was already naked. He came into the shower, bringing a small, unmarked bottle which he set on the window sill.

He leaned his head back beneath the water, wetting down his hair and kindling a burn in my loins. I poured some shampoo into my hand.

Yes, please.

He looked at me and held my gaze while I slid my hands behind his neck and worked the shampoo into his hair, rubbing upward from his nape. His eyelids drooped, then closed as I massaged his scalp.

We had a good time soaping each other up, exploring and tickling and struggling not to laugh aloud. I could have continued that way for a while, but he suddenly changed course.

Rinse.

When all the soap was gone, he took down the little bottle and opened it, pouring a small amount of oil into his hand. He applied this to my chest, rubbing all the way down my torso, which made me salivate. I didn't know what kind of oil it was but it clung instead of rinsing away, and it stayed slippery.

He shared it with me. We slathered each other with it. We were both highly aroused by then and we were touching a lot more, flesh to oily flesh, sliding, with water pouring down our limbs. When I gripped his shoulders I could feel how tight they were.

Backrub. Turn around.

He did, and leaned his arms against the wall. I got some more of the oil and started rubbing his shoulders, the tight spot between the shoulder blades, down along the spine. He gave a tiny moan, and it sent me over the edge.

I took him, hard and fast. Felt his fleeting surprise, then he yielded, leaning flat against the wall while I spent myself.

There was no "Wait," no yearning titillation. Even as I came on like a bull, I was astonished. This was entirely unlike me.

The orgasm was blinding. I held still as it faded, breathing hard. Became aware of my thundering pulse, of Lomen plastered against the wall.

You OK?

For answer he freed himself and turned around. He kissed me hard, burning away my doubts. We traded places, then finally clung together, winding down.

The water hitting my ankles was getting cooler.

Lomen reached for a bar of soap—not the stuff I'd been using, but a rustic-looking tan-colored bar. As soon as the water hit it, I recognized the fragrance.

This was the soap Madóran had made. If I hadn't just spent myself, the smell would have aroused me. As it was it aroused my brain, and I had to demand a long kiss.

The soap quickly dispersed the oil. We finished bathing and shut off the now-cold water, then rubbed each other down with luxurious bath sheets from the linen cupboard.

I was tired, in a good way, and still sort of stunned.

Nap.

Mm.

We dressed, then tiptoed down the hall to Lomen's room. I risked a glance toward the living room but didn't see Amanda.

We tossed our dirty clothes in a corner and collapsed onto the bed together.

I don't know what came over me. I'm not usually...

Shh. Doesn't matter.

He pulled me closer and I closed my eyes. For the first time since Wednesday, we lay quietly together, and I realized this was something I'd been missing.

I woke up smelling sauteeing onions. My stomach growled.

I took a long breath and became aware I was alone in the bed. A moment's grief, then a jumble of memories that made me catch my breath.

Shield, Steven.

I blinked, then obeyed. Shielded twice, for good measure. Sat up.

Lomen wasn't in the room.

I rubbed my face, still waking up.

Where are you?

In the living room. Faranin and Bironan are here.

I tried to remember who they were. Ælven, from the names.

They've come to help us hunt.

Oh, yeah.

Pushing away that depressing thought, I got up, combed my fingers through my still-damp hair, and shuffled out to the living room. Len was talking with Lomen and two others, both doppelgangers of Caeran, though one had a pretty stern expression. They wore the loose, cotton clothing I was getting used to seeing on the ælven. I wondered if Madóran made that, too.

There was a tray with a teapot and mugs on the coffee table. Len waved me toward it and kept talking.

She was explaining Project Ebonwatch, I realized. Explaining my presence.

I poured myself some tea and sat in Amanda's chair. Len was talking about the advantages of building a lab over using an existing building. The biggest plus seemed to be that it could be away from the city but within easy driving distance.

Cheaper in town, I thought, but Caeran always wanted to keep a low profile. Finding land, buying it, building—all these would delay things, but they could be done while we were scrambling to learn the skills we'd need for the research.

I finished my tea and reached for the pot. It was almost empty. I quietly carried it into the kitchen.

Caeran was at the stove, stirring onions and peppers in a skillet. He glanced at me, then nodded toward the counter. I put the teapot there and filled the electric kettle.

"Anything I can do to help?" I said.

"How are you at brewing tea?"

"Uh...in need of training." They used loose tea, I knew that. I had no clue how to do it.

"Never mind. Just chop those scallions, and give me the white ends."

I chopped them, then chopped celery, then sliced up a baguette for garlic bread. I snagged a tiny heel from the baguette, since I'd missed lunch. Really good bread.

"Where are those two going to stay?" I asked, nodding toward the living room.

Caeran shook something into the pan from a glass jar. "Either at Savhoran's apartment, or here. Faranin said the porch is fine for him to rest on; the weather's mild."

"What if it rains?"

"We have an awning that folds out under the pergola."

I thought about offering my place, but the sign on the door made me think twice. I didn't want to ask anyone else to put up with harassment intended for me.

The kettle boiled. Caeran deputized me to stir the veggies while he set a fresh pot of tea brewing. My stomach growled at the aroma rising from the pan.

I helped Caeran until the tea was ready, then lifted the strainer-thingie out of the teapot and put it in the sink. Put the lid on the pot and carried it back to the living room.

"Steve, I'd like you to meet our friends," Len said as I put the pot on the tray. "This is Faranin, and this is Bironan."

Faranin was the stern-looking one. I nodded to both of them. Bironan smiled slightly.

"Steve Harrison is the newest member of the company," Len added. "He's going to be integral to our research efforts."

"Nice to meet you," I said. I couldn't think of anything else. Good luck hunting the alben?

I'd forgotten my mug. As soon as I could do so without being rude, I slipped back to the kitchen for it. Caeran was adding shrimp to the pan.

"This is almost ready. Could you get the dining room ready?"

"Sure. How many places?"

"Just put a stack of plates on the sideboard. We're too many for the dining table."

I pulled some plates out of the cupboard. "Gonna need a bigger boat."

Caeran gave me a quizzical look, then returned his attention to the stove. I fetched out silverware and napkins—cloth; no paper in this house—and put them on the sideboard. Caeran started handing me serving dishes: salad, basket of garlic bread, casserole of rice. He brought the main dish out in a big tureen, then called everyone to help themselves.

I hung back, letting the guests go first, though my stomach protested. Caeran and Lomen both treated Faranin with a subtle deference, making me wonder if he outranked them somehow. Hadn't they told me Caeran was the clan's leader?

Lomen caught my eye and smiled.

You've met almost all of us now. All but Madóran and two others. Well, three others.

Oh?

Mirali's just given birth. A daughter, Nathrali.

I could feel his pride as he said this, almost as if he was the father. For all I knew, he was.

I slapped a quick shield on that thought.

That's cool. About the baby.

Yes, I'm eager to meet her. We'll see them at Evennight.

Caeran, Len, and the two newcomers sat at the dining table. Lomen and I carried our plates to the living room. As we were sitting down, Manda came in from out back and started filling a plate. She curled up in her chair with it, ignoring us.

The dinner was good, but I wasn't as hungry now, and my stomach was getting tight as I thought about the hunt. I ate the salad and the garlic bread, and a few bites of the shrimp—spicy, cajun, really good. I carried the rest into the kitchen and put it in a container, stashed it in the fridge for later. Filled two glasses with chilled water and went back to the living room.

Amanda glanced up at me. I offered her one of the glasses, but she shook her head. I gave it to Lomen and sat next to him, sipping.

I could tell he didn't want me to worry. I also couldn't help worrying, and I knew he knew that. We sat silent, just enjoying being close.

One of these nights I'd like to actually sleep together.

Except that I don't sleep.

Well, you know what I mean.

Yes. We will. Soon.

I watched him polish off everything on his plate. The hunting must involve some physical activity, judging by how hungry he had been that morning. Or maybe just driving the car all night had worn him out. I remembered a long drive I'd made once— Albuquerque to Los Angeles in one night, without stopping. I'd stayed awake on chocolate and caffeinated soda. Not fun.

All too soon, the others got up and started making farewell noises. Amanda stood and reached out a hand for Lomen's plate. He gave it to her and took a long pull at his water.

The curtains over the west window were closed, but I could tell the sun was setting. The light around the edges was golden, and the picture window to the east gave a view of the mountains, all pink with sunset. Amanda came back to the living room and sat staring out that window.

Why did Savhoran keep the car? I thought he had a motorcycle.

He loaned it to Pirian.

I tried picturing Pirian on a bike. Too creepy. Plus, when had he learned to drive it? I'd have bet twenty bucks he didn't have a license.

Nor do I.

I grimaced, and shielded. Lomen grinned at me.

A car pulled up outside. Amanda jumped up and went out the front door. The others came into the living room, and Lomen got up. I couldn't help watching him.

Be careful. All of that.

All of that. I will be back before you wake.

Wake me yourself.

If you wish.

I felt a rush of tingling warmth, as if he'd just run his hands over my torso. I bit my lip.

No fair.

Good night, Steven. Sleep well, when you sleep.

They all went out. I carried our glasses to the kitchen, put Lomen's in the dishwasher and refilled mine.

Len and Caeran were silent. I helped them tidy the kitchen. Did an extra shield before I indulged in speculation: were they talking, the way Lomen talked with me?

Probably.

We were done cleaning up by the time Manda came back in. She looked depressed, and made no objection when Caeran proposed bridge as the evening's entertainment.

Len taught me the basics, and we played a few open hands. I already knew about trick games, having played a lot of Spades in high school, so I picked it up pretty fast.

Then they threw the bidding at me. My brain overloaded fast. Len gave me a cheat sheet that was six pages long, and I stumbled through a few hands. Once the bidding was over, I had no trouble playing out the hand, but I could tell it would take me a while to learn it.

I liked the game. Even when we switched partners and I played with Amanda, who was still in a surly mood. I managed not to annoy her too much.

We played until ten o'clock, then watched the news, then went to bed.

That became our evening routine for the next few days. Dinner with the clan, bridge or poker while they hunted, news and bed. Faranin and Bironan hung out on the back porch a lot. Most mornings they were out there meditating when I got my breakfast.

I didn't see much of Lomen; certainly not as much as I would have liked. He spent most of Sunday catching up on his rest, while I dove into the molecular biology text, trying to get caught up. Then classes on Monday, and on into the week.

It was Thursday morning when Lomen woke me early. He had just come in, and instead of sliding into bed with me, he crouched beside it.

Steven.

I raised my head, startled, blinking.

We found them.

= 9 =

He went off to tell the others, leaving me to stumble out of bed and into some clothes. It was still dark. I got to the kitchen and put the kettle on, then stared at the coffee maker, too asleep to comprehend how to start it.

I heard the front door close. Amanda came in, looking disgustingly awake. She started coffee and pulled yogurt and strawberries out of the fridge. I got the tea brewing and set the timer, having had two lessons from Len during the week.

Voices in the living room. I wandered out and found all the hunters there, including Savhoran and Pirian. The hair on the back of my neck prickled at the sight of him. I almost turned around and went back to the bedroom.

Caeran was there, too, talking with them in ælven. They had filled up the couch and chairs, so I dragged more chairs over from the dining nook and sat in one, as far as possible from Pirian.

Len, in a robe over her nightclothes, brought out the tea tray and started pouring. I stepped into the kitchen, opting for coffee in the hope of waking up faster.

I glanced at the clock on the oven. Five-thirty.

Stifling a groan, I splashed a dollop of cream in my mug and went back out. Sat and listened to Caeran. He shifted to English when Manda came out of the kitchen.

"Pirian has talked to the alben. There are two of them, and they are a couple." He looked at Pirian. "Their names?"

"We did not exchange names. Our conversation was brief."

"Did you ask them not to hunt here?"

"I told them Clan Greystone would prefer they did not."

"And their response?"

Pirian gave a small shrug. "They like it here."

Savhoran turned to him. "Did you invite them to join Clan

113

Ebonwatch?"

Pirian gave him a measuring look. "I did not have opportunity to explain the idea. You are more likely to convince them than I."

"Perhaps we all should meet with them," Bironan said.

"Not here!" said Len.

"No," Caeran said, taking her hand. "They must not come here, or anywhere near our human kindred."

"Were they hunting?" I asked.

Everyone stared at me. I looked at Savhoran.

"Was that where you found them? Were they out hunting?"

"No," Savhoran said. "They are living in a motel on east Central. Lomen sensed their khi."

"And Pirian knocked on their door," Lomen said, looking at Pirian.

There was an undercurrent in the room that I couldn't quite fathom. I looked at Pirian, but his face was neutral. Carefully so, I thought.

I shielded, just because it made me feel safer. Lomen shifted in his seat. Had he felt it?

Could they all tell when I shielded?

There was too much I didn't know.

"Tomorrow night, we will approach them," Caeran said. "I will go and speak to them as Greystone's leader. Lomen, if you will stay here?"

Lomen nodded, and my heart did a little happy skip.

"How do you intend to compel them to leave, if they choose to stay?" Pirian asked.

"I hope we need not compel them. We should be able to persuade them either to go or to adopt the creed."

Savhoran looked up at him. "Do we mention the cure?"

"There is no cure, at present," said Pirian.

Caeran's gaze shifted to him. "We can tell them of our hopes for one."

Pirian did a half-nod, half-shrug. I got the feeling he found the conversation amusing.

The easiest thing would be if the alben would agree to go, but the thought didn't make me happy. It would be good for Albuquerque; bad for Phoenix or Dallas or wherever they went next.

Best alternative? A good old vampire hunt, pitchforks and all?

I found myself uneasily wishing they'd agree to join Clan Ebonwatch. Trouble was, that clan was little more than a theory.

"Even without a cure, the Creed is worth the effort," said Savhoran in a rough voice.

I glanced at Pirian. He didn't radiate agreement.

"You have done well," Caeran said, addressing all of the hunters. "Lomen and Pirian, thank you for locating the alben and making contact with them. We'll meet here tonight and go together to talk to them. Now some of you must seek shelter before dawn."

"And some of us have classes," Manda muttered.

Savhoran and Pirian stood and went out. Manda followed them, and I winced, but Pirian probably already knew about her and Savhoran. For sure he knew about Caeran and Len.

Me and Lomen?

I went back to the kitchen and poured myself more coffee. I'd be buzzing, but I sure wasn't going to get any more sleep.

The strawberries and yogurt were still out on the counter. I helped myself to some and stood staring out the kitchen window into the darkness as I ate.

The conversation in the living room picked up again, back in ælven. Len brought in the teapot, put the kettle on, and went away. Lomen joined me.

That looks good.

There's more. Want some?

I turned to him and saw him smiling in a way that made my arms tingle.

Oh.

I finished the last bite of my yogurt and put the dish in the sink. Lomen headed for his room, and I followed.

He closed the door softly. Dawn was coming; a soft light

seeped around the curtains. Lomen pulled me to him for a kiss.

Mmm. Strawberries.

I laughed and turned toward the bed.

A while later, lying spent and tangled with Lomen, I gradually became aware of the world again. I could hear the conversation in the living room, the gentle rise and fall of ælven cadences.

What are they talking about?

The new house on Madóran's land. Mirali and her child.

Not the alben?

Them, too.

I tried to picture Caeran reasoning with the unknown alben who had committed two rather grisly murders on campus. The thought made me uncomfortable.

What'll we do if they refuse to join Ebonwatch or leave?

Lomen didn't answer immediately. I considered the clan's past experiences dealing with alben, and concluded that it wouldn't be pretty.

The fact that they are willing to talk at all is promising.

Not much comfort. I was glad that Lomen wouldn't be at that night's meeting, and aware that this was a selfish response.

What about a tip to the police? If things don't go well at the meeting, I mean.

The police can't control them, Steven.

My gut sank. We were on our own, then. Or the ælven were. Us feeble humans couldn't help.

How many humans would it take to control an alben? Could an army do it?

Possibly. There was once an ælven who joined a raiding clan in Mongolia. He attained quite a reputation. He was eventually slain, but I believe it took a force of three hundred.

Wow. The cops wouldn't send that many.

Not at first, and if we requested it, they would dismiss us.

As cranks. Yeah.

I buried my nose in his neck. Took a deep breath of him, pine-spice fragrance and our musk and his own delicious scent.

That wouldn't have been you, would it?

No. He committed a major violation of the creed, Steven.

Sorry. I need to learn more about the creed.

It bids us to do no harm if it can be avoided.

I see.

His thumb stroked my arm. I sighed, wishing we could stay like that all day.

So do I, but I had best get moving. I should shower.

I smiled, remembering the shower. He kissed my forehead, then got up, leaving me drowsing.

I hadn't meant to fall asleep. On two cups of coffee I shouldn't have, but I did. I woke up when Lomen came in to get his shoes.

I looked at the clock. "Oh, crap!"

Your first class is at nine, correct?

I have chem lab at eight.

I jumped out of bed and scrambled into some clothes. The bedroom was getting trashed with dirty laundry and my unpacked bag sitting around. I would fix it later. I had a full day.

Manda offered us a ride. I said no thanks, determined to ride my bike as much as possible. Didn't see Lomen again; he had another test midday, so I had lunch alone at the Student Union Building.

By the time I got home—some time that week, Len and Caeran's had become home—I was hot and tired and brain-fried. The molecular biology class was a second-level course, and I was a couple of weeks behind. It would take some work to catch up.

I put away my bike and came in from the garage to find the place deserted. Wonderful smells were coming from the kitchen. I went in to look and found a big pot simmering on the stove: green chile chicken stew.

I volunteered to set the table, and watched Bironan and Faranin covertly, curious how they'd react to the chile, but they took it in stride. I guessed they'd had a lot of opportunities to sample extreme cuisine.

Len was a little agitated. I couldn't blame her. She was quiet a lot, and she and Caeran gazed at each other a lot.

Not long after sunset a car pulled up out front. Savhoran had arrived—without Pirian.

"Is Pirian coming on the bike?" Caeran asked.

"I haven't talked to him since last night," Savhoran said.

Caeran and Faranin exchanged a few words of ælven. Savhoran took out his phone and punched in a call, then waited while it rang.

Not good. I traded a glance with Lomen. I was even more glad he was staying home tonight.

Savhoran frowned and punched at his phone some more. Manda sat next to him, watching him. After a minute he said, "Pirian. Call me," and hung up.

Caeran stood. "We'll go without him."

Len looked up at him, worried. Faranin and Bironan stood. Savhoran bent to say something in Amanda's ear, then the four of them went out.

Len sat staring at the door. I went to the dining nook and started clearing the table. Amanda came and helped. We tidied the nook and the kitchen. Amanda fixed a mug of tea and took it out to Len.

"Let's play poker," she said brightly.

Len came to the table, though she was clearly distracted. Amanda got out the cards and we sat down to another tournament. Lomen obviously liked poker, and he was good at it. I got too ambitious and lost all my chips early, so Amanda elected me dealer and proceeded to pelt me with little details about how it should be done.

Len's heart wasn't in the game. She let her chips trickle away, and didn't seem to care when they were all gone. She shuffled the cards for me and stared at the front door. Then, when we were halfway through a hand, she jumped up.

The door opened. Caeran and the others came in. Len ran a couple of steps toward him.

"They weren't there," he said.

"What about Pirian?" Len asked.

"We can't find him."

Amanda went to Savhoran, abandoning the game. Lomen and I got up and joined the others in the living room.

They talked about whether to go back later to the alben's hotel, or go look for them on campus. No one was sure what to do.

It was a week since I'd found Kimberly. "They're out hunting," I said, to myself mostly, but everyone else stopped talking.

Caeran frowned, then looked at Savhoran. "When did Pirian last hunt?"

Savhoran raised his shoulders. "We do not hunt together. He prefers to go alone."

"Has he been keeping the creed?"

"I cannot say. He does not defer to me."

"You are the head of Clan Ebonwatch."

"In name. But we are not brethren, Caeran. We have no such bond."

Lomen stepped forward. "We should go to the campus."

I wanted to protest. I clenched my jaw and shielded.

"I will go," said Savhoran.

"Yes," Caeran said, "let us go now. Perhaps we can prevent them...Lomen, you will remain here in my stead."

Len looked miserable, but didn't say anything.

"I am willing to go," Lomen said.

"No, I wish to speak to them, if I can. Stay and guard our kin."

They went out again, the four of them. Len stayed on the couch. No one bothered to suggest we go back to the poker game.

Manda turned on the TV and channel surfed. She found a silly movie and left it on. Len sat hugging a cushion, staring at the screen with unseeing eyes.

I quietly cleared away the card game, went and collected a load of laundry and set it going, then sat with Lomen. We watched the movie, then the news. When the talk shows started, I glanced at Lomen, then stuffed the laundry in the dryer and headed for bed, thinking maybe Len needed some girl-talk with

Manda.

Lomen followed me. We slid into bed and held each other. We didn't talk. No use speculating on what was going on with the hunters. We would hear about it when they got back.

I shielded, just for the sake of getting into the habit, then tried not to think about the alben. The memory of finding Kimberly kept coming to me and I kept pushing it away. Finally I drifted to sleep.

I woke when Lomen got out of bed. "They're back," he whispered, pulling on his jeans.

I got up and dressed. It was getting light outside, though it wasn't yet seven.

Caeran, Faranin, and Bironan were in the living room. Len looked like she might have slept on the couch. I glanced at Amanda, who was in her chair with her tablet. She looked all right, so I concluded that Savhoran was OK and had gone to ground for the day.

"What's the news?"

Caeran grimaced. "We didn't find them."

"We searched the entire campus," said Faranin.

"Twice," Bironan added.

"The last hour we went back to their hotel, but they were not there either," Caeran said.

"And Pirian?" Lomen asked. "Still no sign?"

Caeran shook his head. "I left another message on his voicemail."

"Holy shit!" Manda said.

She was staring wide-eyed at her tablet. I moved to look over her shoulder at a photo of a woman, naked, splayed like Da Vinci's Vitruvian man.

"I just found this online," Manda said in a shaky voice. "It's gone viral."

Lomen peered at it, then grabbed the TV controls and in a few seconds had the image on the big screen. It wasn't great quality—obviously snapped on someone's phone—but it was clear enough.

The woman was tied to a chain link fence. Her wrists were bloody, but that was nothing compared to the river of blood that had poured down her torso. Her head was bowed forward, black hair dangling in two dagger points.

"It's Poppy," I said.

"Oh, my god," said Len.

A few tattooed curlicues were visible on the woman's shoulders. Most of the tatt was drenched in her blood.

"You know her?" Caeran asked.

"S-she worked at Zimmerman," Manda said.

Caeran walked toward the screen, peering not at Poppy but at her surroundings. "Where is this?"

Where was there a fence like that? The background was dark, except for some shadowy shapes that looked tree-like and a few distant points of light. I took a couple of steps toward the TV.

"Golf course," I said.

"Oh, crap," said Manda. "North of campus."

Lomen looked at Caeran. "Did you search there?"

"Not that far north."

Caeran headed toward the garage. Faranin rose and followed, with Bironan behind him.

"I'll go with you," said Lomen.

"No. Stay and watch them," Caeran told him, gesturing toward the couch, where Len had curled up around a cushion again.

I picked up the remote from the coffee table and turned off the TV, then took Manda's tablet away from her and shut it off. She let out a gasping sob. I sat next to her and held her while she cried.

Len was crying too, but silently. Lomen went and put an arm around her. She turned and buried her head in his chest.

It took a while for them both to be cried out. When Manda was calm enough, I got up and fetched her a handful of tissues, then went into the kitchen to start tea and coffee.

Lomen joined me. "You knew her?"

"Not really. Not like they did." I nodded toward the living

room. "I saw her at the library a few times, and we'd chat a little, but we weren't friends."

We took mugs of hot stuff to Len and Manda. Lomen asked if they wanted breakfast, but they both said no.

"We should watch the news," Manda said.

She picked up the remote and turned on the TV, then muted it. Images of local politicians filled the screen.

"They won't put that picture on TV," Len said.

"Why not? The whole world's already seen it online."

I sipped a mug of tea and watched the news stories, trying to guess the topics from the images and a little lip-reading.

At 7:30, my phone rang, It was in the bedroom, so I hurried to grab it. Checked the number: campus police.

I took a deep breath before answering.

"Mr. Harrison?" said Buzz-cut's voice.

"Yes?"

"We're at your apartment. Where are you?"

"I'm staying with friends."

"What address?"

I was reluctant to give it to him. I didn't want him barging in and pestering Len and Manda with questions. Refusing wouldn't go over well, though. I gave him the address.

"How long have you been there?"

"A few days."

"When did you last leave?"

"I went to classes yesterday. Came back about five-thirty."

"And you've been there since then?"

"Yes."

"Can anyone there confirm that?"

"Yes. Three others have been here the whole time."

"I'll need their names."

I gave them. Lomen came in and sat on the bed, watching me, which made me realize I was pacing the room. I made myself stop, and sat beside him instead. He laid a hand on my back.

"OK if we come ask you some questions?"

"It's a little early."

"We won't take long."

I gritted my teeth. "Sure, fine."

He hung up, and I put the phone on the night stand. Lomen's arm slid around my shoulders.

You haven't told me of this. How long has he been harassing you?

He just doesn't like me, is all.

Lomen was silent.

I don't want him bugging Len and Manda.

I will talk to him.

That might make things worse.

It won't. I promise you. Let's get you something to eat before he arrives.

We went to the kitchen and made toast and eggs. Manda wandered in.

"The news had a teaser about it. Breaking news, another campus killing. That smells good."

I handed her the piece of toast I'd just buttered. "Where's Len?"

"She went back to bed."

Not a bad idea. Wished I could do the same.

"Listen, Manda, that cop that called you? He's coming over here."

"Jeez, why can't he leave you alone?"

"You don't have to talk to him right now if you don't want to. You could go keep Len company."

She chewed a bite of toast. There was a mulish look in her eye. I hoped she wouldn't decide to give Buzz-cut a piece of her mind. That wouldn't help my cause.

Lomen presented me with a plate of eggs over easy and gently nagged me to eat them. I nabbed the last slice of toast and put two more pieces of bread in the toaster, then started eating while I watched Lomen crack more eggs into the pan.

I didn't know you could cook.

I've picked up a few tricks here and there.

Yeah, but over easy's not easy. Half the time I break the yolks.

It just takes practice.

He handed the next plate to Manda, then said, "Will you excuse me a moment?"

"Sure."

I had finished my eggs, so I rinsed my plate and dug in the fridge for some orange juice. Manda's eyes lit up, and she nodded vigorously, unable to talk because her mouth was full. I poured us each a glass.

The doorbell rang.

Hissing displeasure in case it woke Len, I hurried out to answer it. Buzz-cut and Officer Ulibarri stood outside. I stepped out on the porch with them.

"Hi."

"Can we come in?" said Buzz-cut.

"One of my friends is asleep," I said.

"It's OK," said Officer Ulibarri. "We only have a couple of questions, then we'll get out of your hair."

Buzz-cut shot her a look, which she ignored. She had a black bag slung at her hip, I noticed. I figured it was investigation gear.

Buzz-cut flipped through a much-scribbled-on pocket notebook. He took his time. Finally he held it up and squinted at it.

"Where were you last night between 9:00 p.m. and dawn?"

"Here," I said.

"You didn't go out?"

"No. We played poker."

He handed me a thin stack of photos. "Look through there, tell me if you know any of those people."

There were six pictures, all young women. The third one was Kimberly.

I frowned. "That's Kimberly Darrow."

"Got it in one. What about the others?"

I stared at him, wondering if this was some kind of head game. Probably it was.

Going back to the photos, I dismissed the next one and moved it to the bottom of the stack, and found myself looking at Poppy.

Poppy, alive and smiling. Damn.

"Know her?"

"She works at the library on campus," I said. "Her name is Poppy. I don't know the last name."

"When did you last see her?"

I was about to play it cool when I realized that it was a trick question.

"I just saw a picture that looked like her," I said. "Someone posted it online. Has she been murdered?"

Buzz-cut grimaced. "Looks like. So when did you last see her in person?"

I thought about it. "Last Friday."

"You sure about that?"

I looked at him. "Yeah, I'm sure."

He gestured to the photos. "What about the last one?"

I looked at it. Hispanic girl. Pretty, looked shy, and rang a very vague bell. I frowned.

"She looks familiar..."

"What's her name?"

"I don't know. I don't know her, but I've seen her picture before."

Officer Ulibarri reached for the photos. "Thanks."

The door opened and Lomen stepped out. "Is there a problem?"

I shielded, just out of surprise. He looked like Mr. Straight Nerd. He had his hair pulled back into a tight knot at the nape of his neck. He was wearing a striped long-sleeved button-down shirt tucked into his jeans, and a pair of dark-framed glasses.

Buzz-cut looked him up and down.

"Um, this is Officer ... Renniger, and Officer Ulibarri," I said.

Lomen stuck out a hand straight at Buzz-cut. "Lomen Greystone."

Buzz-cut shook hands. His eyes narrowed.

Lomen shook hands with Officer Ulibarri. "How can we help you?"

She smiled. "We were just asking Mr. Harrison some questions."

"Can you tell us where he was last night?" said Buzz-cut.

Lomen turned his head to look at him. "He was here. We were playing cards."

"He didn't step out?"

"No, we stayed in all night. What's this about?"

"Just confirming a couple of things," said Officer Ulibarri. "Thanks for your time."

She moved to go, but Buzz-cut stayed put. "How long have you known him?" he asked Lomen.

Lomen looked faintly surprised. "A few months. Why?"

I felt a touch on my wrist and glanced aside to see Officer Ulibarri offering me a business card. She was looking at me intently.

I took the card and nodded a thank you, then stashed it in my pocket.

Manda burst out the front door. "Steve, they've got that picture on the news, only they..."

She looked at Buzz-cut, then flung her arms around me.

= 10 =

Startled, I froze.

Lomen?

Just play along.

I brought a hand up to Manda's back and whispered in her ear, "Did Lomen put you up to this?"

She nodded and kept clinging. I was acutely aware of Buzz-cut's gaze. I squeezed Manda's shoulders, then let go, taking a step toward the policeman.

"Is there anything else you need, Officers?" Lomen asked.

Buzz-cut watched me with hooded eyes. "Guess not right now."

I turned to the door. Manda followed me. I let her go in first.

Lomen lingered behind. I was about to go back out when he stepped in and closed the door. He headed for the kitchen and we followed.

"Thank you, Amanda," he said in a low voice. "I think that was helpful."

Helpful?!

Shh.

I grabbed a mug and reached for the coffee. Heard the sound of a car pulling away.

"My pleasure," Manda said. "That cop's a jerk. He's got no business treating Steve the way he does."

I thought about the card in my pocket. Instinct made me keep it to myself.

"I agree," Lomen said.

"As if we didn't have enough problems," Manda added, reaching for the fridge.

The coffee tasted acid. I left it on the counter, went to the bathroom, and splashed some cold water on my face. Hoped the day wouldn't get any worse.

I decided to deal with the laundry, needing to do something to help calm myself down. I pulled the load out of the dryer and then stood in the laundry room sorting socks.

You're angry.

Yeah, I am.

What did I do wrong?

I threw a pair of underwear back in the basket and swallowed.

I'm not ashamed of who I am.

Nor am I.

And I won't pretend to be someone I'm not.

Lomen didn't answer right away. I picked up the shorts again and frowned at them. Were they mine, or his?

I see. I apologize.

My annoyance evaporated, leaving behind a vague unhappiness.

I know you were just trying to help.

That policeman is prejudiced.

Yeah, I noticed.

The garage door opened. I looked up and saw the Lexus pulling in.

They're back.

I took the laundry basket to Lomen's room and left it by the dresser. Went out to the living room, where Caeran and the others were gathered, except for Len. She must still be asleep.

Lomen looked up at me from the far end of the couch, apology in his eyes. He'd dispensed with the glasses.

"The police had the area blocked off," Caeran said.

He looked strained. He must have been pretty tired by then.

"We were able to sense their reactions, but there were too many people for us to discern whether the alben's khi was present."

"It must have been them," Manda said. "Same M.O.'s, combined this time."

"Yes. The police were thinking the same thing."

"What about the motel?" Lomen asked.

"We went by again, but they were not there. They may have moved."

Lomen frowned. "If they're in a different motel, we can find them by their khi. They won't be able to leave in daylight."

Caeran sighed. "It is worth looking. However, we need a rest."

"I'll go," Lomen said.

"Not alone," said Faranin.

I'll go with you.

No.

He said it with enough force that I shielded instinctively.

I'm sorry, Steven. It's too dangerous for you.

They can't do anything to me in daylight, right?

They could still control you.

From a distance? Through a door?

A short distance, yes. A door probably won't make a difference.

I'll stay in the car. You and I are the only ones who've had any rest.

Lomen pursed his lips. Caeran was watching him.

I shielded again.

Can they hear us?

No, but they can tell that we're talking.

Lomen straightened in his seat. "Steven and I could drive up Central. If I sense the alben's khi, we'll call."

Caeran shook his head. "Better if we all go. They will not move before nightfall. We have time to rest."

It made sense. I was still disappointed. I wanted to do something. I was pretty sure Poppy had been grabbed at random, but having two acquaintances murdered in less than a month made for a certain level of anxiety.

From the corner of my eye, I saw Manda stifling a yawn. I stepped over to her chair.

"Want a ride to your apartment?"

She brightened. "Great idea. I'll get my wallet."

I looked up at Lomen. "We could go to my place. Faranin and Bironan can rest here."

"We can easily rest outside," said Bironan.

"More comfortable inside, isn't it?" I said.

Lomen stood. I went to get my keys from the bedroom, and grabbed my pack as well. By the time I got back Manda was waiting by the door to the garage.

Caeran handed his keys to Lomen. "Come back by four."

"It'll be before then," I told him. "I have an afternoon class."

"I'm skipping mine," said Manda, yawning again.

We headed out. Lomen drove south and turned into an apartment complex. We waited in the car, watching Manda run up the stairs to a second-floor apartment and disappear inside.

"Your place?" Lomen asked softly.

"Yeah."

We didn't talk while he drove. I was too stressed, I realized. Buzz-cut had both pissed me off and alarmed me, which was probably his intention.

Maybe Albuquerque wasn't any better than Cruces.

My tension increased as we got closer to my apartment. I was bracing for finding something awful. A burning cross, maybe.

There was nothing unusual to be seen. Lomen parked at the curb and we got out. I checked the mail—it had been a few days —and pulled out a handful of junk mail.

I started toward the apartment. Lomen touched my arm, and stepped past me when I paused. He walked slowly, looking right and left. Looking for what? Booby-traps?

Khi.

Realization hit me. He was looking for the alben, or for Pirian.

Did Pirian know where I lived? A shiver surprised me, and I shielded.

Nothing here. Only the police.

Figures.

I unlocked the door and we went in. The place was as still as a tomb. I dumped the mail on my desk and sorted through it. There was a printed notice of my course changes, otherwise it was all junk. I tossed all but the course changes in the wastebasket, then sat on the couch.

Tired. I rubbed my eyes. I'd slept part of the night, but the morning had been stressful. Lomen sat beside me and lightly rested a hand on my back, rubbing along my spine with his thumb.

May I?

I leaned forward, letting him rub my back. I hadn't realized how tense my muscles were. He massaged with just enough pressure to unlock the knots. It felt so good I started salivating.

Ever heard of Ten Thousand Waves?

No.

It's a Japanese spa. Let's go there.

Now?

I laughed. *It's in Santa Fe.*

Ah.

I sighed. *What a mess.*

It will get better.

How? Caeran's going to try to talk to them, and they're going to laugh in his face. They've made it clear they don't care what he thinks.

They may care what all of us think.

I realized I was staring at the rug. *Do you want to fight them?*

No.

But you will.

If I must.

Shit.

Lomen dug a little harder into my shoulder muscles. I closed my eyes.

I want to keep you safe, Steven. That's my goal in all this.

Who's going to keep you safe? I can't, apparently.

I'll be careful. I've no ambition to be a hero.

But you are a hero. You saved Manda, that day in the library.

No—you saved *her. You went in first, and startled Kanna into fleeing. If she hadn't run—well, I shudder to think what might have happened.*

I thought back to that day at Zimmerman. Summer afternoon, I was trolling for books, and I noticed a woman watching Manda with an expression I didn't like. And then following her into the restroom. And I'd gone in after them.

I'd had no idea what I was looking at. The alben—Kanna—could easily have killed me.

I failed Amanda that day. I was supposed to be guarding her. It is you who are the hero.

You couldn't have known she was already in the building.

I should have detected her. She masked her khi well.

Don't beat yourself up about it. She's dead, right?

Yes.

Let's just worry about the ones that are alive. How are we going to stop them?

He switched from my shoulders to between my shoulder blades. I was starting to zone.

It is possible for an ælven to control another. Success is more likely with two, or preferably three.

Caeran, Lomen, Savhoran, Faranin, Bironan. Barely enough to control two alben, by that standard.

Where does Pirian fit in?

I wish I knew.

Could they have killed him?

Possibly. I don't think he's dead, however. We would probably have sensed an ælven death.

You're that connected?

We are always aware of the khi around us. A change like that, we would probably sense.

Well, if Pirian's not dead, where the hell is he?

With them, perhaps.

Shit.

So...if he's gone rogue...

We are dealing with three alben instead of two.

Great.

I straightened, aware that the backrub was putting me to sleep. Lomen's hands fell away. I turned to face him and took his near hand in mine.

"Thank you."

He laced his fingers through mine, and my heart did a slow flip. I'd wanted more than a short-term thing. Was this becoming more?

Lomen's hand squeezed mine.

I had forgotten what a comfort it is to have a lover. It had been a very long time, for me.

There's no one in the clan...?

No. When we were in Europe, we met other ælven from time to time. For a while we allied ourselves with another clan, and I knew a couple of them, but it was centuries ago.

Centuries.

I reached up to touch his face. His jaw was perfectly smooth. I realized they were all like that: Caeran, Faranin, even Savhoran. And I hadn't seen any razors in the bathroom other than mine and a pink one that was probably Manda's.

You don't have to shave, do you?

No.

Dammit.

He grinned.

Caeran's son had very light facial hair. He almost never shaved, at least when we knew him.

Lucky him.

It was at a time when most men wore beards. There were occasions when it was a disadvantage to him.

So did you know Shakespeare?

My remark had been half-flippant, but he answered it seriously.

We tended to avoid human society, for the most part. Caeran's marriage was an exception.

Oh, man. I swallowed. "You thirsty?"

"Now that you mention it."

I stood, reluctant to let go of his hand. Gradually our fingers unlaced. I shoved my hands in my pockets as I went to the kitchen, and found Officer Ulibarri's card.

What had she wanted? The look she had given me was non-trivial.

I filled two glasses with cold water. The clock on the stove said 2:15. I hadn't realized it was that late.

I went back to the living room and handed Lomen a glass. "I'll have to start thinking about getting to class soon."

"Shall I drop you on campus, or take you back for your bike?"

"You can drop me. I'll be fine walking."

His silence made me expect to find him waiting after my class. I couldn't work up to being indignant about it—not after all the crap that had been happening.

I took out my laptop and got online, then got out the card and shot Officer Ulibarri a text:

> THANKS 4 UNDERSTANDING.

It wasn't two minutes before she sent back an answer:

> I WANTED TO APOLOGIZE FOR MY
> PARTNER'S BEHAVIOR. HE'S SENIOR TO ME
> AND I CAN'T DO MUCH ABOUT IT, BUT HE IS
> OUT OF LINE. THE DNA CLEARED YOU DAYS
> AGO.

So they'd run my DNA. My anger rose at Buzz-cut's harassment, but something else niggled at me.

What had they compared my DNA to? If they had a sample then Kimberly had probably been raped, though they might have just found a stray hair.

"Holy fucking shit," I whispered.

Lomen gave me an inquiring look.

"The police have a sample of alben DNA."

= 11 =

My brain started buzzing. Could we get the sample away from the cops? Not without breaking a bunch of laws and risking deep trouble.

Lomen shook his head.

It's already been analyzed. The data could be in a dozen places.

I could get a job with the police. I could get in and destroy the sample, find all the copies of the analysis —

Steven, they must have samples from last year, too. It's too late.

My heart sank. I knew he was right.

This is bad. If someone starts messing with those samples and realizes they're looking at another species...

They would not be likely to connect it to us.

I looked at him, thinking how amazing he was, how much more skilled than any human, and how much more vulnerable. I had to save him. All of them—all the ælven. We had to find that cure.

Project Ebonwatch was even more important than we'd thought, and time was of the essence. I didn't like the helpless feeling of knowing how much I had to learn before I could begin to be of use.

I put aside my laptop and put my arms around Lomen. I just wanted to feel his heart beating next to mine. We made love, reassuring each other, reaffirming our connection.

Finally I looked at the clock. "I've got to go."

Lomen drove me to campus and dropped me near the building where I had my genetics class. I liked the prof—a deep-voiced, no-nonsense woman with masses of curly dark hair—and actually enjoyed the next hour and a half. When I came out, Lomen was waiting under the trees by the door.

We walked to Len & Caeran's, crossing Central to the residential areas and then turning east. I noticed more yellow leaves on the trees, more leaves down in the street. Fall weather, state fair weather. A memory from high school came to me—marching band—riding up in school buses to march in the state fair parade. I smiled.

Evennight is not long away.

Are they still planning to have it ... up north?

I don't know.

Or were all bets off until the alben were found?

Cold impatience filled me. I thought of following the hunters, finding out which Route 66 sleazebag motel the alben were crashing in, phoning in an anonymous tip to the police.

You would be sending the police to certain death.

I stopped walking. Resentment, partly because I knew he was right, morphed into irrational anger.

I wish you wouldn't snoop on my thoughts all the time.

Lomen stopped suddenly, as if I'd struck him a blow. He turned to face me. I was already sorry, but the look in his eyes made it worse.

"I will do my best to stop. You might want to keep practicing your shielding."

Lomen—

He turned and kept walking. The silence in my head was thundering; he'd shut me out.

Shit.

I hurried to catch up to him as he turned the corner on to Len and Caeran's block. "I'm sorry. I didn't mean that."

"Your instinct was correct. We have become too enmeshed, too quickly. A step back would do us good."

But I didn't want a step back.

This was the Lomen I'd seen the morning I found Kimberly and called Manda. Aloof, cold. Giving me a chance to walk away, he'd said. Or maybe walking away himself.

"Don't leave," I whispered, but he had already turned up the path to the door of Len and Caeran's house. A few butterflies rose from the bushes as he passed.

I stopped halfway up the path and shielded three times. Stood there trying to get zen. I had to settle for not quite panicked.

Everyone was in the living room except Manda and Savhoran. The sun was still up; they wouldn't leave their apartment until sunset, another hour or so.

Lomen was talking quietly with Caeran, who looked up at me as I came in. I felt a blush coming in hot and went to the kitchen to get a glass of water.

This was not good. I needed to talk to Lomen, apologize some more, work things out. I shielded again, swallowed a swig of water.

Len came into the kitchen. "Want to help with dinner?"

"Sure," I said, grateful for the distraction.

She set me to chopping onions. They stung my eyes, tempting me to give in to a good cry. I ignored that and kept my thoughts off of Lomen by going over that day's class in my head. I had some homework for that, and needed to catch up on a lot of reading.

Just don't think about it. That was a plan.

Len was stirring something on the stove. She threw the onions into the pot and gave me some cooked chicken to shred. The smell of the sautéeing onions woke up my brain, which informed me I was hungry. I'd forgotten lunch again.

A pungent smell, vaguely reminiscent of marijuana smoke, tickled my senses. Len was chopping roasted green chile on another cutting board. She added that to the onions, and when I was done with the chicken she threw that in along with some broth.

"That needs to stew for a bit. Want a glass of tea?"

I nodded. She fixed iced tea for us while I washed my hands and tidied up the kitchen. We went out back, leaving the ælven to their conversation.

"What happened?" she said softly when we were sitting with our glasses on the patio.

I swallowed a mouthful of tea. "Just a misunderstanding. I said something stupid. I need to apologize some more."

She gazed out at the yard. "They take their time over

decisions," she said. "They have all the time in the world, so they forget that we want to feel secure."

That seemed like a non sequitur. I sat pondering it, trying to apply it to my situation.

"I have something for you," Len said, getting up. She left her glass on a table. "Be right back."

I stared at the garden, trying to resist feeling miserable. Lomen would forgive me. It was just a thoughtless whine, I hadn't really meant it. He had to know that.

Len came back and handed me a couple of sheets of copy paper. "This is just the beginning. It's long."

It was a copy of a handwritten poem. At the top of the first page it said "Creed of the Ælven, translation by Lenore Whiting."

"So you found time for it."

"For starting it. The whole thing's going to take me a while, but it's good for me. I had to ask Caeran about how to translate some words. There are nuances."

I started reading.

> *Walk many paths, leaving no mark behind but of beauty.*
> *Honor the ældar and spirits who watch over all.*

Most of it seemed idealistic and a bit unreal. I was reading about an alien culture, I reminded myself.

One line really caught me, though:

> *Find your way back, when you falter, and seek to atone.*

I sat staring at that, a hollow feeling in my heart. Had I screwed up irreparably? If I found a way to atone, would Lomen forgive me?

This was their code of ethics. My culture didn't have much of one, compared with this.

"What do you do about atonement?" I asked Len.

"We're not required to atone. We're not ælven."

"Not even as a member of the clan?"

She grimaced slightly. "I've offered atonement a couple of times. Caeran insists I'm not obligated, but it does seem to make them more comfortable. They feel responsible for my actions, having accepted me into the clan. So it's kind of a grey area."

"Have you ever offered atonement to Caeran?"

"I've never needed to. It's not that bad, is it?"

"I don't know." I put the pages down and drank some tea.

A big part of the problem was that I was ignorant. I could have mortally offended Lomen without realizing it.

We needed to talk.

Len went back to the kitchen. After a couple of minutes, I followed. She gave me some cheese to grate, then lettuce and tomatoes to chop while she assembled a pan of rolled enchiladas. By the time she put that in the oven my stomach was grumbling.

I wandered out to the living room where the ælven were talking in their own language. Waited a while trying to catch Lomen's eye, but he ignored me. Finally I gave up and went back to his room.

I sat at the desk with my genetics text and stared at the screen, not seeing the words. Lomen was going to go out hunting again, without saying a word to me. Without giving me a chance to atone.

He could be killed.

Not likely, I told myself, but still it was possible. The alben were murderers—multiple murderers. They did not acknowledge human law, true—but neither did they acknowledge the ælven creed. They were outlaws in either culture.

A soft knock at the door made me look up, heart leaping with hope. Len stuck her head in.

"Did you want to keep this?" She held out the copy of her translation.

I swallowed disappointment and came to take it from her. "Yeah. Thanks."

"Dinner's ready."

I stuffed the creed into my pack and followed her to the dining room. The four ælven had already served themselves and were sitting around the dining table. Len and I took our plates to the living room.

Len turned on the TV. Caeran looked up, but she just gave him a flat stare and he went back to his conversation.

Poppy was the top story on the news. They had cropped the picture of her to just show her head, but that brought the whole image back to me. I wondered who had snapped it and posted it, and whether they were in jail now.

The story had no content. UNM student found murdered. We all knew that.

I couldn't eat more than a few bites of my dinner, though it was excellent. I took my plate to the kitchen, covered it with plastic, and stuck it in the fridge. I'd try again later, maybe.

I tidied up the kitchen, rinsing dishes and sticking them in the washer, putting away the leftover enchilada sauce and scrubbing the pot. Wiped down the stove and the counters. Filled the kettle and started it heating for tea.

Nothing left to do.

I heard the scrape of chairs from the dining nook. Busied myself wiping down the sink, but they didn't come in. Instead, I heard them saying goodbye to Len.

I stepped into the living room in time to see Lomen go into the garage. He didn't look back.

Bironan sat on the couch, frowning at the TV which was still on, playing a game show now. He glanced at me.

I headed for the bathroom. Washed my face and brushed my teeth. I knew I wouldn't be able to study, so I went back to the living room and sat in Manda's chair, staring stupidly at the TV.

Had the other three gone to Manda's to get Savhoran, or were they going against the alben alone? Three against two—not great odds, from what they'd told me. Not enough for control.

The night outside darkened until I couldn't see the front yard for the brightness of the porch light. Bironan picked up a magazine and flipped through it, ignoring the TV and me both. Len was in the kitchen doing the rest of the dishes.

I heard a noise outside that made me stare at the window.

Bironan heard it too—he looked, then jumped up from the couch and retreated to the back of the room.

The front curtains were open, and through the picture window I saw a white-haired figure stagger up the path, heading for the door. Pirian.

"Len!" I called, even as two heavy thumps fell on the front door, followed by a more muffled thump. I went to open it.

Pirian stared at me dully, then sank to his knees in the doorway. He would have pitched onto his face if I hadn't caught him. His coat was wet.

Wet with blood.

= 12 =

I looked over my shoulder at Bironan. "Help me!"

The ælven shook his head, white-faced. "I dare not—his blood is a danger to me—"

The curse. Fucking hell.

"Just get some blankets out of that chest and put them on the floor." I jerked my head toward the cedar chest under the window where Manda stashed her bedding during the day.

Len appeared in the doorway of the kitchen, already on the phone. I dragged Pirian through the front door and kicked it shut.

Bironan spread a cheap Mexican blanket on the living room floor and laid a sheet over it, then retreated again, backing away as I edged Pirian toward the bedding. Len hung up and came to help me.

"Get his feet. Can you lift them?"

She did. "Caeran and the others are coming. He's going to call Savhoran."

I heard the back door slam. Bironan, escaping the mess.

Len glanced that way. "Can't blame him."

"No. A little farther—OK, set him down."

My arms ached from manhandling Pirian's dead weight. Blood from his clothes started seeping into the bedding.

"I'll get some bandages," Len said.

"I'll get water."

"Not from the kitchen! Let's just use the front bathroom. Keep it as contained as possible."

"Jesus."

She was right. For the ælven, this was like having an AIDS patient bleed all over your house. No wonder Bironan ran.

I was covered in blood. I couldn't get the curse, I told myself, but it was hard to believe it when I was bathed in contamination.

My heart was beating hard. I kicked off my shoes and followed Len to the front bathroom. She turned on the water in the sink and I rinsed off the worst of the gore. My clothes were a mess, though.

Len was ransacking the cupboards. She handed me a towel and I rubbed my arms down with it, then took it out to the living room.

Pirian was out cold. I looked for a wound but didn't see one. His jacket and the shirt he had on underneath it were soaked. The blood seemed to be coming from everywhere.

I stuffed the towel along one side of his torso and went back for another one. Grabbed one off the rack without touching anything else in the bathroom. Len had an armful of first aid stuff and followed me back out with it.

"Spirits!" she said as she dropped the bandages on Manda's chair. "What happened to him?"

"I don't know. He passed out right after I opened the door."

"Get his shirt off. We've got to stop the bleeding."

I wrestled him out of his jacket, which was no easy task. I lifted his shoulders with one arm and pulled up his shirt with the other hand.

Len gasped.

His chest was a mass of cuts. While I was struggling to remove his shirt, Len ran back to the bathroom and returned with a stack of towels. She laid one over Pirian's chest. Blood started seeping into it at once.

She reached toward the towel.

"No, let me," I said, grabbing two more towels to stuff along his sides. "I'm already a mess."

"OK, yeah. Put some pressure on it. See if you can stop the bleeding. He's still breathing, right?"

"Barely."

With both hands, I pressed the towel down between his armpits. From what I could tell, the cuts started there and continued down his chest. After about thirty seconds I moved lower, putting pressure on the next few inches.

Len was busy unwrapping a roll of gauze, softly cussing to herself.

I had a few seconds to think about what might have happened, and I didn't like what I came up with.

I worked my way down Pirian's chest and returned to the top. The bleeding might have slowed a bit. I kept pressing on the towel until Len came and knelt beside me.

"OK, lift it. Gently."

I carefully pulled the towel away. Blood started seeping again here and there, but more slowly than before.

"Sweet spirits!" Len whispered.

I swallowed. "It's ælven, isn't it?"

She nodded, then started cutting strips of gauze and laying them over the lines of curved and swooping letters that were slowly oozing blood. I gently pressed the gauze down.

"What does it say?"

She shook her head, lips pressed together and tears starting in her eyes. We kept working, adding a second layer of gauze while the blood reddened the first.

The front door opened. I looked over my shoulder and saw Lomen, eyes wide, coming toward me.

"Steven!"

My heart lurched with fear.

"Stay back! Don't touch me!"

I'd shouted louder than I'd meant to. Lomen froze.

"It's not my blood," I added, my voice shaking. "It's Pirian's!"

Caeran stepped up behind him. "Come away."

"Bironan's in the back yard," I said.

Caeran nodded, then took Lomen's arm and drew him back, gently closing the front door between us.

"I'll be right back," Len said, getting up. "Keep going."

She'd added a third layer of the gauze. I gently pressed it down, feeling the blood rise up against my fingers. Something very sharp must have made those graceful cuts.

I heard Len banging around in the bathroom again. She came back with a box of thick gauze pads, four inches square, individually wrapped. She dumped the packages on the floor and started ripping them open.

"Pull it down," she told me when she had three of the pads in her hand.

I folded down the saturated gauze from the top part of Pirian's chest. She laid the pads over the exposed cuts and taped the top edge down with first aid tape, then opened three more pads. I folded down the gauze again and she added the new row, taping its top edge to the first.

She gestured for me to move the towels away from Pirian's sides. I did, and we saw that the cuts didn't extend around there, so she was able to tape down the bandage on both sides. We continued working down Pirian's chest until we reached the waistband of his pants. The cuts continued below it.

I looked up at Len. She nodded, grimacing. I undid Pirian's pants and pulled them down.

The cuts extended almost down to his groin. I was silently grateful they went no farther.

I wiped up the worst of the blood with a towel, draping another over his loins for Len's sake. If she noticed the gesture to modesty she didn't acknowledge it. She was all business, taping the last of the gauze pads over the lowest cuts, then putting a hand on Pirian's brow and peering at his face.

"He's cold. Can you—no, you need to clean up. I'll get him a blanket and make some tea."

I looked at the heap of bloody towels we'd amassed. "Should I wash these?"

"Yeah, but you'd better shower first. Then we'll work on cleaning up."

"How thorough do we have to be?"

"I have no idea. Better to be safe than sorry, though."

She scrubbed her hands and forearms down in the bathroom, then turned it over to me. I stripped off my bloodstained clothes and left them in a pile not touching anything else, then got in the shower and scrubbed every inch of myself, twice. I kept thinking of Lomen as I bathed, of the look of horror on his face, and of

Bironan's terror of contact with Pirian's blood.

How bad was it? Could I now be a "carrier" of the curse? Would it be unsafe for an ælven to touch me?

It couldn't be that bad. Caeran and the others had no problem being around Manda, sharing meals with her and so on. But maybe she'd never been in contact with infected blood.

I needed to know more. As usual.

I dried myself, wrapped a towel around my waist, and padded down the hall to Lomen's room, being careful not to step on any bloodstains. Put on shorts and a t-shirt and returned to the living room.

Pirian looked like crap. His usual pallor was rosy by comparison to his current hue. I checked to make sure he was breathing, then poked my head in the kitchen.

"Should I wash the towels and stuff?"

"Yeah," Len said. "Put in some bleach."

I laid out the least gory towel on the floor and started piling the others on top of it. Added Pirian's clothes, and then mine. The bleach might ruin them, but oh well. Clothes were replaceable.

I heard the Lexus start up in the garage. Len came in with a mug in her hand.

"They leaving?" I asked.

She nodded. "Caeran's taking them up to Madóran's place. He'll bring Madóran back. This is more than I can handle."

I swallowed dismay. I needed to talk to Lomen, and he was leaving.

I carried the bundle to the laundry room, hoping to get a glimpse of Lomen, but the car had already pulled out. Depressed, I stuffed everything into the washer and started it going. Went back to the bathroom to wash my hands yet again.

I heard the front door close, voices in the living room. Manda and Savhoran had arrived. As I came out, Manda was pushing the coffee table away from the couch. She got a sheet out of the chest and spread it over the leather.

Savhoran turned to me. "Help me carry him."

I started to protest, then my brain caught up. Savhoran had

nothing to lose. Gratitude and relief filled me.

I lifted Pirian's shoulders while Savhoran took his legs. We got him onto the couch, and Len covered him with a blanket, then propped him up with a couple of cushions. She held the tea mug to his lips. He frowned and mumbled something, but didn't drink.

Savhoran came and sat in Manda's chair, laid a hand on Pirian's shoulder.

"Pirian," he said softly, and continued in ælven. The words were beautiful to listen to. I decided I had to learn this language.

Pirian's eyes shot open and he took a gasping breath. He grabbed Savhoran's hand.

Savhoran gave a grunt, then pulled away. Pirian had a death grip on his wrist.

Manda made a little sound of dismay and started toward them.

"No!" Savhoran said, flinging his free hand out toward her. He stood up, wrenched his arm away from Pirian, and stumbled backward.

I caught him, steering him away from the bloody bedding still on the floor. We ended up against a wall, Savhoran gasping for breath. Manda came and wrapped herself around him.

"What happened?" Len said.

"Khi," Savhoran said. He gulped, then took a deep breath. "Pirian needs khi. The alben fed on his. He just tried to take mine."

"No one touch him," Len said sharply, looking from me to Manda.

"Oh, no problem," Manda said, shooting Pirian a dark look.

"I should be able to control him," said Savhoran. "He is very weak. He just caught me off guard. If the three of you form a circle, we can feed him khi without risking him harming any of us."

Len looked at me. I would have liked nothing better than to bow out. Pirian had abandoned the clan, or so it seemed, by not showing up when he was expected. And he still gave me the creeps.

But Savhoran had spoken to him with compassion. And he'd suffered—I didn't want to think about how he'd suffered, how he must still be suffering. If the clan wanted to help him, I had to support that.

"I'm in," I said. "But I don't know what to do."

"We'll show you." Len turned to Manda. "You don't have to."

Manda grimaced. "No, I'll help."

We brought some chairs from the dining nook and arranged them near Manda's chair. Savhoran sat there while the three of us made a little circle holding hands, with Manda in the middle. Len put one hand on Savhoran's shoulder and indicated I should do the same. Savhoran closed his eyes and spoke in ælven. Some kind of prayer, I figured.

He held a hand over Pirian's forehead without touching it. My hands got hot, holding Manda's hand and on Savhoran's shoulder. Pirian moved restlessly, then subsided.

We sat there a long time. I felt like we were floating. I thought about Lomen, wondering when I'd see him again.

When. Not if.

Len started humming softly. I didn't recognize the tune, but it gave me something to focus on. It was peaceful, sitting there, drifting. I closed my eyes and listened and tried not to think about anything.

Finally she stopped humming, and I felt Savhoran straighten. We dropped hands.

"I think that is enough for now," Savhoran said. He sounded weary.

I felt lightheaded and a little dizzy. I stretched my back and wiggled stiff shoulders. Savhoran got up and went into the kitchen with Manda.

Len sat in Manda's chair and held a hand in the air over Pirian's forehead, as Savhoran had done. She frowned and leaned back.

"Well, I don't think he'll die immediately. He's still terribly weak."

"Loss of blood?"

"More the loss of khi. She really did a number on him. It's amazing that he managed to get here."

She. The alben female. No question that it was the same one, then.

Why hadn't she killed him? Because he was ælven, sort of? Had she let him go, or had he escaped?

Len joined the others in the kitchen. I moved the first load of laundry to the dryer and started a second—the bedding that had been on the floor, and a couple of stray towels. Washed my hands again, then went to work on the floor and the bathroom.

Len didn't keep any heavy-duty cleaning sprays in the house; she mostly just used vinegar. I figured that wouldn't cut it in this case, so I put some bleach in a spray bottle from the laundry room, added some water, and went to work. I sprayed and rubbed down every surface that had come in contact with blood, including the whole bathroom, sink and shower, and the laundry room. By then I was seriously in need of some fresh air, so I went out back.

The moon was up, hanging gibbous in a black sky. Waxing or waning? I couldn't tell. I had never really cared much about that kind of thing, but I knew that Len did.

I wondered where Lomen was. Halfway to Mora County, probably. I was tempted to call him, but the conversation we needed to have wouldn't be good over the phone.

Maybe he'd already written me off. Maybe I was too much of a pain for him to put up with.

Stop it, I told myself.

I should just go to bed and get some rest. What the hell time was it, anyway?

I heard the screen door from the kitchen open and close. Savhoran joined me on the lawn, looking up at the moon.

"Thank you for helping my clan-brother."

I turned to look at him, saw only the shadowed edges of his face. "Is he?"

"Until he declares himself otherwise."

Or you do.

"He came here seeking help," Savhoran said, a little stiffly. "You gave it. On his behalf, accept my thanks."

I nodded, aware that the ælven took this stuff seriously.

"You think he can be redeemed? If he survives, I mean."

Savhoran's brow creased. Weariness, worry—maybe hunger, too. "I hope so. I cannot afford to lose him, if Clan Ebonwatch is to continue."

"Do you *like* Pirian?"

A wry smile curved his lips. "No more than you. But I pity him. He has borne this curse for centuries. Little wonder it has made him bitter."

I swallowed. I knew that Savhoran drank human blood, but that didn't bother me. He obviously cared, obviously hated having to do it. Would he stop caring, as the years went on? Would he become like Pirian, a predator who made my hackles rise?

"We should go in," he said gently, and something in his voice reminded me of Lomen, which gave me a twinge of emotional pain. He headed for the house, and I followed.

The kitchen smelled like chocolate. Len had made some hot cocoa, New Mexican style with vanilla and a pinch of red chile. The four of us sat in the dining nook with mugs.

Pirian hadn't moved. I looked at him, realizing I wasn't as terrified of him as I had been. He was in rough shape at the moment. I could almost pity him, especially when I remembered the mess of cuts on his torso.

"What do the cuts say, Len?" I asked quietly.

She frowned. "It starts with 'You are mine.' I don't know all the words."

"She did this to the last guy, too, probably," I said. "Caeran said the cops were freaked out about the knives."

"Yeah, probably."

"Which means the police have a sample of alben script."

"Oh, crap!" Manda muttered.

"And a sample of alben DNA. We've got to fast-track Project

Ebonwatch as much as possible."

"We're still a minimum of two years away from starting any meaningful work," Len said.

"Are we? What if we don't wait on the classes? I don't mean skip them, but start working ahead. We can get texts for the future classes, for the research we need to do. We don't need the degrees, just the learning."

"And the practice. We've got to do the lab work."

"So we ramp up the lab."

Len gazed at me, lips pursed, then nodded. "Yeah. I'll talk to Caeran about fixing the location."

"And we might consider enlisting some help."

She shook her head. "No one outside the clan."

"I was outside. You've got that confidentiality agreement. Maybe we can pick up someone with more experience."

"Humans in general don't have a great track record for keeping promises."

"You took a chance on me."

"Because of Lomen."

Oh.

They'd figured they had me by the nuts. I felt a flare of resentment, but let it go. It was basically true, after all.

I finished my cocoa and took my mug to the kitchen. The clock said eleven. I ought to study, but instead I just went to bed.

First night in a while I had slept alone. How easily I'd been spoiled. I lay there feeling sorry for myself and thinking about Lomen until I fell into a restless sleep.

My alarm woke me. I fumbled to turn it off, dragged on some clothes and went out to scare up some breakfast. The living room was dark, curtains drawn over all the windows and only one lamp on in the corner. A stranger looked up at me from Manda's chair and I caught my breath.

He was ælven, but unlike the Clan Greystone guys he did not look like a clone of Caeran. His hair was black and long, down to his waist, and he wore it loose. Fine features, pale skin but with a golden tint as if he'd been in the sun. Blue eyes. He smiled and my heart flipped over.

"You must be Steven," he said in a rich, deep voice.

I nodded.

He stood and came toward me, extending a hand. He wore a kind of loose caftan, floor-length, that clung a bit to his slender frame. His movements were graceful, like a dancer's.

"I am Madóran. Thank you for your presence of mind in helping Pirian. Lenore has told me what happened."

I looked at his hand. "Maybe you shouldn't touch me. I was covered in his blood."

Madóran shifted, bringing up both hands and running them through the air around my head, shoulders, and down my body. His fingers were long. I felt a tingle, like a hint of static electricity.

"I sense no trace of the curse in your khi. I think you need not worry."

I stood staring at him. He was gorgeous, and my body was reacting. I felt a flush climbing up my neck.

"Um," I said, and ducked into the kitchen.

Jeez. Stupid.

He didn't follow. I felt like an idiot as I put cereal in a bowl and ate it without tasting it. Had he noticed my reaction to him? Probably.

I shielded, belatedly. He'd probably notice that, too.

God, these ælven. I'd never be able to look at a human again.

I felt guilty for being attracted to him, even though Lomen and I hadn't made any promises. Just the thought of being with someone else—though the temptation was strong—made me feel disloyal.

That wasn't something I'd felt before, in any relationship. Jealousy, yeah. Guilt, no. But then, I was usually the one who wanted more of a commitment.

I rinsed my dishes and put them in the washer. Ran a hand through my uncombed hair, then stepped out into the living room.

Len was sitting with Madóran beside the couch. Pirian was propped up on a heap of cushions, and his eyes were open. He was sipping cautiously at a mug of tea. He looked up as I came in, and said something in ælven to Len.

She came over to me. "Pirian would like to talk to you."

A stab of fear ran through me. I told myself he couldn't hurt me, not in his current state, and besides, Len and Madóran wouldn't let him.

I walked over and took the chair Len had been sitting in. Madóran glanced at me. I saw that he had a hand on Pirian's wrist.

Pirian looked better. Still pale, and still not well, but not like a corpse. He met my gaze.

"I owe you thanks," he said.

I gave a nod, not trusting myself to speak. My primary reaction to him was still a wish to get far away, fast.

"I did not betray Clan Greystone," he said.

Madóran murmured something to him in ælven and he closed his eyes. That little bit of talking had exhausted him.

I got up and headed toward Lomen's room. Len was standing by the kitchen doorway, looking a little forlorn, so I stopped.

"Where's Caeran?" I asked.

"He went to try to get a better look at—where Poppy—"

I nodded. "Savhoran and Manda go home?"

"Yeah."

I glanced toward Pirian. "Looks like he'll live."

"Now that Madóran is here. We nearly lost him."

Didn't seem to me like it would have been a huge loss, but I shoved that thought deep. They were dying out; they needed every salvageable gene they could muster. If Pirian's *were* salvageable, which we didn't know yet. As a person, he hadn't impressed me.

But by damn, if I could find a way to make his DNA viable for the continuation of the species, I'd do it. I wanted the ælven to survive.

These ælven, these individuals that I'd met, would outlast me by a long way—by centuries—yet they were doomed if we didn't successfully intervene to preserve the species. They had multiple problems: the curse (which needed a real name), their low birth rate, possibly a scarcity of females (I needed more data there), the tendency to commit suicide after living a long time, and the various pressures resulting from the dominance of humans on the planet. Maybe others that I didn't know about as well.

I heard the door to the garage open. Len darted through the living room to meet Caeran, and I followed, keeping my distance from the couch. Caeran came in, looking grim.

"Everything OK?" I asked.

He grimaced, and headed for the kitchen. Len and I hovered in his wake.

Caeran didn't answer until he'd poured himself some tea and taken a sip. "I went to the latest murder scene. There are fewer police there today."

"You found khi?"

"Yes. Both of the alben were there."

I nodded. Our conclusions confirmed.

"And so was Pirian."

= 13 =

"Pirian was in on the murder?" Len whispered.

"He was present," Caeran said. "I don't know that he participated."

I could believe it. And we'd helped save his life. Sonofabitch.

Poppy's flashing grin came to mind. I'd seen her a week ago. She hadn't deserved that horrible death.

I muttered a curse.

"He does have much to answer for, when he is able," Caeran said.

I headed back to Lomen's room. I didn't want to look at Pirian.

How did the ælven handle criminals? There was stuff in Len's creed translation about atonement. Nothing about punishment.

I took out my laptop and made a quick list of homework I had to do over the weekend. Added reading a couple of the books I'd picked up to the list. The book I'd checked out from the library—the last time I'd seen Poppy.

I sat staring at the screen and thinking about Lomen. When would he be coming back?

Telling myself to chill out, I dove into the homework. A couple of hours later I set the computer aside and went to the kitchen looking for lunch.

Curtains had been hung over both the doorways into the kitchen, one from the hall and one from the dining nook. I assumed it was to keep light from getting through if someone opened the back door from the kitchen. Madóran was stirring a small pot of something on the stove that smelled salty and looked like soup with a lot of spinach in it.

The sleeves of his caftan were rolled up above the elbow. Something about his forearms made my mouth water.

He looked up at me and smiled. "Are you hungry? There is

chicken salad in the fridge." He saw me looking at the pot and added, "This is for Pirian."

I turned away, not wanting to think about Pirian. Got out the bowl of chicken salad and scooped some onto a plate. There was a loaf of fresh-baked bread on the counter, and I carved off a chunk of that, then retired with my plate to the patio.

Len and Caeran were there, talking quietly. Caeran looked up as I came out.

"Do you have time to talk?"

I nodded, mouth full of bread.

"Good. We have much to discuss."

Len picked up two empty plates from a side table, making room for my lunch. She took them into the kitchen and came back with a pitcher of iced tea and three glasses.

"What are you going to do about Pirian?" I asked Caeran.

"Hear his explanation, first of all."

Len glanced at me. "Madóran says he's too weak, still."

"Nice for him," I said.

"He will explain," Caeran said. He was wearing his head-of-the-clan expression, a grim face of endurance.

"Does the creed require atonement for doing harm to someone other than an ælven?" I asked.

"The creed requires us to treat all living beings with respect," Caeran said. "If harm is done, atonement must follow."

"What kind of atonement makes up for killing a human?"

Caeran's face got grimmer. "That is for the one atoning to decide."

The criminal got to choose his own punishment? That was convenient.

I didn't say it out loud, but Caeran must have sensed the direction of my thoughts.

"If an ælven refuses to atone, or offers insufficient atonement, a council of adjudication may be called," he said.

"Adjudication? The ælven have laws?"

Len shook her head, but it was Caeran who answered. "Not like your body of law. The creed serves that function for us, and enforcement is generally left to the conscience. But there are occasions when someone's peers—their family or clan—disagree with their decisions. In those cases, a representative group is chosen to negotiate with the offender until all agree upon a satisfactory atonement."

"What if the offender doesn't agree?"

"He is given a choice: he may accept the atonement offered by the council, or be banished."

"Cast out," Len said softly. "Forever."

I wondered if being cast out would bother someone like Pirian. Seemed to me he lived on the fringes already.

"The alben were cast out of ælvenkind long ago," Caeran said. "If Pirian cannot adequately explain and atone for his actions, he will be named alben."

"There are some who say it was unjust to cast them out," said a deep voice behind me.

I looked around and saw Madóran coming out of the kitchen, a glass in his hand. He reached for the pitcher of tea, but Len jumped up to pour for him. The crackle of ice in the glass was the only sound for a moment.

I watched him drink, a swallow moving that long throat. Behind him, the garden and one of the pergola's carved pillars—carved by him, I remembered—made me think of lush places in other countries. I reached for my own tea, wanting distraction.

"That is an old argument," Caeran said.

Madóran nodded, black hair rippling over one shoulder. "A very old one."

He pulled up a chair to join us, his face more serious than I had previously seen it. "Here is what I have learned from Pirian so far, as I was healing him. I have his leave to share it with you." He set his glass on the table by my plate.

"Pirian spoke privately with the two alben on two occasions before the recent killing. They invited him to join them, and he was persuaded to do so."

Caeran let out an exasperated sigh.

"He was present at the killing, and fed from the victim,

though it was mainly the alben male who fed upon her. When she was dead, the alben turned their attention to Pirian. He became their new victim."

Len made a small sound and shook her head.

"They took him to a place he had not been before—he believes it to be another motel. The male controlled him, while the female..." Madóran frowned. "She fed upon his khi, taking pleasure in causing him pain while doing so. I have heard of such perversions among the alben before, but they are rare."

I struggled to comprehend what he was saying. The female had sucked away Pirian's khi while she was carving poetry into his torso? Sick, sick, sick.

"How did he escape?" Caeran asked.

"When she had all but drained him of khi, she turned to her partner. While they coupled, Pirian found the strength to escape."

"How did he manage to get here?" Len asked.

"I am afraid he controlled a human driver, a vehicle for hire..."

"Taxi," I said.

Madóran's gaze shifted to me. "Yes."

"To bring him here?" Len said, looking horrified. "Jeez, the cops will be here any minute! I'm surprised we haven't seen them already!"

Madóran shook his head. "I doubt they will come. Pirian placed fear in the mind of the driver. He will most likely seek to avoid thinking of the event."

"That's not right!" Len said. "He can't *do* that!"

"He will atone for that as well as the rest," Caeran said.

She turned on him. "You're taking him back? I can't believe you're even considering it!"

"If he offers atonement—"

"I'm sorry, he doesn't belong in this clan!" Len got up and paced a few steps along the patio. I'd never seen her so mad.

"He is not of our clan," Caeran said, watching her. "He is Ebonwatch."

"I don't care," Len said. "I don't want him around!"

"Len," I said, keeping my voice gentle, "You just helped save his life."

"That's different," she said, turning to me with angry eyes. "A healer is obligated to save a life. That doesn't mean I want him in my family!"

Caeran reached a hand toward her. "He is not—"

"Or anywhere near it!"

"Lenore," said Madóran quietly.

She stopped her pacing and turned to look at him. He leaned forward, resting his elbows on his knees and looking up at her.

"I think this may be the making of Pirian."

Len's frown deepened. I felt myself frowning, too, and and realized I didn't want to hear that Pirian could be redeemed.

"It has given him a disgust of the alben and the curse that he did not feel before," Madóran said. "He is angry with himself for being deceived, and for causing needless pain. And he is bitterly angry at the two who used him."

Len's chest rose and fell with sharp breaths. "I suppose you want to try and save them, too!"

"More DNA for the gene pool," I said, keeping my tone unemotional.

"Well, you can't do it," she said, ignoring me. "They're broken. They're hooked on causing pain and the feeling of power they get from it. That can't be fixed."

"I fear you are right," said Madóran.

Len rounded on me. "As for DNA, go get a sample if you dare! But they can't be allowed to keep murdering."

"There's only one way to stop them," Caeran said.

Len stared at him, tears starting in her eyes. "I know."

Caeran looked at Madóran. "We need to take counsel with the others."

Madóran nodded.

"Hunting the alben will be difficult," Caeran added. "They were elusive before, and now they know we will seek them."

"I suggest waiting for Pirian to recover. He will likely insist on leading the hunt."

"After Evennight, then."

"Yes."

Evennight. The equinox. It was soon, I knew. There was supposed to be a ceremony.

"That brings another issue to mind," said Madóran. "Mirali has asked that Savhoran not attend the Evennight celebration."

Caeran frowned. "That is unkind."

"But not unreasonable, in her view. I declined to forbid Savhoran's attendance, but I promised to convey Mirali's request."

"Thereby leaving the decision to him? But what choice has she left him? None."

"Weren't he and Manda going to do something at Evennight?" I asked. "A … handfasting?"

"Cup-bond," Len said. "Yes, they are. You can't ask them not to come, Madóran."

"It is not I who ask it. I will offer them an alternative, however. A cup-bonding ceremony here, with my blessing."

Len sighed. "She'll be disappointed."

"Maybe," Madóran said, "but I suspect Savhoran will be relieved. Mirali is not the only member of the clan who makes him uncomfortable."

"He makes *them* uncomfortable, you mean."

"Their unease discomfits him. Savhoran is painfully aware of their dread, having felt it himself until recently."

"Dammit," Len muttered, and stepped off the patio, marching toward the back of the yard. Caeran got up and followed her.

I watched them, acutely aware of Madóran a few feet away and afraid to look at him. I did a shield before my jumbled emotions got broadcast to the whole neighborhood.

I picked up my glass and drank some tea. "Did I just hear you and Caeran proclaim a death sentence?"

"You heard us agree that it might be needful. We will not act until all of Greystone has spoken."

"And Ebonwatch?"

"Yes, since they are kin-clans. Pirian's opinion we know.

Savhoran may object."

"Banishment isn't an option?"

"Not when the well-being of others is at stake. If we do not kill these alben, they will continue to torture and kill others, both human and ælven. Len is correct. They are beyond rehabilitation."

I couldn't argue with that. Also, it would be a very good thing if they were kept from leaving their DNA all over the place and carving paragraphs of their language into their victims for the cops to find and analyze.

"How do you atone for killing an ælven?" I asked softly, watching Len and Caeran who appeared to be having a heavy discussion under the birch trees at the back of the yard.

"Atonement is chosen by the offender. Each situation is unique."

I wasn't satisfied by that answer, but I wasn't going to push it. Len leaned against a tree and Caeran took her hand.

"I have known only a few ælven who had to make such atonements," Madóran said. "One spent a century in seclusion, writing down everything she remembered of the one she had killed. Another built a hospital for humans and saved many hundreds of their lives."

"What about the other alben here? The campus killers from last year and this summer? Kanna and..."

"Gehmanin," Madóran whispered.

"How were their deaths atoned for?"

He was silent for long enough that I glanced at him to see if he'd heard me. His face was filled with such sorrow that I caught my breath.

"I do not know how their deaths were atoned for. It may not have been done yet."

"You're not going to demand that the killers atone?"

He turned to me, surprised. "I? Caeran is the clan's leader."

"But they all look up to you. They all speak of you with reverence."

A slight flush crossed his cheeks, gone as fast as it appeared.

"It is not my place to demand their atonement."

"If no one demands atonement for such a...a transgression, and none is made, then what happens?"

Madóran shook his head slowly. "I have never known such a case. Atonement is important to the soul of the transgressor. Ælven do not neglect it."

"Except when there's disagreement, and a council is called."

"A council of adjudication. Yes. But even in those cases, atonement has been offered. It was just believed insufficient."

He met my gaze, and those grey eyes seemed to look right into my heart. I reached for my tea.

"Pardon all my questions. I'm not criticizing, I'm just trying to understand."

"I know." I could feel his smile. "You are a relentless inquirer. You will be an asset to Ebonwatch."

The shift in his tone—a trace of affection—sent a tingle through me. I took a bigger gulp of tea than I intended, swallowed hard, and felt the chill sink into my chest.

"Can I ask you a different question?" I said when I could breathe again.

"Of course."

I looked at my hands. "I know you said my khi was OK, but I'm wondering if exposure to infected blood could make me a carrier. I wouldn't want to endanger anyone."

Like Lomen. I slid a little shield into my thoughts.

"We do not know exactly how the curse is transmitted," Madóran said, "but here is what I understand. It can be passed from ælven to ælven. I have never heard of it passing to or from a human. It apparently passes through close contact—I believe your current term is transmission of bodily fluids—but exposure does not always result in infection."

Madóran shifted in his chair and I looked up. His face was troubled. "Caeran and Savhoran were both exposed in fights with Gehmanin," he said, "but so far Caeran has not fallen under the curse."

So far.

I looked at Caeran, now speaking earnestly to Len, still holding her hand. He was under a lot of pressure. I'd forgotten the added stress of being exposed to the curse.

"Does it take a long time to incubate?"

"My impression is that it can, although for Savhoran it took only a few months."

This was not good news. If Caeran eventually came down with the curse, that would leave as a gene base for Project Ebonwatch only Lomen, Faranin, Bironan, Madóran, and the three ælven I hadn't met: Mirali, her baby, and her partner. We'd need more—a lot more—to preserve the species.

I hadn't actually talked to any of the ælven about that goal, except a little to Lomen. I wondered if I should present the idea to Madóran. He was the healer, after all—the one who might best understand the implications.

Might be better to propose it in a company meeting. If there ever was one. If we ever got all the fires put out enough to actually organize the research effort.

It occurred to me that if I had access to cryogenic storage, I could take DNA samples from the two alben (after they'd been hunted down) and store them for future use. Gene therapy might someday help the ælven population issue.

We could even harvest the female's ovaries. Cold thought; I didn't like that I'd come up with it. Sometimes my brain was a heartless SOB.

I allowed myself a moment of picturing that procedure. Or would her eggs produce children afflicted with the curse? Did the disease impact the DNA of the victim, or did it manifest elsewhere?

It wasn't worth pursuing imaginary vengeance. I had a vague idea that Madóran wouldn't approve of such thoughts, and anyway the problem of saving the ælven was more interesting.

I wondered if a human female could serve as a surrogate parent for an ælven child. Could that help with the low ælven birth rate? Or would the child somehow end up mortal?

In vitro fertilization. Add that to my list of things to learn.

Too many ideas. I shook my head to clear it of the what-ifs. I needed to focus, to zero in on what was most important right now.

I could feel Madóran watching me. I glanced at him. He was smiling slightly.

"You are thinking deep thoughts," he said.

I sighed. "Just trying to figure out the best way I can help."

"You will find it."

Something was niggling at me; something I'd talked about lately. Not the alben. Not Pirian. Something about ælven and humans. I frowned, watching Caeran and Len still deep in their heart-to-heart.

Caeran's son rarely had to shave.

I drew a deep breath. Looked at Madóran, who still watched me intently.

"Have the ælven ever tried breeding humans with high ælven content?" I asked.

He blinked. "I do not understand."

"The child of an ælven and a human is mortal. If that child breeds with another ælven, is their offspring more like an ælven? Longer-lived, maybe?"

Madóran's eyes widened. "I do not believe such a thing has ever been attempted."

I looked back at Caeran and Len. "Might be worth a try."

"It would be wrong to impose such a requirement on anyone."

"Oh, they'd have to participate voluntarily, of course. But maybe they could be offered incentives."

That sounded so cold. Would I need incentives to mate with an ælven? Granted, females weren't my cuppa, but for a good cause, I'd be willing to give it the old college try.

"It's easier for ælven to have kids with humans than with each other, right?" I asked.

"In some cases. Human females can conceive with ælven males."

"What about ælven females?"

Madóran shook his head. "Our physiognomy is different. The ælven female … this is rather technical."

"I don't mind."

He gave me a long, almost skeptical look. "Very well. Conception occurs differently in humans than in ælven. The human female is always open to the seed of a male. If she carries a fertile egg, she will likely conceive."

I waited. Madóran seemed to be searching for words.

"An ælven female is ordinarily not open to conception. Her body has a barrier that no seed can pass. When she couples, her partner's seed is blocked by this barrier. She—they both—experience pleasure, but they do not conceive."

"Wow, most humans would love that!"

He smiled wryly. "Our problems are opposite. Humans seek to avoid conception. Ælven yearn for it."

"How does it happen, then?"

He spoke in a low, almost reverent voice. "Very rarely, during the ecstasy of coupling, the barrier in the female's body opens and draws in her partner, binding them together physically for a time. This permits the male's seed to impregnate her."

Bound together physically? I had a vague memory of hearing about something like that, but not in humans. Dogs, maybe?

"And a human male can't … doesn't …"

"I have never heard of a human male achieving conception with an ælven female. I believe it is impossible."

OK, scratch that. But a breeding program still might work. And human females could participate, which was good if ælven females were scarce.

How many generations would it take to achieve immortality? Or was that possible? Maybe high-ælven-content humans would still be mortal, just longer-lived. Like in Tolkein.

But there were those half-elvens. They got to choose whether to be mortal. Convenient.

I wondered if Tolkein had known any ælven. Looking at Madóran, I could imagine that he had.

"These questions stray from the subject of the alben's curse,"

Madóran said softly.

"Yeah. I've been thinking about the ælven's future, too." I met his gaze. "You're a healer, and you've been around a very long time. Do you think the ælven are in danger of becoming extinct?"

He leaned his head back, appraising me, then slowly nodded. "I have feared so for a good while."

"Well, it might be worth trying the breeding thing. Might buy you some time, if nothing else."

He laughed softly. "And it took a human to think of this. How dull-witted we are."

"No, you're scary smart. This just didn't occur to you. Heck, humans have only really understood genetics for a couple of centuries."

A corner of his mouth twitched into a smile. "And it might take a few more for the ælven to pay attention."

"Nah, all you need to do is come out of the woods now and then."

His smile faded to a sad shadow of itself. "We shelter in the woods of a purpose. They are our refuge."

"And I don't blame you. But I'd still like to help you. There's a lot going on right now, so it would probably be better to wait, but down the road a ways I'd be interested in organizing that breeding program. Totally voluntary, of course."

"You would only see the beginning of such a program, not its final result."

"That's OK."

Madóran gazed at me, his expression hard to read. A shadow of a smile hovered on his lips.

"You are remarkable, Steven. A man of many ideas. Caeran was right."

Not too many people had ever referred to me as a man before, rather than a boy. I felt myself blushing, and glanced toward Caeran. He and Len were coming toward us, crossing the lawn hand in hand.

"What do you mean? What did he say about me?" I whispered.

Madóran leaned toward me and laid his hand over mine.
That you would lead us out of darkness. You and Lenore.

= 14 =

I drew a sharp breath, overwhelmed by a sudden awareness of Madóran. He hadn't opened himself completely, not the way Lomen shared with me, but it was enough to make me shiver, and it gave me an instant hard-on.

I shielded hastily. Probably did no good.

Madóran drew back and reached for his tea. He disappeared from my mind as fast as he'd come.

I was shaken. His soul, which had scarcely brushed my awareness, was as wondrous as Lomen's, and completely different.

Len stopped in front of Madóran and stood waiting for his attention. He put down his glass and looked at her.

"I have a plan," she said.

Madóran nodded. Caeran, standing a little to one side, watched them both.

"We'll host Manda and Savhoran's cup-bonding here on the night before Evennight. That will be our Evennight celebration. We'll do a feast, and a ceremony—the whole nine yards. Will you preside?"

"I would be honored."

"Then afterward I'll drive you home so you can do a ceremony for Mirali and the others, and I'll come back right away."

Madóran glanced at Caeran, then looked back at Len. "Will that not be tiring for you?"

She shrugged. "Someone has to stay here with Steve and Manda."

"Savhoran will be here."

"He can't help during the day. We talked," she nodded toward Caeran, "and we think it's better to have an ælven here at all times."

171

"But then you will be alone on your drive home," Madóran said.

"I will ask one of the others to accompany her," Caeran said.

Lomen!

Shut up, I told my heart.

"That one would miss the Evennight celebration." Madóran looked at Len. "Unless you are willing to stay for it?"

Len shook her head. "If Savhoran isn't welcome, then I won't attend."

Madóran closed his eyes, looking weary. After a moment he opened them again.

"And is Pirian welcome at your celebration?"

Len's face was unhappy, but she nodded. "He can come, assuming he's well enough."

And he behaves himself. I didn't need telepathy to read that thought.

Madóran sighed. "I suppose this compromise will serve, though I regret anyone having to miss Evennight."

"We may find an alternative to that," Caeran said.

"But not to the two separate celebrations. It bodes poorly for the unity of Greystone."

Caeran nodded. "I intend to discuss this with Mirali. If she cannot abide the fact that Ebonwatch is our kin-clan, she may wish to change clans."

I sucked a sharp breath. Mirali was the clan's only ælven female, as far as I knew.

"We would hate to lose her," Madóran said.

"Yes. I hope she can find tolerance within her heart."

They would lose her child and her partner, too, if she left. It would create a devastating hole in the clan. Could they recruit more ælven somehow? Had they kept in touch with anyone back in Europe? Caeran's mentioning the possibility of Mirali switching clans implied that there were other clans to switch to.

Which implied that there was a bigger gene pool to draw on. How big, though? If they were threatened with extinction, that meant the birth rate was way lower than the death rate. Or the death/curse rate.

Were the ælven scattered all over the world? How many were left?

"I must see to Pirian," Madóran said, rising. "Lenore?"

She stared hard at him, then sighed and followed him indoors. I looked at Caeran.

"Hell of a week," I said.

His lips twitched into a faint smile. "Yes."

I stood, collected the lunch dishes, and went into the kitchen. Len was nowhere in sight. Madóran was at the stove, ladling the green soup into a bowl. He glanced up at me, then opened a drawer and took out a spoon.

"I thought they didn't eat regular food," I said quietly.

"Mostly they do not, but they crave greens after feeding. It aids their digestion."

"But Pirian hasn't...hunted."

"He fed from the human victim, before he became a victim himself."

Poppy. Shit.

Madóran carried the bowl out to the living room. I cleaned up the dishes and tidied the kitchen. Caeran came in with the tea pitcher, stuck it in the fridge.

"Do you have any yard work that needs doing?" I asked him. "I could use some exercise."

"Not at the moment."

"Then I guess I'll ride my bike down to my place. I should check the mail."

"I could drive you."

I shook my head. "Thanks, but I really need the workout."

"Take your phone."

"Right."

I went to Lomen's room to collect my keys and a gimmie hat, then went out to the living room. Len was there, watching Madóran feed soup to Pirian.

He still looked like crap. His black eyes locked on mine. At that moment I'd have been happy to beat the shit out of him.

I went to the garage, feeling his gaze on me. The hair on the back of my neck rose.

I got on the bike and pumped hard to the intersection with Lead. I hadn't been back to my apartment in over a week. I wondered if I would find any more charming surprises. The thought made me tense, and I pedaled down the hill even though I didn't need to.

No burned crosses on the lawn, no new signs on the door. I emptied the mailbox and carried the heap inside to sort it. Brought my bike in, too, and locked the door. Yes, I felt paranoid.

I looked around at my college-student furnishings, surprised at how stark the place seemed. I'd been living with the ælven for a couple of weeks now, and was getting used to the way they decorated. They liked lavish ornamentation, often incorporating botanicals—lush vines, leaves, and flowers—and animals. A celebration of life.

As opposed to my décor, which was more a celebration of economy.

I sighed, feeling lonely. Except for the sound of traffic outside, the place was silent.

I missed Lomen.

Here, away from all the telepaths, it was safe to think whatever I wanted. The thought uppermost in my mind was that I had gotten myself into a weird and fairly scary situation. It didn't help that I was powerless against the alben who threatened the happiness of my new family.

Because that's basically what they were. Family. Clan, they called it. What it meant was, more than just friends. We looked out for each other. We had connections; intimate ones.

I got myself a glass of water and sat on the couch to sort the mail. Mostly junk, as usual. I recognized my sister's handwriting on a card-shaped envelope. Set it aside until I'd looked through all the rest. There was an electric bill I was almost late in paying; I dealt with it, then opened my sister's card.

It was a birthday card. "Happy Birthday, Brother," with a football player with a cake tucked into his elbow.

I'd completely forgotten my birthday. It had been a few days ago. I was legal now. I'd always planned to celebrate by going out to a bar and getting carded.

In the past, when I'd been dating, I'd made sure my current squeeze knew about my birthday. It hadn't even occurred to me to tell Lomen. Maybe because it was kind of ludicrous to demand recognition of my twenty-one years from someone who was several centuries older?

I swallowed and set the card aside. Nice of Ruth to remember. I should send her a note.

Was I really going to spend my life with the ælven, trying to solve their problems? Was that really my best choice?

The alternative was to come back to my second-hand furniture and my empty bed and try to forget them. Start over. Alone.

No. They were too amazing, too exhilarating. I was hooked, just like the alben, only where they were hooked on darkness, I was hooked on light.

Every time one of the ælven spoke in my mind, even Caeran in his gentle way, it thrilled me to the core. I was in awe of their beauty, their grace. And Lomen—if I had to die tomorrow, one more night with him would make it worth it.

Except he was in Mora somewhere. I'd forgotten the name of the town.

I swallowed the longing and looked for something else to think about. Picked up Ruth's card again and opened it. She'd written a couple of lines under the stupid football joke:

> *Mom broke her foot stepping off a curb. She's doing fine*
> *but misses her water aerobics class. Dad's thinking about*
> *running for the City Council. Miss you.*
>
> *Love, Ruth*

I got out some paper and an envelope and wrote her a short note thanking her and hoping she was well. Hoped Mom would be better soon. Didn't send a message to Dad; if he was running for political office, the last thing he'd want would be to hear from his gay son. I'm sure he wouldn't have minded if I'd dropped off the face of the planet.

Which was sort of what I'd tried to do, where my family was concerned. I really didn't fit in with the rest of them. Maybe I was a changeling.

Ruth was practicing her Christian charity by writing to me. She liked to think she loved me but in fact we didn't know each other that well. She was destined for marriage and motherhood, though she talked about going to nursing school after high school. I suspected she secretly wanted to be engaged by the time she graduated so she could skip college.

I hoped she'd find her dream football player, and that he'd do something useful after his knees blew out, maybe selling cars or insurance. The idea of being around to witness any of it made me depressed.

I would never, ever tell my family about the ælven, not even the smallest detail. They would think I'd joined a hippie commune or something.

Maybe I had.

Smiling, I took the junk mail to the recycling bin, then tidied the living room. Scrounged up some stamps for the electric bill and the note to Ruth, wheeled out my bike, locked up, and left. I dropped the mail at the post office, then rode home.

The curtains were drawn tight over the front window. The garage door opened as I rode into the driveway and dismounted; someone had been watching for me. I put my bike away and went into the house, pausing just inside the living room to let my eyes adjust.

The kitchen windows were covered, now, and the house was darker. Without vision, I was more aware of Pirian's presence in the room: a heaviness off to my right, where the couch was. That discomfort that made me want to flee. I'd always assumed it was his attitude that bugged me, but now I wondered if it was something else.

We weren't alone; there was at least one ælven in the room as well. I recognized a slight tingling sensation that felt good. It was familiar, but I hadn't consciously noticed it before.

I was beginning to see a little, silhouettes of Madóran and Len near the couch. They hadn't greeted me, and assuming the silence was intentional I kept my mouth shut and walked quietly down the hall to Lomen's room.

My hand went to the light switch, then I decided against it. I sat on the bed and felt gingerly around on the nightstand. Found Lomen's candle but no matches. Damn.

Well, fine. I took out my phone and woke it up. The screen was plenty bright enough for me to confirm that there was no box of matches, nor a lighter, anywhere in the room.

Giving up, I left the phone on the bed, took out a change of clothes, and headed for the bathroom to shower. I tormented myself a little by using Lomen's soap, the smell of evergreen and spice and the hot water waking memories that made me stifle more than one groan.

He'd be back soon. The crisis was over; Madóran had pronounced me, and I presumed the house, free of infected blood. No reason why Lomen couldn't come back right away instead of waiting for Evennight.

When was Evennight, anyway?

I dried off and dressed, then went back to my phone to surf up the equinox. It was Friday. A week away.

I could offer to drive up and fetch Lomen, except I didn't have a car. Kind of doubtful that Caeran would want to lend me the Lexus. Besides, I didn't know exactly where Lomen was.

Something made me aware of someone in the hallway, either a sound or that tingly sensation. I looked up, shielding, and saw a silhouette in the doorway.

"I am going out to run an errand," Caeran said softly. "Would you like to come along?"

"Sure."

The darkness in the house was a little oppressive. I told myself I could study later and followed Caeran to the garage.

After the house and even the feeble light in the garage, the daylight was blinding. I wished I'd grabbed my shades. Caeran seemed not to be bothered, and I realized I'd never seen him, or any ælven, wearing sunglasses.

He drove east, and at first I thought he was going to cruise the cheap hotels on Central looking for the alben, but he turned north again and headed for the freeway. Watching him reminded me of Lomen, which made me lonely. I gazed at the Sandia Mountains, remembering hiking up there with one of my exes.

Caeran drove to an electronics store. Hadn't expected that. I followed him into the computer department and over to a display of tablets.

"Which kind does Amanda use?" he asked.

I pointed out the model, then let myself get distracted by the sexy, state-of-the-art ones. My phone was a couple of years old. I told myself firmly that it was fine for at least a couple more. Stuff changed so fast, and I couldn't afford cutting edge.

"Is that one better?" Caeran asked, looking over my shoulder.

"Not really. It's got some nice features, but the other one's fine."

Caeran pulled three boxed tablets like the one I was looking at from the shelf. "You will need the best available tools as we go forward with Ebonwatch."

I put down the demo and followed him to the checkout, feeling like I should decline, except he wasn't just buying one for me. He paid cash for the tablets and the extended warranties.

As I helped take the boxes to the car, I wondered if he always carried that much money. Might make him a target for muggers.

But then, a human mugger probably wouldn't stand much chance against an ælven. They could do everything the alben did, they just chose not to.

Good thing they had that creed.

"It is time we set up our laboratory," Caeran said as he started the car. "Pirian and the alben have distracted us, but there is little we can do about them at present. Tomorrow I intend to view some properties that might work for the lab. I'd like you to come along, if you're willing. Your opinion would be helpful."

"Sure."

He drove to a grocery store. After insisting that we put the tablets in the trunk, I followed him around as he shopped. He was picky; top-quality stuff: organic produce, whole-grain breads, fancy cheese. He invited me to add anything I wanted to the cart.

"Do you cook?"

"Bachelor cooking," I said. "You guys outclass me by a mile. I'm happy to wash the dishes."

I did grab a carton of plain yogurt, and Caeran asked me to pick out some ice cream since he didn't much care about sweets. Following his lead, I chose top-shelf brands, a half-gallon each of Dutch chocolate, coffee, and butter pecan.

The afternoon was fading by the time we headed home. A storm front was coming in from the west, making it dark early. It would be a good night to stay in.

I helped carry everything inside, and noticed that a fire was going in the living room fireplace. Caeran turned on the kitchen light and we put away the groceries, then he started making dinner. I offered to help, but he waved me away.

"Get your tablet set up. The others are for Len and Manda."

He didn't have to tell me twice. I grabbed one of the tablets and headed for Lomen's room, where I could turn on the light to work on setting up software and transferring files. Before I knew it, there was a soft knock on the door: Len, calling me to dinner.

Candles were burning on the table in the dining nook, their golden glow the only light in the room besides the fireplace. "We would have eaten out back," Len said, setting a platter of broiled salmon on the table, "but it's getting windy."

Caeran brought out rice pilaf and spinach to go with the fish. "Madóran," he said gently. "Time to eat."

The healer looked up from his post by the couch, then stood and stretched. With a last glance at his patient he went down the hall, and a couple of minutes later joined us at the table.

"Is he any better?" Caeran asked in a low voice.

"Still very weak," Madóran said. "It will take time. He is stable, at least, and in less pain."

"Will you need Len tomorrow, or may I take her to view possible sites for the laboratory?"

Madóran looked at Len. "By all means, go," he told her. "I do not mean to keep you bound here."

"But if you need my help—"

"You can help when you return. We will be fine."

She hesitated, and I wondered if she was worried that Pirian would do something awful to Madóran while we were away. I didn't think he was capable, frankly, but I was no expert.

"Maybe Savhoran and Manda could be here tomorrow," I said. "Are they coming tonight?"

"Yes," Caeran said. "That is a good suggestion."

While we ate, Caeran talked quietly about the properties he wanted to look at. Some were just vacant land, some had buildings. All of them were outside the city, east of the mountains. It would be a significant commute for us as long as we lived in town. I almost mentioned that, but then I remembered that after three years or so we'd be mostly done with college; certainly with regular classes. We could move out of the city, finish our degrees up by telecommuting. I had a feeling Caeran wanted to get away from Albuquerque.

If they bought land and built, that whole process could take a year or more anyway. Caeran was talking about a large lab, with a separate structure for offices and another that would be a small dorm, essentially, where people working in the lab could grab a shower or a meal or crash for a while without having to drive back to town.

"Manda and Len have drawn up a list of equipment we'll need," Caeran said. "If you don't mind, Steven, I'd like you to look it over and add anything they might have missed."

"Can you give me a little budgeting guidance? I mean, an electron microscope would be nice, but..."

"I believe that's already on the list."

I took a breath. "I need a maximum, because I'm sure I can go over it."

"All right. Try to stay under ten million dollars."

I stared, wondering if he was joking. He didn't look like he was.

Madóran shot Caeran an amused glance, then turned to me. "Financial resources are not an issue. Please ask for everything you can imagine needing. We will let you know if anything you request is beyond our means."

Cryogenic freezer? DNA sequencing analyzer?

Holy cats.

"I'll think about it," I said.

Pirian made a small noise. Madóran instantly rose and went to him.

That signaled the end of the meal; Caeran and Len stood. I helped clear away the dinner things. Len fixed a plate for Manda in case she hadn't already eaten, and put it in the oven to keep warm.

I pulled the curtain aside to peek out the kitchen window. The storm had robbed us of a sunset; the sky was ragged, trees swaying. I let the curtain fall and started in on the dishes.

I was just finishing up in the kitchen when a knock fell on the front door, followed by the doorbell. It was Manda and Savhoran. Caeran took them to the table.

"You hungry?" I asked Manda.

She nodded, so I fetched her plate, and brought out tea for the rest of us. Savhoran thanked me with a silent smile. While Manda was eating, Caeran quietly told them what he'd learned that day at the scene of Poppy's murder.

Manda dropped her fork with a clatter that made me wince. Madóran looked up at her from his chair by the couch. She cussed under her breath, and Savhoran took her hand.

"I'm afraid there's more bad news," Caeran said, and told them about Mirali's request that Savhoran not attend the Evennight celebration.

Savhoran's face was unreadable. Manda looked ready to explode.

"We've got a plan, though," I said hastily, looking at Len.

She explained her alternate-Evennight idea, though she didn't sound excited about driving Madóran home.

"I could do that, if you want," I offered.

Len looked at me. "Actually, I'd rather not see Mirali, so if you don't mind..."

"I don't. I'd need directions, though."

"Madóran can direct you," Caeran said, watching me.

My motivation was probably obvious, but no one commented on it.

Manda was still simmering. "You know, it's pretty insulting of Mirali to ask that," she said.

Caeran nodded. "I will speak to her about it."

"Are there more Greystones?" I asked.

They all looked at me.

"Back in Europe, I mean—or did all of you come over?"

"What does that have to do with anything?" Manda said.

"Just thinking ahead," I said, glancing at Caeran.

"There are others," he said quietly. "Greystone is kin-clan to a larger clan. We were given the name when we chose to come here."

"So Greystone is just you guys, but you have connections elsewhere," I said.

"Yes."

Those were the people Mirali would go back to, if she left Greystone. They were also, possibly, a genetic safety net. I wanted to ask how many there were, but it seemed like the wrong time.

Madóran came to the table and greeted Savhoran and Manda. "There is broth with greens, if you wish it," he told Savhoan.

Savhoran shook his head, lips tight.

"He needs to hunt," Manda said in a low voice. "We just came over to find out how that one was doing." She jerked a thumb in Pirian's direction, frowning again.

"In another day or two, he will be stronger," Madóran said.

"Good, 'cause we've got questions."

"Maybe you'll be able to ask some of them tomorrow,"

Caeran said. He told them about our going to look at land tomorrow, and asked if they'd spend the day with Madóran and Pirian.

"Of course," Savhoran said. Manda frowned, but he looked at her and she gave in with a sigh. "Pirian is still my clan-brother," Savhoran added. "I will gladly spend the day with him."

"Well, if we're going to do that, you'd better hunt." Manda got up. "Thanks for the dinner," she said to Caeran.

"Wait," I said, and she turned.

I fetched the last of the new tablets and gave it to her. "Caeran got us these."

She brightened. "Cool! Thanks, Caeran! You want my old one?"

"Give it to Lomen," he said.

She and Savhoran left. Madóran returned to the couch to sit by Pirian, and Len and Caeran went to their room, leaving me alone at the table. I sat finishing my tea, thinking about the next few days.

The house was kind of weird, dark all the time. I could hole up in Lomen's room and study, or maybe ride down to my apartment and work there.

Evennight was Friday. I figured Thursday night would be our celebration. I had only one class on Friday, not too bad to skip it if I drove Madóran home that day. I could stay for the ceremony up north, so Lomen wouldn't have to miss it.

A log rolled off the fire, knocking the screen out of line and landing half on the brick hearth, scattering bits of coal onto the wood floor. I jumped up and went to the fireplace, grabbed a pair of tongs that were long and awkward, and managed to get the log back into the fire.

I brushed the flecks of coal off the oak and onto the brick. One was caught in a crack between two of the floorboards. I picked it up and yelped; it was hot—sizzled against my skin. I threw it into the fire and cussed, sticking my thumb in my mouth.

Before I could stand, I heard Madóran's footsteps. He knelt beside me, saying softly, "Let me see."

"It's all right, I can get some ice," I said, but he took my hand and cupped both of his around it.

I held still, caught by the wonder of him. His presence—his, khi, I suppose—enveloped me like a warm blanket. He didn't speak to me but he was there with me.

The pain of the burn had vanished the moment he touched me. His hands were cool on mine, like a stream on a hot day. I closed my eyes, quietly reveling in the contact. I forgot to shield, forgot everything except how amazing he was.

Old, old soul. Deep heart, gentle but surprisingly strong. A heart that could care for a killer, though killing was opposite to his purpose.

Gradually I became aware of a shift in his attention. My hand was healed; I knew it because he knew it. His hands were warmer, now, which would have made the burn react if it hadn't been completely cured. I should thank him, but I was drifting in a state of bliss and afraid to lose it by moving, by speaking.

I felt a smile flash through his khi. My soul shivered in response.

I was on the verge of giving myself to him. The thought made me draw back, made me open my eyes.

His face was lit golden by firelight, flames dancing in his eyes. I smelled pine and spice, warmed by the fire and the heat of his flesh. His smile as he gazed at me sent a tingle through me.

Oh, how I wanted to throw my heart open.

I shouldn't ... I ...

He withdrew, not quite completely for which I was grateful, because it would have felt like a door slamming. Still, the bliss vanished, and only a tiny thread of contact remained.

Of course. Forgive me, Steven. I would never wish to hurt Lomen, or you.

He gave my hands a gentle squeeze, let go, and returned to the couch and to Pirian.

It took me a few breaths to calm down enough to stand and go to my room.

Lomen's room. Oh, jeez, I wished he was there.

= 15 =

I hid in the bedroom the rest of the evening, except for a short trip to the bathroom to get ready for bed. I tried to study but that was pretty hopeless. The text looked better on the tablet than on my phone, but I mostly just stared at it without seeing the words.

I slept poorly. Had a lot of weird dreams. Luckily I didn't remember any of them the next morning.

I woke before dawn, hearing the front door close. Must be Manda and Savhoran coming back. I drowsed for another half hour, by which time my brain was clamoring at me enough that I gave up and got dressed.

Caeran had bought a mess of fruit at the grocery store. I picked out a cantaloupe and a couple of oranges and sliced them up, leaving the majority on the cutting board while I carried a dish of fruit and a cup of yogurt out to the back patio.

It was chilly. I ate, then went back inside to make tea and coffee. A pot was simmering on the stove: the green soup, reheating. While I was filling the kettle, Savhoran came in and helped himself to some.

Which meant that his hunting had been successful. I wondered what sort of person he'd fed from, what he'd given them as atonement. Man, that must be hard to live with.

I shielded, hoping he hadn't caught that. If he did, he gave no sign.

Even now, fresh from feeding, he didn't give me the creeps the way Pirian did. Was his atonement what made the difference?

Madóran came into the kitchen. I paid close attention to measuring the coffee while he helped himself to the fruit.

I really had nothing to freak out about. I told myself not to be a dick.

Madóran was friendly but didn't push the least bit. Still, I was glad when Len and Caeran came in, crowding the kitchen enough that I had an excuse to leave. I took a mug of coffee to my room and studied—more successfully this time—until Len came to fetch me.

I grabbed a hat, my shades, and my phone and followed her to the garage. Caeran was already in the car.

"Is Manda coming with us?" I asked as I climbed in the back seat.

"No, she wants to study," Len said.

And to hang out with Savhoran, I figured. Sounded like she didn't get to see as much of him as she'd like.

Caeran drove to the freeway and headed east, through Tijeras Canyon. Some of the trees there were already starting to turn.

Out of the house, away from the darkened rooms, I began to relax. The weather was clear, and as we drove away from the city I remembered how beautiful the east side of the Sandias was. In contrast to the stark, rugged stone of the west face, the lee side had more gradual slopes that were covered in pine, with patches of oak and, higher up, aspens. Those weren't a blaze of gold quite yet, but it wouldn't be long.

Caeran drove south on highway 14, winding through the Manzano Mountains, a lesser chain than the Sandias. Still beautiful woods.

Len was giving him directions from her tablet. I didn't pay much attention. Soon Caeran pulled off next to a gate that was chained shut.

A hand-painted sign on a board wired to the gate screamed "KEEP OUT!" Beyond, a rutted dirt driveway led down to what looked like a farm: an open, relatively flat meadow, piñon trees scattered along its edges, a one-story house on the south side.

"This is it," Len said.

Caeran got out of the car and stood gazing at the property. Len got out too, and I followed.

"I had hoped for more woods," Caeran said.

"I don't think this is the right area for us," Len said. "Did you see that sign about land grants? This is old Spanish grant country. They don't take kindly to gringos moving in."

Caeran gave her an amused look. "Gringos?"

"You're a gringo, sweetie. Same as me."

I walked over to the gate. "I've heard of newly built houses being burned down in places like this."

Len nodded. "Yeah."

"We would not permit that," Caeran said. "But I do not wish you two and Manda to have to deal with hostile neighbors. We will try elsewhere."

We piled back in the car and continued south, passing through a couple of tiny villages. I saw farms, ranches, signs advertising firewood or hay, signs in Spanish. After a while we turned west and started climbing into the mountains. The roads got progressively rougher, and the cloud of dust that kicked up behind us foretold mud in wet weather.

We passed an area that had burned fairly recently. All that was left were the tall, black spikes of tree trunks. A few plants were starting to come back, so it had been maybe a year or two, but nothing taller than a bush was green. When we passed back into living forest, I felt relieved.

The property that was available in the area turned out to be twenty acres of undeveloped forest. Sunflowers grew along the roadside. We got out and walked among the trees: mixed pine and juniper. Dry grasses, knee high, brushed against us, leaving hopeful seeds in our clothing.

Caeran stood gazing up through the trees at the sky. "The land is good, but it's rather far from the city."

"Long commute," I said, nodding.

"No utilities," Len added. "We'd have to drill a well and set up a solar array."

"Yes," Caeran said, "though neither of those is a problem. I am more concerned about the distance."

"It's pretty," Len said, bending to pick a little purple flower.

"We'll keep this one in mind."

Caeran headed back to the car. Reluctantly, Len and I followed. I would have loved to spend more time walking there, but there were other properties to look at.

We retraced our route back to the highway and north again, past the burn and the villages and the Spanish grant land. We crossed under the freeway and were now on the back side of the Sandias.

The highway wound through the little town of Cedar Crest. I'd driven through it a couple of times before, on the way to hikes and once on a visit to the former mining town and current hippie art scene of Madrid. We didn't go that far.

First stop was to the east, another farm-like property much like the first one but without the Spanish grant issue. Caeran wasn't hot for it, so we moved on.

Driving further north, we turned off into a community of fairly fancy houses, spaced well apart.

"How large are the lots here?" Caeran asked.

"Ten acres," Len said. "We're looking at two adjacent ones."

She directed him toward the northwest by a fairly winding route. We had a fine view of the antenna farm on Sandia Crest. That would mean good Internet reception, for what it was worth.

After about fifteen minutes, we turned onto a short street that ended in a cul-de-sac. Len pulled up a map of lots on her tablet, and we got out and walked around. The area was hilly, with a dense forest of mixed piñon and juniper. Rocky underfoot. Chamisa bushes were in bloom, and I sneezed, wishing for antihistamines.

"Can't see the neighbors," Len commented. "That's good."

"This is the one that's zoned residential?" Caeran asked.

"Yeah. We might have to pull some strings to build the lab—there are covenants."

"If we combined the two lots and built right in the center, perhaps that would do."

"Take some legal finagling. Manda would know what we need."

Caeran turned to me. "Steven? What do you think?"

I looked around at the hills. "You'd probably have to berm some of the buildings. Where's the center spot?"

We consulted Len's tablet and GPS, and found the center of

the two lots. It happened to fall in the steepest part, with a dry wash running almost exactly down the property line. It would take a lot of earth-moving, and some erosion control, to get it ready for buildings.

We left it on the list and got back in the car. Drove back out to the highway and back south. Turned right on the road that went up to Sandia Crest, which made me curious. There were a few houses in the area, but not many as far as I knew.

We drove up for a while. Len directed Caeran to turn on a side road that was almost invisible. It wasn't paved, but it was well-graded and recently graveled. It started to climb, and a ponderosa forest closed in around us.

I rolled down my window, wanting to smell the pines. This forest reminded me of the Gila Wilderness, one of my favorite childhood stomping grounds. Clumps of oak grew beneath the evergreens, some of the leaves going orange already. I inhaled deeply, not quite hanging my head out the window like a dog. As we wound higher into the mountains, the air got perceptibly cooler, with a hint of the damp forest scent that I had always loved.

"Look for a lot number sign that says '64'," Len told us.

She spotted it first, just a small sign by the road, no driveway. Caeran pulled the car over to the side of the road and turned on the hazards. We piled out.

I walked a few steps onto the land and stopped to take a deep breath. Tall pines swayed gently and I heard the rushing-water sound of wind in the trees. I closed my eyes.

Footsteps moved past me, crunching on dry needles in the grass. After a moment I followed.

The grass here was greener though it was definitely drying out with the approach of autumn. We walked westward up a gentle slope and before long reached a small meadow ringed by pines. A stand of aspens, just starting to get a tinge of gold on the edges of their fluttering leaves, stood at the north end.

"Oh," Len said, sounding enchanted.

Caeran turned to me. "What do you think? Big enough for the

lab?"

"Um."

My first thought was that it would be a shame to fill that beautiful place with buildings. Knowing the ælven, though, the buildings would be just as beautiful. I made myself focus on the question.

"I don't think the lab needs to be huge. It will be me, Len, Lomen...you?"

"Probably not me, but as you suggested, we should recruit one other if we can."

"So maybe one big room, one smaller room, some storage and space for an office. Don't need a reception area—or do we?"

"No. The house will serve if we ever need to entertain."

"So, a house. How many will live there?"

"Those working at the lab, and possibly one or two others. Manda, for instance."

"Office for Manda, then. And the house: four bedrooms? Five? That's kind of big."

Len grinned. "Wait 'til you see Madóran's house."

"We could do worse than use Madóran's house as a model," Caeran said.

"It wouldn't fit here, though," said Len.

"The lot is thirty acres."

We walked westward, uphill, leaving the sunny meadow behind. The wonderful vanilla smell of the ponderosas filled the air. I took long, deep breaths, savoring the forest.

Could I live here? Oh, yes.

I found myself wishing I could share this with Lomen. Wanting to lie in that meadow, with the smell of dry leaves around us and aspen leaves flickering against blue sky above.

We found another meadow, a smaller one, after walking about five minutes. The sound of water was more pronounced, and when Len gave a cry of delight I saw why: a little stream ran down one side of the meadow, trending northward.

Caeran watched her run over to it, smiling fondly. He seemed more relaxed than I'd seen him in a while.

"If we site the house here, would you mind walking to the lab?" he asked me.

Duh. "Uh, no."

"Even in the snow?"

"I've got a down coat." Left over from the one season I dated a skier. I'd been too much a novice for him.

We strolled over to join Len by the stream, then we all followed it uphill for a while. Just when I was wondering if we'd strayed off the lot, we found the water's source: a spring, bubbling up from a rocky hollow in the hillside. More aspens stood around it, along with scrub oak and other bushes I couldn't identify. The slope got noticeably steeper beyond the spring.

"Is this on the property?" I asked.

"If it isn't, we will buy this land as well," Caeran said.

"Might be on forest land," Len said.

"Then we will seek permission to use it."

"It's gorgeous," I said, staring at the water rising out of the mountain's heart. Like most desert rats, I'm sentimental about water.

"I think we've seen enough," Caeran said.

Len stepped toward him. "There's one more property."

"We'll look at it."

The walk downhill seemed shorter. We got in the car and headed back to the village. The other property Len had us visit was closer to it and smaller. It was pretty, but there were neighboring houses within sight. We didn't have to discuss it.

We got back in the car, but instead of starting it, Caeran pulled out his phone and asked Len to give him the number of the agent selling the previous lot. Right then and there, he offered to buy the land at its listed price. He also asked if any adjoining property was available. I could just picture the real estate agent salivating.

We were thirsty, so we stopped at the local grocery store for drinks. This would be our neighborhood store, I thought, admiring a fairly extensive wine section.

I could buy some, I realized. On impulse, I grabbed a bottle of champagne and took it to the register with my bottle of water. The cashier asked to see my ID and wished me a happy birthday, which got me a raised eyebrow from Len.

"You must be very thirsty," Caeran said as we walked out.

"It's for celebrating, right?"

He smiled. "Good idea, though perhaps a little premature. I have yet to sign the purchase."

"We could stop on our way home," Len said. "The agent's here in Cedar Crest."

"They won't have the paperwork ready, I think, but yes—let's stop and say hello."

The real estate office was in a tiny strip mall with half a dozen store fronts. The agent, a thirty-something who introduced himself as Tony Gutierrez, was delighted to see us and came close to fawning over Caeran. He offered us all chairs and coffee, and passed around the listings for two neighboring pieces of land. Caeran ended up signing a purchase agreement for the original lot and writing out a down-payment check for an amount that made me feel faint.

We were doing it. We were building a compound—a commune, maybe—in a gorgeous forest in the mountains. I had trouble believing it was real.

Driving home, Caeran chatted with Len about finding an architect and where to put a solar array. I sat thinking about that beautiful land, which I couldn't wait to see again.

In less than half an hour, we were home. The commute would be livable, though I'd probably have to get a car. A buzz of excitement had lodged in my chest, and I wished Lomen was in Albuquerque instead of miles away.

Going back into the darkened house knocked my mood down a couple of notches, and even as I stepped inside I noticed tension in the living room. A pair of candles on the coffee table lit the room. Pirian was sitting up, albeit in a slumped attitude. A mug of tea sat untouched before him.

Savhoran stood on the other side of the table, glowering. Madóran, in Manda's chair, looked calm and watchful. Manda wasn't in the room.

"Pirian," Caeran said. "How are you feeling?"

"Persecuted."

His voice was raspy. He still looked like crap, although Madóran wasn't hovering the way he had the previous day.

"We are discussing a matter of atonement," Savhoran said.

"I did not kill the human."

"You participated in her death."

Oh, man. I slunk to the kitchen to put my champagne in the fridge.

The back door opened and Manda came in. The look she gave me told me this had been going on for a while.

She got out a glass and filled it with water. "Any luck?" she murmured.

I nodded, answering in a low voice. "Caeran put money down on some land."

Her face lit with interest.

Someone said something sharp in ælven in the other room. Manda glanced sidelong toward the doorway, then invited me to escape to the back patio with a sideways nod. I followed her out, relieved to be in the sunlight again.

"They've been arguing all day," Manda said, stretching out in a chair. "They're going around in circles, I think. Pirian is just being stubborn."

"And Savhoran is standing his ground."

"Uh-huh. He's in the right: the creed is clear about atonement."

If Pirian left over this disagreement, the others would consider him alben. Maybe he wouldn't care.

But we'd lose access to his genes. That was worth caring about, even though he was infected.

I wondered idly if we could get a cryo-freezer small enough to fit somewhere in the house, and if we could sneak a sample of Pirian's DNA. I had vague recollections that hair wasn't viable, but if it had a follicle attached....

"So tell me about this land," Manda said, turning in her chair to face me.

I told her, trying not to rave too much about how beautiful it was. She listened, and when I'd finished she asked, "What about water rights?"

"Caeran asked the real estate guy about that. He's going to check about the spring. We'll have to drill a well anyway; the spring doesn't have enough volume to serve the lab and the house."

"What's the water like on neighboring properties?"

"We didn't talk about that."

"I'll call." She took a swig of water. "It'll be hard on Savhoran."

"Why? I figure they all will love it. No humans crawling all over."

"But that's the problem. He'll have to come to the city to hunt. He already has to be careful."

Whenever I thought about Savhoran's life, I was struck by how bleak it must be. He really was courageous, to be able to face it. Good thing he had Manda.

"You all set for your cup-bonding?"

She gave a huff of laughter. "Nervous. Pretty ridiculous, considering how simple a ceremony it is."

"Maybe, but it's a big step, right?"

She nodded. "I just hope I can help him enough."

The note of doubt in her voice was disconcerting. Usually, she exuded complete confidence.

The sun was dipping toward the horizon. It would be up for a while yet, but my stomach was starting to growl. No lunch. The discussion was still going on in the living room.

"Should we maybe start some dinner?" I asked.

"Yeah, probably a good idea. I don't think they're going to stop. Can you cook?"

"A little."

"Then I'm your sous chef. All I'm good for is chopping stuff."

We went inside and I ransacked the cupboards for something I could handle cooking. Fell back on the bachelor's standby:

pasta. I grabbed an onion and some miscellaneous veggies out of the fridge, and while Manda put together a salad, I put water on to boil, then sliced up the onion and set it sautéeing. Threw in some tomatoes and zucchini then poked around in the spice cupboard and found basil, Italian herb mix, and garlic powder. With all of those, my veggie mess started turning into a sauce.

I put the pasta on to boil, then grabbed a stack of plates and started toward the dining nook. Manda called me back.

"Pirian's hungry. We should probably eat out back."

"Oh. OK." I put the plates on the counter, out of her way. "How's he going to hunt? He's still pretty weak."

"I think that's part of what they're discussing. Savhoran could take him out, but he's …" She lowered her voice. "He wants to make sure Pirian offers proper atonement."

"And Pirian doesn't want to?" I whispered.

"He says he doesn't have anything to offer."

"Like a gift, you mean."

"Yeah. Which is a good point, but I get the feeling he doesn't see atonement as necessary, not the way the others do."

"He hasn't been following the creed the way they do."

"Right. Hard to go back, I guess."

I nabbed a slice of carrot from the salad bowl. "Didn't he accept Savhoran's authority when he joined Ebonwatch? Savhoran's the clan leader, right?"

"Yeah," Manda said slowly. "I'm not so sure how seriously Pirian takes that, either."

I stirred the sauce and crunched the carrot, trying to imagine Pirian's point of view. Wasn't very successful. To me it seemed obvious that staying in Ebonwatch would be to his advantage, but force of habit might be keeping him from seeing that.

I opened a bottle of the wine I'd brought from my apartment and set it on the counter by the salad. When the pasta was done, Manda called the others to the kitchen to dish up. I heard Len telling Madóran that she'd sit with Pirian for a while.

I got some Romano cheese out of the fridge and got out the grater. Madóran came in, looking tired. I was about to ask him when he had slept last, then I remembered and bit back the question. He glanced at me and smiled.

Shield, shield, shield. Maybe it didn't do any good. I did it anyway; they probably found my random thoughts distracting, if not annoying.

I waited until everyone else had food, then fixed myself a plate and a glass of wine and joined them on the patio. The sun was setting, and the light slanted in on us, but it was pleasantly warm with a cool breeze blowing. It would be a beautiful evening.

Except for some poor human, somewhere in Albuquerque. It would be a sucky evening for him or her, though I hoped Savhoran would keep it from being downright horrific.

I put that thought aside and settled in to eat, taking the chair next to Manda. Madóran and Caeran were subdued, though after a while Caeran started telling Madóran about the land, and they both cheered up a bit. They talked about how Madóran had built his own house—brick by adobe brick, apparently, over about half a century—and it sounded like Caeran was considering having the ælven build their own place on the new land.

It wouldn't work. They didn't know how, and even if they learned fast and spent untold fortunes on equipment, they wouldn't be able to do the modern construction needed for the lab as fast as we wanted. The house could be hand-built, but it would take time and it would still have to pass an inspection, which it sounded like Caeran wanted to avoid. I was getting the impression he wanted to keep the lab compound off the grid as much as possible.

I decided not to point out the problems with that until later. There was enough stress in the air for now.

Madóran kept glancing toward the house, and when he was about halfway through his dinner he got up. "Len needs to eat."

"So do you," Manda said. "Sit down and finish."

"But—"

"I'll go. I'm done."

And she was. She stood up, brandishing her empty plate, and

went into the kitchen.

Madóran sat down and picked up his fork. His brow was furrowed, making him look tired. Caeran, sitting beyond him, caught my eye. I looked away and focused on my salad for a while.

Shield. And don't think about anything.

Len came out with a plate of food and sat next to Caeran. They were silent, so I figured they were talking.

I realized I felt cold. Looking up, I saw that the sun had set. That fast, it was getting chilly.

I finished my salad, thought about getting seconds on pasta, then decided what I really wanted was a hot beverage. I stood, and Madóran looked up at me.

"Think I'll make some tea," I said. "Would you like some?"

"Yes, thank you."

"Want more to eat?"

"No. It was very good."

I held out a hand for his plate and he gave it to me. Our hands didn't touch, but I still felt a tingle. I went inside, put the kettle on, and puttered in the kitchen until it boiled.

Savhoran came in as I was pouring the water into the teapot. He looked weary.

"Tea?" I offered, and he nodded.

I took down mugs for everyone except Pirian. He might still have that mug of cold tea sitting there. I wasn't going to look.

"You going out tonight?" I asked Savhoran quietly while we waited for the tea to steep.

"I think we must. He needs sustenance. His khi is better, but he is still weak."

I nodded. Losing a mess of blood will do that to you.

I watched Savhoran, who seemed lost in thought. Not happy thoughts, from his expression.

"Is it going to work?"

He looked at me blankly.

"Ebonwatch. The clan."

He sighed. "I don't know."

"Wish I could help."

A smile ghosted across his face. "Thanks."

"You need more members."

The timer started beeping. I shut it off and took the infuser out of the teapot. Poured a mug of tea and handed it to Savhoran.

"But recruiting is a problem," I added.

"Yes."

"Would it be worth seeking out others? Do any of you have friends who...."

"Not here. Back in Europe, but finding them would be difficult."

"They all left their clans?"

He gave me a direct look. "When you are struck by the curse, your clan does not want you."

Ouch. I nodded in sympathy. He headed for the living room.

I carried tea out to Len and Caeran, then went back for the other two mugs. Madóran followed me in. My heart started beating faster.

I shielded, then dared a look at him as I handed him a mug. He sipped it cautiously. He still looked beat; even more so now.

Manda came in from the living room and set two mugs in the sink. "They're going out now," she said. "You could lie on the couch if you wanted, Madóran."

"I thought I would rest a while in Len's office."

"There's no bed in there," I said. "Want to use Lomen's room? I need to study, I can do that out here."

He turned to me with a grateful smile. "If you don't mind, that would be a great relief."

I put down my tea. "I'll just grab my laptop."

Madóran followed me down the hall and stood sipping his tea while I gathered up my computer, earbuds, power supply. I heard the front door close and footsteps slowly going down the path to the street, where Manda's car was parked. Finished collecting my stuff and headed for the hall.

Thank you, Steven.

I froze. It wasn't that overwhelming intimacy that had blown me away before—in fact, I think he was being careful not to be too intimate—but just the contact itself made my heart leap. I had missed it, I realized; Lomen had spoiled me.

I swallowed.

Of course. I hope you get some good rest.

Madóran smiled as I went out. The door closed gently behind me, but a thread of contact remained. A gift, I realized.

I set up my computer in the dining nook. Manda was in her chair with her tablet, already studying. I heard Len and Caeran come in and start cleaning up the dinner dishes. The kettle whistled and immediately stopped.

Len brought me my tea, which I'd forgotten in the kitchen. I opened my biology homework and then sat staring at the screen, unable to focus. I put in my earbuds, but didn't turn on any music. I was useless.

I tried not to think about what I'd rather be doing. Instead I sat pretty much thinking nothing, my mind wandering over all that had happened in the last few days, always returning to that tiny thread of khi connecting me with Madóran, fragile and precious. A treasure.

Did these people even realize how much he gave them? They all respected him, and I hadn't exaggerated when I'd said they revered him. But did they remember all the gifts he gave them, large and small? Half the artwork and furniture in the house—and parts of the house itself—had been made by him. The ælven were all amazingly talented, but for multiple talent and sheer artistry, Madóran outshone them all.

I had to stop dwelling on it. There were no answers to my questions, or at least none that I could demand.

I drank some tea. It was already cooling. With an effort, I managed to finish three of my molecular biology problems before my brain refused to do any more.

I closed the laptop and took out my earbuds. Leaving them on the table, I took my tea to the kitchen to warm it up in the microwave. Caeran didn't like using it; he said it disrupted khi. I suddenly believed him, because while it was running I couldn't sense the connection with Madóran. I was afraid I'd lost it, but when the microwave shut off I found it again, and felt ridiculously relieved.

I took my tea out on the patio. It was full dark, now, but I didn't bother to turn on the light. Easing into a chair, I wondered where the hunters were and whether they were continuing to negotiate.

Pirian was unpredictable, possibly unreliable. Part of me would be glad if he left, though I'd feel sorry for Savhoran. Pirian hadn't been a great clan-brother for him, but he might be better than none.

Movement caught my eye; something jumped down into the yard from the wall at the back right corner. At first I thought it was a cat, then it rose and resolved into a human form.

No—not human. But definitely female.

I took a sharp breath.

Madóran—someone—

Blinding pain seared through my head.

= 16 =

My body went limp, out of my control. I heard my mug hit the concrete and shatter.

The female—the alben—was coming. I couldn't move, but I could tell she was getting closer.

The pain in my head didn't stop. There was something that should have helped, but I couldn't concentrate enough to remember what it was.

Where is he?

Her voice was like nails on a chalkboard. With it came her anger, impatience, and something more—arousal?

I was horrified.

She must not have expected an answer. She'd certainly made it impossible for me to give her one.

Fire crawled through my brain. There was something familiar about it, a nasty, prickling undertone that I'd felt before.

From Pirian, when he spoke to me.

The thought reminded me of what this alben had done to him, the mass of cuts on his chest.

I was going to die, I realized. In a very nasty way.

A loud bang behind me. The pain suddenly vanished.

I heard a grunt, masculine, and then another bang. Caeran's voice called out in ælven, a command.

I saw the silhouette of the alben pause, maybe five yards away. So close!

Caeran strode into the yard. The alben shifted, then turned and ran staggering back the way she came. Caeran followed, but stopped as she went over the wall.

The air around him glowed. The buzz of khi was everywhere. I closed my eyes as a shudder went through me.

Steven.

I felt a shadow move beside me. Looked up at Madóran. He

reached his hands toward me, then paused.

May I?

I nodded. He put his hands on either side of my head, and filled me with light.

Echoes of pain that I hadn't known were still there faded. Warmth and love were all that I knew. Madóran's healing spread through me, following paths I now realized the alben had blazed though my mind.

She had searched me, while I was helpless. Looking for Pirian.

Let me see.

For a moment I didn't understand, then I realized Madóran was asking me to let go of a barrier I didn't even know I had raised. I had to take a couple of deep breaths before I could relax enough to drop it. The warmth filled that last, frightened corner of me, the part of myself that I had instinctively protected.

You are becoming skilled at controlling your thoughts.

It was praise. I was too numb to respond.

Come inside.

Madóran took his hands from my head, only to offer them to help me stand. I felt shaky enough to be grateful.

Caeran came back and opened the kitchen door for us. Broken pottery crunched beneath my feet.

Never mind. We will deal with it later.

Madóran led me to Lomen's room and gently urged me to lie on the bed. He sat beside me, taking my hand.

This should never have happened, Steven. Forgive our carelessness.

Not your fault.

We assumed that because she had fed, she would not be a danger to you. We were wrong.

I was having trouble stringing thoughts together. Shock?

Yes. Rest now. You will recover.

Don't leave.

I won't.

I closed my eyes and lay basking in Madóran's khi. Stray thoughts flicked through me. Madóran had already been tired. What was this costing him?

The alben was looking for Pirian. Did he know?

Caeran came and had a short conversation with Madóran in ælven. I didn't have the energy to be offended at being excluded. Ælven business; I probably couldn't help even if I'd wanted to.

I was such a wimp. Totally useless. Couldn't even defend myself.

Hush. No human can withstand such an attack. Many ælven could not.

I was still frightened, I realized. I wanted to cry in Madóran's arms. Wow, crazy reaction!

Cry if you need to. It's all right.

So kind. The tears came with that thought, quiet release flowing down my face, into my hair. I didn't care.

I was safe. Alive, not about to die.

After a while my nose stuffed up and I had to blow it. Madóran helped me, then silently advised me to lie down again.

He stayed beside me, not talking, just there. Exactly what I needed. Now and then a wave of fear would go through me, and he would chase it away with a wave of healing. Gradually I relaxed, and drifted into sleep.

I was running. I had to be somewhere, and I was late, and there were alben after me, several of them. My dread increased with every step, but I couldn't stop, and I couldn't yell for help.

Steven. You are safe.

I gave a little gasp and opened my eyes. Soft light filled the room. Madóran had lit Lomen's candle.

Forgive me for waking you.

No ... thank you. Bad dream.

My head ached. I sat up, and Madóran handed me a glass of water. I chugged it, then put a hand to my temple.

May I?

He took the glass and set it aside, then placed cool hands on my temples. I sighed with relief.

Did she ... damage something?

No. It is the shock. Your body is unharmed.

Faculties a different issue. His hands fell away.

Mind-numbing fear was the problem. It was all too familiar. I'd been there before, years ago. High school bullies: adult bodies capable of killing, driven by adolescent minds. I shook my head to get rid of the memory.

No one should have to feel that way.

I met Madóran's gaze and gave him a tired smile. *Thank you.*

He reached up and brushed my hair back from my temple. A caress, this time.

Oh, sweet heaven.

I closed my eyes, which was maybe a mistake, because it made me aware of the pine/spice aroma in the room. No doubt he sensed my physical reaction.

The ache of desire overwhelmed all other feelings. I looked at him, reached up to touch his hair. I'd been wanting to do that since I first saw him. It was soft and fine, black as midnight.

He smiled, leaning into my touch a little. That did away with what was left of my self-control.

I kissed him hungrily. He answered, gentle and warm, accepting. Leaving me the lead.

A small part of me protested, but it was too late. I needed this. I'd make amends later. Atone, somehow.

He let me spend my tension, then showed me ways to pleasure him that I'd never imagined. The headiness of double-awareness filled me with delight and joy and relief. I was safe. Safe, and loved.

Madóran was completely unlike Lomen. He was fluid, changeable, subtle and wonderfully generous. Not that Lomen was the opposite, but he was more direct, rather masculine and straightforward.

When we were both spent we lay still. I listened to Madóran's heartbeat, strong and slow.

Sleep a little more. We will be leaving shortly.

Leaving?

We are going to Guadalupita. It will be safer there, now that the alben are aware of this place.

Oh.

I didn't bother trying to hide my dismay. He must know all about my feelings—all of them, contradictory and foolish and afraid, everything.

Going to Guadalupita. That was the name I'd forgotten; the name of the town where Madóran lived.

I'd be seeing Lomen in a few hours.

= 17 =

I sat up, rubbing my face. I'd never get back to sleep, not now.

Madóran's fingers traced a pattern on my back.

It will be all right, Steven.

I tensed, then turned and caught his hand, kissing his fingertips to show I wasn't angry.

I have to figure this out for myself.

Yes. You will.

His smile was full of fondness. Clearly, he didn't mind my feelings for Lomen. That made the guilt worse, somehow. I stood, then bent to kiss his forehead.

Thank you—for the healing—for everything.

My pleasure.

I'd better get ready, if we're leaving.

I pulled on a t-shirt and shorts, then went out. Madóran followed me, wearing his caftan again. Easy to put on, a caftan. And to take off.

I tiptoed into the darkened living room, but it was empty.

Savhoran and Pirian left earlier so as to arrive before dawn. Amanda went with them.

Poor Manda. At least she was with Savhoran. It didn't sound like a fun drive, though.

I gathered my computer stuff and took it back to the bedroom, which smelled of sex and beeswax. Ignoring that as best I could, I put the computer and my new tablet in my backpack, then got out my bag and stuffed some clothes into it.

Do I have time for a shower?

I expect so.

No clock in the room. I lifted the window curtain and saw that it was still dark outside.

The time didn't matter so much, I guessed. We would leave when we were all ready, which might mean they were waiting on me.

Len is sleeping.

Good.

I got out some clean clothes. Madóran, standing in the doorway, stepped out of my way. I paused, wanting to show my gratitude even though I'd already thanked him, wanting to kiss him but not daring. Wanting to avoid even thinking about asking him to join me in the shower.

I did a nod that turned into an almost-bow. Weird, but he smiled and nodded back.

I took a long, hot shower. I did not use Madóran's soap.

By the time I came out, someone was cooking breakfast. My body informed me that it was definitely ready to eat.

I went across to the bedroom, intending to tidy it up, but Madóran had beat me to it. The bed was made, the candle was out and a faint light was coming through the curtains. My bag and backpack were gone—loaded in the car, I assumed. I tossed my laundry in the closet and went out to get breakfast.

"How are you feeling?" Caeran asked me as I joined them at the table.

I glanced at him, looking for irony, but if he meant any he hid it well. "Much better, thanks to Madóran."

I looked at the healer and my heart did a slow flip. I could have gone back to bed with him right then.

I focused on my eggs and toast for a minute. They were watching me, I knew.

"And you, Madóran?" Caeran asked. "Did you manage to get any rest?"

"I am well-rested, thank you."

A memory hit me and I looked up at him. "She attacked you, too!"

"Only briefly. Caeran took the brunt of her rage."

"I was hoping the two of us could subdue her, but we were unprepared," Caeran said.

I was kind of glad they hadn't managed to do that. What would we have done with her? Tied her up and sat on her?

"After Evennight, we will return here and lay a trap for her," Caeran continued. "If we catch her, the male will probably follow."

And then ....

No one filled in the blanks. At least their deaths would be merciful, or so I assumed. Unless Pirian was involved.

I looked at Len, wondering how she was feeling. Her plans for Evennight had been disrupted yet again. We were headed to Madóran's, and we'd stay there until Friday and have one Evennight celebration with everyone all together. Mirali would be there, perhaps. So would Savhoran, and she'd just have to live with that.

Unless Madódran did some fancy tap-dancing. I looked at him, wondering if he ever felt pulled in different directions.

His gaze flicked in my direction, and a slight smile curved his lips.

OK, fine. Dumb question.

I drank a deep swallow of tea and finished my breakfast without making any more conversation. We threw all the dishes in the dishwasher and turned it on, then locked up the house and got in the Lexus. Len took the shotgun seat. I sat in the back with Madóran.

The sky behind the mountains was glowing pale gold. Sunrise came late in Albuquerque because of the Sandias to the east. Before the sun cleared the mountain range, Caeran had reached the freeway and turned west.

Not much conversation in the car. Caeran and Len were probably talking in mindspeech. I could have done the same with Madóran but I really was trying to be good, and fair, and as honest as possible.

I still felt rotten. I'd done a selfish thing. Involved Madóran in my selfishness, though he didn't seem to mind it much.

I glanced at him. He was looking out the window.

I shielded, hoping he'd understand that I just needed some space to think things through.

Caeran stopped to fill the gas tank, then turned north on I-25 and we were off for Guadalupita. The sun rose on my right. I put on my shades and sat pondering how to explain to Lomen.

I wanted to offer him atonement. Trouble was, I didn't understand the concept that well. The hunters, Savhoran anyway, offered gifts of atonement—often things they had made according to Savhoran—to the humans they fed from. I didn't think that would work in my case; there wasn't anything I could give Lomen that he didn't have or couldn't get.

My handicraft skills were limited mostly to things a bachelor needed for getting by: enough sewing to mend clothing, a small repertoire of edible and not-too-complicated recipes. I knew seven different ways to fix a toilet with a paperclip, but I couldn't wire a lamp.

I closed my eyes. I'd think of something. I had several hours.

I woke up when the car stopped.

Blinking, I sat up and looked around. We were at a gas station. Len opened her door and looked back at me. "Pit stop," she said, and got out.

I'd been slouched against the door and my neck was stiff. I rolled my shoulders, trying to loosen up.

Madóran headed into the convenience store. Caeran was already pumping gas. I got out and offered to help, but he shook his head.

"Where are we?"

"Las Vegas."

"Still a ways from Guadalupita?"

"An hour or so."

I went into the store, used the bathroom, and looked for something to drink. Nothing was interesting, so I grabbed a bottle of water.

An hour until I saw Lomen. An hour to figure out what to say to him, what to offer besides my apology. I walked up and down the aisles, looking hopelessly at canned food, chips, candy, maps, boxes of tissue. Useless human stuff.

Near the door was freezer chest full of ice cream. My favorite toffee ice cream bars were in there. Suddenly I wanted to get

Lomen one of those. So what if it was insignificant? It was a gesture.

One that would melt during an hour-long car ride.

Frowning, I refused to admit defeat. I wanted to share this little thing with Lomen—this small pleasure that was part of me. I prowled through the store again and found a picnic-sized styrofoam cooler. I took that and the ice cream bar and my water to the register and asked the clerk to ring up a bag of ice as well.

Outside, I got the ice out of the big freezer, opened the bag, and dumped as much as would fit into the cooler. Then I buried the ice cream bar in the middle of all the ice, emptied the excess on the pavement, and threw away the bag.

No one commented as I carried the cooler back to the car and tucked it into the trunk among the luggage. I got back in my seat and opened my water. Caeran drove north on a small state highway.

The land was pretty. I had never been this way; my experience of northern New Mexico was limited to Santa Fe and one unfortunate skiing trip to Taos. I gazed at the wooded hillsides, mostly piñon with some pines and deciduous mixed in. Meadows filled with tall grass and wildflowers, sunflowers and purple asters and a bunch more I didn't know by name, were interspersed with forest.

As we drove north, the pines appeared more frequently. The town of Mora had a river and an old mill. I would have liked to explore, but we didn't stop. We turned onto a smaller road and continued north.

I was starting to get hungry by the time Caeran slowed and turned onto a driveway. A carved owl peered down at us from a fencepost, and I recognized it as Madóran's work.

"Where's the town?" I asked. "Farther up the road?"

Len chuckled and turned in her seat to grin at me. "You missed it. It was the post office back there."

I vaguely remembered driving past a couple of buildings standing together, but I certainly hadn't registered them as a town.

"Guadalupita is not so much a town as a collection of land grants," Madóran said. "I was already living here by the time the other colonists reached the area. They kindly gave me a grant of my own."

The driveway was dirt but well-graded. To our right was a fence, to the left an open meadow.

"Hope you have nice neighbors," I said.

"I own the two neighboring grants as well. I bought out their owners many years ago."

Holy wow. Spanish grants, the original ones anyway, were not small. They were intended as farmsteads.

Madóran gazed out of the window, smiling. Glad to be home.

We drove for several minutes before we reached the house. Caeran parked next to Manda's car and we all got out. I stood gazing at the house, which was *huge.* The front *portal* was twice as long as the front of Len and Caeran's house.

Caeran opened the trunk. Madóran extracted a small leather bag, then stepped onto the wooden *portal* and went to the door.

I swallowed, remembering that Lomen was here. I got my backpack, my bag, and my cooler out of the trunk, and followed the others inside.

The entryway was as big as Len and Caeran's living room and was filled with plants. The far wall, facing west, was glass, but shaded by another *portal.*

We went through a doorway on the right and into a greatroom. It was beautiful, filled with hand-carved furniture and rugs and artwork. A kiva fireplace in one corner promised cozy winter evenings. The far end of the room held a dining table that could probably seat a dozen.

Madóran led us to a door at the back of the room that gave out onto a *plazuela,* the classic inner courtyard of the traditional hacienda. This one was a lush garden, with a fountain and flowering bushes and vines and shaded by huge cottonwood trees that were going golden. A deep *portal* ran all around it, protecting the inner windows of the hacienda from the sun, with partial glass walls that looked like they might slide to fully enclose the *portal* in cold weather.

This might have started out as a hand-built one-room adobe house, but it was more like a mansion now. It must be worth at least a million dollars.

Madóran led us along the north *portal*, chatting with Len and Caeran about "their" room. He paused at a door near the corner with the western side of the hacienda.

"I think—yes, this room is unoccupied. You may have it, Steven."

He pushed open the door to a small but luxurious bedroom, with more Madóran-made furniture and its own kiva fireplace. I went in and set my stuff on the bed.

"This is great. Thanks."

"We'll put some lunch together shortly—you're probably hungry."

"Yeah. Let me know if I can help."

He smiled, then walked on with Len and Caeran, turning the corner and heading along the west *portal*. I watched them go into a room at the southwest corner, then stood gazing at the garden.

No wonder Len and Manda always talked about this place. It was beautiful. A haven.

I could see the fountain through my open door. Birds played and squabbled in the water. I watched them for a while, then decided I should unpack.

There was no table, only a nightstand. I put my pack on top of the dresser and put my clothes in the drawers, then looked at the cooler.

Stupid idea. The ice cream might have melted anyway, or maybe the wrapper was soggy.

Pretty feeble, Steve.

I set the cooler on the floor behind the door, telling myself I'd deal with it later. I was too tense to study, so I sat on the bed and zoned out on the birds some more.

I should go find Lomen and just make a clean breast of it. Better to talk to him alone than with everyone else listening.

Listening! Jeez!

I shielded, wondering if I had broadcast my anxiety to the whole clan. What a putz.

I heard voices and footsteps coming along the *portal*. Panic stabbed me and I jumped up and went to the dresser, fussing with my pack, taking out my computer gear. Movement made me look toward the door.

For a second my heart contracted, then I recognized Faranin and Bironan. They stopped, looking at me in surprise.

"We did not know you had arrived," Bironan said.

"Just a little while ago."

"We are to be neighbors, then," said Faranin. "We are sharing the library, next door."

"Library?"

Bironan smiled. "Come and see. You are welcome to read any of the books."

They opened the door to the west of mine, which accessed a big, L-shaped room that took up the whole corner of the house. One side was full of bookshelves and a work table, the other side had two big couches that were probably beds at night, and more bookshelves. Chairs—comfy ones around the fireplace and straight-backed ones around the work table—made it a homey library, and tall, stained-glass windows on the north wall let in muted daylight.

"Nice," I said, understating.

"We heard that you encountered the alben female," Faranin said. "I trust you are unharmed."

I swallowed. "I think so. Thanks."

His face hardened. "She will be dealt with."

Boy, I sure never wanted these guys angry at me.

"Well, guess I'll get ready for lunch," I said. "Thanks for the welcome."

I went back out, heading for my room. Down the *portal*, I saw another ælven that I took for Caeran going into one of the rooms. He looked at me.

"Steven!"

Not Caeran. My heart started pounding.

Lomen hurried toward me. I shielded, trying to find the right words to say to him.

He caught me in a tight hug.

Forgive me. I should have been there.

I froze. He held me at arm's length.

Are you injured?

No, but—come in here.

I stepped into my room and he came in after me. I closed the door, then took a couple of steps away, struggling for the right words.

What's wrong?

He wasn't pushing. I knew that if he wanted to, he could read what was wrong straight out of my head. Peel me open like the alben had.

Don't think about that.

I turned to face him. His eyes were troubled, watching me.

I owe you an apology.

Why?

I took a deep breath. No way to soften it.

I slept with Madóran.

He stared at me for a long moment, then a corner of his mouth curved upward.

He's marvelous, isn't he?

My jaw dropped. Lomen's smile widened.

You thought I would be angry.

Well...yeah. I mean, after the fuss I made about wanting long-term...

He gathered me into his arms and banished all my fretful fears. His warmth was different from Madóran's, but every bit as potent. With a long sigh, I relaxed for the first time that day. He stroked my hair.

When I heard the alben had attacked you, I was so afraid...

I'm all right. Madóran was right there. And Caeran. They got her off me right away.

I'm glad.

He leaned back to look at me, brushed my hair back from my face.

She did you harm, though.

Madóran said there was no damage.

No, but you were not frightened like this before.

I'll get over it. With your help.

He pulled me close again and I basked in it. Just to stand there in his arms was wonderful.

My gaze fell on the cooler by the door. I chuckled.

I brought you something.

I slid from his embrace and picked up the cooler, put it on the nightstand and opened it. The ice hadn't melted much. I dug out the ice cream bar—package only slightly waterlogged—and presented it to him.

Ice cream?

That's my favorite kind. I wanted you to have one.

His smile held both amusement and affection. He accepted the bar with a little bow.

I thank you.

I was thinking I should offer you atonement. Stupid, I know.

Not stupid at all. You honor me, though you owed me no atonement.

I shrugged, embarrassed. Gestured to the bar.

Well, anyway, I hope you like it.

Will you share it with me?

Um, sure.

His eyes narrowed with glee. He unwrapped the bar, took a bite, chewed a couple of times, then reached for me.

His kiss was an explosion of sensations: toffee, love, cold, himself, sweetness. We made short work of the ice cream and a fast mess of the bed. Still lying there glowing when a knock on the door made me jump.

"Steve? Lunch is ready." Len's voice.

"OK. Be right there."

My voice was about an octave higher than normal. I hoped she hadn't noticed.

We got dressed and tidied the bed, then Lomen led me out into the garden, crossing it diagonally and going in another door that turned out to be the kitchen. A little table by the window was already full: Len, Caeran, Manda, Faranin, and Bironan were crowded around it.

Madóran looked up from the counter, glanced from Lomen to me, and smiled. "Settling in?"

"Yeah," I said, feeling a blush start up my neck.

"There is tuna salad. Come and help yourselves."

We did, and took our plates out to the garden, where there were chairs and low tables spaced around the *portal*. Madóran joined us.

We ate in silence at first. I felt embarrassed, though neither of them gave me any reason.

I'd had sex with both of them in the past twenty-four hours. Apparently they both thought that was just fine.

My expectations of how they would react had been based on human culture, and were completely bogus. Long lives made you more tolerant, I guessed. I would have expected the opposite, but again that was based on humans, who got more set in their ways the older they grew.

The oldest humans were still little more than children to these guys, though. If the ælven went through that set-in-ways phase, they must grow out of it again.

They really were an alien species. A beautiful, glorious, completely non-human species.

I was getting full after the ice cream, and poked at the last of my salad. Tried to think of something to say.

"So we're staying through Evennight, right? Just one ceremony?"

Madóran sighed. "Len still wants two."

"Kind of silly, now that we're all here. Doesn't she see that?"

"She sees it. She is still unhappy with Mirali."

"Not like her to be so stubborn."

Madóran glanced at Lomen. "Len and Mirali have never gotten along well. Mirali once … I do not want to say she attacked Len, but that is what it amounts to."

I stared at him. "She *attacked* Len?"

"It was defensive. She was ill, and unexpectedly encountered a human stranger. Her reaction was disproportionate, but understandable."

"Len did forgive her," Lomen said.

"Yes, but there has been unease between them ever since."

Wow. I wondered what this defensive attack had been like. If it was anything like what the alben had done to me, I didn't blame Len for being touchy.

"Want me to talk to her?" I offered.

"What would you say?" Madóran asked.

"That the clan needs to be united, and not squabble."

"She will point out that Mirali began the dispute."

"Mirali needs to be tolerant, too. She doesn't have the right to say who can attend Evennight and who can't, right?"

"True."

"So it's her choice. If she doesn't want to be around Savhoran —and Pirian?"

Madóran nodded.

"—and Pirian, then she doesn't have to attend the ceremony." I took another bite of chicken and chewed it, thinking. "Does Pirian want to be there?"

"I believe he is looking forward to it, yes."

"He said as much when they arrived this morning," said Lomen.

I looked at Madóran. "Are they staying here?"

"Yes."

"And Mirali, too?"

"No, she and her family are in the new house."

I remembered something about a house being built. Hadn't paid much attention.

I put down my plate, which still had a couple of bites of salad on it. "Sorry, I took too much. It's wonderful, I'm just stuffed."

Lomen scraped my leftovers onto his plate and kept eating. Madóran smiled fondly at him, which gave me an unexpected twinge of jealousy.

I clamped down on that fast. No way could I indulge in that

kind of selfishness, not when they were both being so generous.

I had a lot to learn.

Bironan and Faranin came out of the kitchen on their way back to the library. Smiles and nods were exchanged. I couldn't help wondering if those two were lovers. None of my business, really.

Lomen picked up my plate and headed for the kitchen. Madóran was still eating, slowly savoring each bite as he gazed at his garden.

"Good to be home?"

He smiled at me. "Yes."

"You've been doing a lot for other people lately. Me included. Is there anything I can do for you?"

He paused, chewing another bite, finally swallowing. "Yes. Do talk to Lenore about Evennight. I think she may listen to you more than to me, just now."

"Glad to," I said.

He ate the last bite of his salad. I stood and offered to take his plate. He handed it to me with a look so fond I felt another blush starting. I smiled back and went into the kitchen.

Lomen and Caeran were at the table, talking. Manda had disappeared somewhere, gone to hang with Savhoran, maybe. I joined Len at the double sink, one side of which was full of sudsy water and dishes.

I handed her Madóran's plate. "No dishwasher, eh?"

"Madóran's not much into gadgets. We only talked him into the microwave because I wanted something to heat up my tea."

She nodded toward a small microwave on the counter, its sleek black incongruous against the Spanish-style blue and white tiles.

"Shall I rinse?" I offered.

"Thanks."

We worked in silence for a while. The two at the table were talking in ælven. I wondered how much of it Len understood.

"Don't be surprised if you have nightmares," Len said softly.

"Already had one."

She paused and looked at me. "I'm really sorry she got to you. We were trying so hard to protect you."

That surprised me. "To protect all of us, you mean."

"Well, yeah. But Manda and I—we knew what might happen. Knew how to watch out, at least. I should have warned you not to go outside after dark, even in the back yard."

"You couldn't have known she'd come in the yard."

"Yeah, I could. Manda saw an alben drop right into the *plazuela* there." She gestured toward the window.

That was unnerving. A wave of fear went through me, leaving me tingling.

"That one knew about this place, right? I mean, the two in Albuquerque don't, so ..."

"They probably do. From Pirian. And they're hunting him. They can track him by his khi."

Crap.

"Does Mirali know that?"

"Oh, yeah. She's apoplectic."

I finished rinsing a plate and set it in the dish rack to dry. "You still mad at her?"

"I still think she's wrong."

"Yeah, but I can see her point of view."

Len glared at me. "You agree with her?"

"I didn't say that."

I wasn't doing a very good job at peacemaking.

"Look, we should just have one Evennight ceremony. Mirali doesn't have to be there if she's uncomfortable."

"Well, Savhoran shouldn't have to worry about her comfort."

"I agree. One ceremony, everyone's invited. No one has to come."

She gave me a long look. "Yeah, OK. Madóran shouldn't have to do it twice."

"Yeah."

"But she'll be pissed."

I was about to say that was her problem, but it was really the clan's problem. As long as there was conflict between the protective mother and the sufferers of the disease-without-a-name, the clan would be in danger of breaking up. Technically it was two clans, but kin-clans, whatever that meant. And a clan with two members wasn't much more than an idea.

I tried to think of a way to make them all happy. I couldn't figure one out. It seemed like an impasse, but I wasn't ready to give up.

What did they each need?

Mirali needed to know her child was safe.

Savhoran needed acceptance, respect.

Pirian . . . I wasn't sure what Pirian needed. He wanted vengeance, but that had nothing to do with Mirali.

There should be a way to find a compromise. Maybe that was something humans actually did better than ælven. We were more contentious, and naturally more impatient. Maybe we were better at making deals that everyone could live with and getting on with things.

I set the last dish in the drain, then asked Len where to find a glass and filled it with water. The garden drew me, despite the image Len had given me of an alben violating its peacefulness. I told myself that couldn't happen in the daytime, and went out to find a chair in the shade.

Madóran was still there, sitting with eyes closed. Not wanting to disturb him, I chose a seat that was shaded by trees, and sat down to ponder the problem some more.

Mirali was afraid. Maybe she didn't understand how the curse was transmitted.

Of course, they didn't know for sure. That's one of the things we'd be looking for as we studied the disease-without-a-name.

Dammit, it needed a damn name.

It was the disease that was really the problem. The source of all our woes.

I wondered, if we could offer the two alben back in Albuquerque a cure, would they take it? Or were they too addicted to their perverse pleasures?

Ugh.

Didn't matter anyway; a cure was years if not decades away, and the clan wouldn't tolerate the alben's activities that long.

A raucous squabble in the fountain drew my attention. Some scrub jays had gotten into it, splashing with great vigor and arguing with great volume. I saw Madóran lean forward to watch them, and since he wasn't meditating I decided to ask him a question.

"Lunch was great," I said as I joined him. "Did you make it?"

"With Amanda's help. Just leftovers, but thank you."

"I'll take your leftovers any day."

He chuckled.

"Mind if I pick your brain?"

He gazed at me. "That is an odd expression."

"Sorry—I just want to ask you a couple of questions."

"Of course."

"What can you tell me about the curse? The nature of the disease, I mean. I want to figure out a name for it."

"We have always just called it the curse."

"Yeah, but that won't look so good on a grant application. Can you tell me about what it does in the body? Is it blood-borne?"

"It alters the blood."

"Alters it?"

"Weakens it. The hunger is a result of that. The blood no longer sustains the body as it should. As if it were hollow, suddenly."

I mused about that. "So the curse might be doing something to the digestive system, too. Well, it must—because they can't eat normal food any more, right?"

"They can eat it, but it doesn't satisfy them. They don't really digest it. Mainly it just makes them uncomfortable."

"Except for the greens."

"Yes, they do need greens, but they only want them after feeding."

Greens contained a lot of iron. Something to do with blood-iron levels? Iron absorption?

Hollow blood.

Blood was "hemo" in Greek, as in hemoglobin.

I pulled out my phone to surf up the Greek for "hollow." I heard a door close and glanced up to see Manda coming across the *plazuela*.

"I hope you brought your charger," she said, flopping into a chair next to Madóran.

"I did. You don't happen to know Greek, do you?"

"Not me. I'm the business kid, remember?"

Len and Caeran came out of the kitchen, hand in hand, reminding me that I hadn't told Madóran that Len had agreed to one Evennight ceremony.

"What do you need Greek for?" Manda asked.

"We need a scientific name for the curse."

"Cursus albenius."

"Mmmm . . . not quite."

Len looked at Caeran. "You know Greek?"

"No. I'd have thought Madóran would."

Madóran turned his head to look at me. "What do you wish to say?"

"'Hollow', for 'hollow blood'."

"'Koilos'."

I frowned, trying to extrapolate structure rules from other medical terms. "Hemo-koilos."

"It would be koilohaemia," said Madóran.

"That's a mouthful," Manda said. "How about 'Steve's anemia'?"

"Harrison's anemia," Len said. "You use the last name."

"No, I like koilohaemia," I said.

"It can be both."

"As long as I can pronounce one of them," Manda said. She got up and went into the kitchen.

Madóran looked at me. "So. Now it has a name."

"Name it, then you can defeat it." I looked at Caeran. "Good thing we're getting started on the lab. We don't want to do any of the research at UNM, or they'll want control of our results."

His eyes widened slightly. "I hadn't thought of that."

"We can use them to learn technique—how to use the equipment, how to do the research—but we shouldn't actually do it there."

"Get me that list of the equipment you'll need."

"I will."

"A man of many ideas," Madóran murmured, smiling.

Caeran and Len continued down the *portal* and went through a door in the west wall, and I saw that Lomen had been behind them, leaning against the wall. My heart did a little happy bounce at seeing him. He smiled.

"You talked to Len," Madóran said.

"Yeah. She's OK with just having one ceremony." I had a thought and sat up straighter. "Hey, would you mind introducing me to Mirali?"

"You will meet her at the celebration."

"What if she doesn't come? I'd like to meet her ahead of time, if you don't mind. I bet the prospect of a human stranger at the party just adds to her discomfort."

"We could walk over to the new house, certainly. I cannot promise that Mirali will agree to see you. She is . . . somewhat prejudiced against humans, I fear."

Given what we were doing to the planet, I could hardly blame her.

"Well, I'd like to meet her and admire the baby. Is now a good time?"

Madóran shrugged. "As good as any."

"May I come along?" Lomen asked.

"Fine by me," I said.

"Of course," Madóran said, rising.

We went along the south *portal* to a utility room from which a side door opened onto a lush vegetable garden. It was half an acre at least, and well-tended.

"Wow. Nice!"

Madóran smiled. "I enjoy gardening, and of course food one grows oneself always tastes best."

He led the way past the garden and through a large orchard—

mostly apples, from what I could tell. We walked through dappled shade, with the smell of the fruit rising around us.

"Don't tell me you come close to eating this many apples."

He laughed. "Oh, no. I let neighbors pick the fruit and keep most of the harvest as their payment."

It was peaceful, walking with these two men I admired—no, loved. I loved them both. I didn't care if they picked up on that thought. It was true.

Despite the fear and havoc created by the alben, despite the tension of needing to find a cure for koilohaemia (preferably yesterday), I felt more fulfilled and more at peace than I ever remembered feeling before. I had found not just one person, but a whole family who respected me for who I was, and who valued me. It was as if I had finally found my true home.

The apples gave way to a field of raspberries. They were mostly done, but a few late berries clung under the leaves. Madóran invited me to eat as many as I liked, so I grabbed the ones I spotted—warm from the sunshine, sweet and tart on the tongue—and shared them with Lomen as we passed between rows of bushes. Beyond was another orchard, this one not bearing fruit at the moment. The leaves looked a little like peaches, if I was remembering right.

A house came into view: single-story adobe, small, with a wing still under construction. Similar in style to Madóran's hacienda, with all possibility of eventually getting that big. For now, it was just a modest house.

Some tall cottonwoods stood west of it, shading it from behind. I heard running water; there was a river back there among the trees.

Madóran stepped onto the *portal* and knocked on the front door. After a longish pause, it was opened by a male ælven, plainly one of Caeran's kin by his brown hair and green eyes. He shot me an unsettled look, then turned a questioning gaze on Madóran.

"Greetings, Nathrin." Madóran gestured to me. "I have a guest, Steven Harrison, who would like to meet Mirali."

I bowed slightly, the way I'd seen Lomen do. Nathrin sized me up with a longer look, then answered.

"I will find out if she is comfortable receiving visitors. May I ask you to wait?"

Madóran nodded, and Nathrin closed the door. I traded a glance with Lomen.

Don't mind Nathrin. They are still afraid.

Still?

Since we journeyed here. It was a difficult time. Mirali was very ill and we feared we would lose both her and her child.

Well, I'm glad that didn't happen.

Madóran strode a few steps away, along the *portal*. I looked at Lomen.

Did I say something to make him mad?

He is giving us privacy, I believe. He knows we are talking.

Can't he hear us?

Mindspeech between ælven is quite rare.

I gazed after Madóran, suddenly feeling bad. I'd assumed the ælven could all talk with each other this way.

We learn instinctively to shield our thoughts long before we can talk. It is a habit few of us can overcome.

Except with humans.

Most humans do not know how to shield. Your thoughts are open, and we can answer if we choose.

Why doesn't your shield interfere with that?

I believe it is because your khi does not trigger our defensive reflexes. We can influence you through khi, and that includes being able to converse with you.

I couldn't help the shiver that went through me. Yeah, I'd been influenced pretty hard.

Speaking of shielding, you might want to do so now. It would be polite to Mirali and Nathrin if you kept your thoughts quiet.

I promptly shielded, then walked after Madóran.

"Lomen tells me you couldn't hear our conversation. I didn't realize that. I'm sorry."

He smiled. "No need to apologize."

The door opened again. Madóran returned to it and I followed.

"You may come in," Nathrin told us.

I brought up the rear, shielding my thoughts again for good measure. The house was simply furnished, though there were Madóran touches here and there: a carved door, a low table, and in the room where Mirali awaited us, a pottery urn and mug on a tale beside her.

She looked up, green eyes wide and defiant. It was the first time I had seen Caeran's features on a female. I had expected small and frail, but she was majestic, nearly the same size as her partner.

She had her baby in her arms, and had apparently recently been feeding it. A blue and green shawl draped her shoulders. The baby was wrapped in similar colors, so that its pale face glowed against the darker tones.

"Mirali," said Madóran, bowing. "I am glad to see you looking well. May I introduce Steven Harrison? He is a new friend of ours."

I bowed to her. "I am honored to meet you."

She shot Madóran a glance that looked like annoyance to me, then put on a tolerant smile. "Hello."

"Congratulations on your beautiful baby," I said. "Is it a girl?"

She nodded, and her eyes softened a bit. "Her name is Nathrali."

A girl. Good for the clan's future.

"May you grow strong and wise, Nathrali," I said softly.

The baby opened her eyes and looked straight at me. I was surprised. Not that I was an expert, but I thought newborns didn't learn to focus like that for a while. But that was humans; aelven might be different.

I smiled at her. She stared back for a minute, then turned and burrowed against her mother's chest.

"Evennight will be her first celebration with the clan, right?" I said. "Same for me."

Mirali's eyes narrowed. She looked as if she were thinking of what to say.

"Yes," Nathrin said.

Mirali looked at him. I could have sworn they were talking in mindspeech.

"I doubt we will be there," Mirali said.

"Because Savhoran and Pirian are here?" I said. Madóran shifted beside me; I paid no attention. "You know, just being in a room with them won't endanger you or Nathrali."

"You cannot know that."

"Madóran tells me the disease is blood-borne, and probably only transmitted through contact with bodily fluids."

She looked at Madóran. He nodded.

"That is my belief."

"We're going to find a cure," I said brashly.

She tilted her head back. "Before the ceremony?"

"Of course not. You're right, it will take years, but we will find one. Before Nathrali is grown up," I said, again taking a risk.

"A laudable goal," Mirali said. Her tone told me she didn't buy it.

"Look, come to the ceremony. You can stand on one side, and Savhoran and Pirian on the opposite. Fair enough?"

Her gaze shifted from me to Madóran. "One wonders why a human concerns himself so with our customs."

"His concern is for our well-being, Mirali."

"How refreshing."

"My concern is for your survival. All of you." I glanced at Nathrin. "Your best chance is if you stay together."

Nathrin said nothing, but a fleeting smile of exasperation crossed his face. Aha! He had been arguing the same thing.

"You see, until a couple of weeks ago I didn't know the ælven existed," I went on. "You're a miracle to me. I want you to survive, to prosper. I'll do what I can to help."

"Steven has committed his life to curing the curse," Lomen said.

Mirali's eyes widened. "Why would you do this for us? You say you knew nothing of us a short while ago."

"I …" I shrugged. "You're the best thing I've ever found." I glanced at Madóran, hoping I wasn't sticking my foot in my mouth. "I want to be around you as much as I can. All of you."

"All of us?" Mirali said quietly. "Even Pirian?"

Had she lifted that from my thoughts? But I had shielded. Maybe she just counted on my being afraid of him. Well, I was, but it was more complicated than that.

"Pirian is struggling to figure out which way to go," I said. "I know what that's like. If I can help him, I will."

She gazed at me, then at her partner. I shot another glance at Madóran. He smiled, then gave a tiny nod toward the door.

"Thank you for allowing me to visit. I hope to see you again soon," I said, backing away.

Mirali watched me go, her green eyes thoughtful. Nathrin showed us out, and as I passed him in the doorway he offered his hand.

"Thank you for visiting."

The ælven didn't shake hands much; I knew he was honoring me. I grasped his hand briefly and smiled.

"I'm glad I got to meet you."

He nodded. "We will meet again."

Nathrin turned to Madóran and said something in ælven. Madóran answered briefly, then we walked back toward the hacienda.

That brief exchange in ælven had made me realize that they had all spoken English for my sake during the visit, even Mirali. That little courtesy made me feel self-conscious; I'd required them to speak in a foreign language. I hadn't meant to impose on them in such a way.

"You did well, Steven," Madóran said.

"Hope I didn't say anything stupid."

"No. I think you impressed them."

"And Mirali is difficult to impress," said Lomen, grinning.

As we walked back, I found myself thinking about Pirian. Not that I wanted to—I'd rather have nothing to do with him—but what I'd told Mirali was true. I knew what it was like to have to decide between two cultures, two ways of life. He hadn't volunteered for the curse. He was facing a tough choice: commit to Ebonwatch and follow the creed, or go alben and be alone. Either way he had to give something up.

We got back to the hacienda and Madóran paused at the veggie garden to pick some stuff for dinner. I offered to help, with the caveat that I couldn't tell a carrot from a turnip. Madóran laughed.

"How would you like to carry the basket?"

He got a big wicker basket and a broad-brimmed straw hat for me from the utility room. Lomen excused himself, saying he wanted to study. I watched him go into the hacienda.

"Not a gardener, either?"

"He is competent, but I think it holds no passion for him."

I followed Madóran around as he pulled things out of the ground and clipped green stuff. He showed me how to pull carrots, and how to rescue them when I broke off the tops. The joy he took in his garden was contagious. I found myself smiling as I coaxed a fat carrot out of the ground.

"I've never done any gardening," I said. "You really love it, don't you?"

"Like many tasks, it can be a meditation. In this case, since one is growing food, a very potent one."

"Is that how you feel about all the things you do? I mean the carving, and the pottery..."

"They are all meditations, yes. Making useful objects, and making them beautiful, focuses one on life's blessings. Of course, it is also a way to pass the time. I lived here for more than a century before the colonists arrived, alone except for the occasional traveler who stopped to ask shelter."

"Or the occasional brigand who wanted to rob you?"

Madóran paused and looked up at me with a grin. "Very few of those. I dealt summarily with the first two or three, and word got around."

I raised my eyebrows. "Do I want to know how you dealt with them? No, I don't think I do."

"I did them no harm," he said mildly, lifting a head of lettuce from the ground.

"Just scared the bejeezes out of them?"

He smiled as he put the lettuce into the basket and got to his feet. "I think that is enough. Thank you for your help."

"My pleasure. Thanks for putting up with my questions."

"Your questions remind me of all I have to be grateful for."

He stood smiling at me, a slight breeze stirring his hair around his face. A strand blew across his cheek, and without thinking I reached to brush it back.

The tingle of his khi flashed through me as I touched his face. I stood marveling, just enjoying the sensation for itself. Truly amazing, these ælven.

I have another question.

Yes?

You and Lomen can't talk with mindspeech.

True.

But I can talk with each of you. If I talk to both of you at once, can you hear each other through me?

An interesting question. I believe the answer is "no," but I have never attempted it.

Could we try it sometime? Just to see?

I am willing.

Thanks.

You are a fount of curiosity, Steven. It is quite refreshing.

We went into the house and took the vegetables to the kitchen, where Madóran started washing them. I got myself a glass of water.

"Think I'll go study for a while, if you don't mind. Unless you want help with dinner?"

"No, no. Not for a while yet. Go and fill your mind."

I crossed the *plazuela* to my room. Lomen was sitting in the shade by the fountain; he glanced up at me and I smiled a hello.

Studying in that beautiful garden. What a hardship. I decided to join him.

I fetched my tablet and pulled up a chair so I could share the small table beside Lomen. "OK?"

He smiled. "Fine."

I brought up my genetics text and caught up on all my reading for the course. I would miss a week's worth of classes. Ouch.

I got out my phone and texted all my professors, explaining that I was out of town on family business—I smiled at that—and asking for the assignments for the week. Maybe someday I'd catch up.

School wasn't such an urgent thing for me any more. I had quit worrying about what degree to take. I'd get one, sure—but it wasn't the first priority now. First priority was learning the skills I needed to conquer koilohaemia.

I sat musing about it. Hollow blood. I wondered if it really was a form of anemia.

"Does Madóran have a microscope?" I asked.

Lomen looked up from his book. "I don't know. I doubt it."

I sighed. "Have to wait until we're back in town."

"What do you want it for?"

"I want to look at a sample of alben—well, of infected blood. Savhoran would give me one, right?"

"Probably, but please be careful with it."

"Oh, absolutely. I'd just need a drop to put on a slide."

The worry in his voice reminded me that for him, too, the disease was a real threat. He might not be as obsessive as Mirali but he was just as concerned, and rightly so.

I would be *damn* careful with any samples I took. Gloves and isolation, the works. Just treat it like plutonium.

I turned to my chemistry homework. It went fast in that pleasant place. Occasionally a door would open and someone would walk around the *portal*, usually on the way to the kitchen. The birds twittered and fussed in the fountain. The air was perfect.

After a while I realized I was staring at the tablet with my thoughts a million miles away. Zoning. Time to give up on studying.

I got up, and Lomen gave me an enquiring look.

"Think I'll take a nap," I said.

I took my water glass to my room and stretched out on the bed. It smelled like Lomen and me, which made me smile.

I must have conked out right away, because it seemed like only a minute had passed when Lomen knocked on the door, calling me to dinner. I got up and rubbed my eyes, combed my fingers through my hair, and headed for the kitchen.

It was late; the sun must be setting, because the whole *plazuela* was shaded and a bit chilly. I followed Lomen across it and into the kitchen, which was full of fantastic smells.

"Ah, good," Madóran said as we came in. "You can carry. We are dining in the great room."

He indicated a platter of roast beef and bowls of spinach and carrots. Lomen and I collected them and went through a door at the far end of the kitchen, which opened into the plant-filled entryway. In the greatroom, Manda and Bironan were setting the long table, putting out wine glasses and lighting candles. We added our burdens to the potatoes and salad that were already there. It looked like a feast.

There were eight of us at dinner. Talk was mostly about the Evennight celebration. While Madóran told the others about our visit to Mirali, I asked Manda how Savhoran was doing.

"Fine. He's been resting all day, which is good. He needs to catch up."

"And Pirian?"

She shrugged. "The same, I assume."

"You'd be happier if he wasn't around."

"Wouldn't you?"

"Partly. But the ælven need all the DNA they can muster."

"Even diseased DNA?"

"Might be of use. And maybe Madóran is right—maybe Pirian will change."

Manda sighed. "I ought to cut him more slack. He pretty much saved my life, once. Not that he meant to."

I turned to her, astonished. "Pirian saved your life?"

"Let's not talk about it over dinner. I'll tell you later."

She reached for the wine. I thought about what Len had said —that she and Manda both knew what to watch out for. They had both been attacked by alben. Now I had joined the club.

Occupational hazard, I told myself. From now on, we'd be better organized, and there wouldn't be any more alben encounters.

I hoped.

"You and Savhoran still going to do your..."

"Cup-bond? Yeah. We'll do it after the Evennight ceremony, that way Mirali can leave if she wants to."

"That's nice of you."

"Savhoran's idea. He's morbidly sensitive about his condition and how the others react to him." She glanced toward Faranin and Bironan, and lowered her voice. "He's always worrying that they'll banish him."

"They can't, can they? What do you mean, 'banish'?"

"Caeran could, as clan leader. Greystone is superior to Ebonwatch. Even though Ebonwatch existed millennia ago, this iteration is new, and subordinate to Clan Greystone, which means Caeran can tell them what to do in certain circumstances."

"Caeran wouldn't banish Savhoran."

She gave me a skeptical look and stabbed a carrot. "Anything's possible."

I looked up to find Caeran watching me. He smiled slightly and said something to Madóran.

The meal was leisurely. Conversation ranged over multiple topics, but by tacit agreement we didn't talk about the alben. We did talk about the lab. Caeran wanted to design the compound during the winter and start construction by spring.

The wine went around frequently, and at one point I realized I was getting bleary. I switched to water for a while.

Finally Len got up and started clearing away plates. I offered to help, and Lomen helped carry the dishes and the leftovers to the kitchen. Len put on a kettle for tea and asked me if I wanted coffee.

"No, tea's fine."

She smiled. "You're getting acclimated."

"Less caffeine. I'd like to get a good night's sleep. So quiet out here."

"Yeah. You'll sleep well."

She gave me and Lomen bowls of nuts and fruit to take back to the greatroom. Savhoran and Pirian had joined the table, which caught me off guard. I snuck a look at Pirian while I set a bowl of fruit in front of Madóran.

He looked less haggard; merely unwell. The anger that I'd felt toward him earlier had changed to confusion. Had he really saved Manda's life?

Savhoran was sitting across the table from him, with a glass of wine in front of him, listening to Caeran with a serious expression.

"The most important thing is that we all work together," Caeran was saying. "To that end, we will have one Evennight ceremony. Clan Greystone will stand on one side of the circle, and Clan Ebonwatch on the other."

That produced an unbalanced image in my mind, one that smacked of segregation. It probably wouldn't look that bad; Greystone would be more like three quarters of the circle to Ebonwatch's quarter, and I would be in there somewhere. Maybe I could be a buffer, like a no-man's land.

I slid back into my chair, catching Lomen's eye as I did so. "That way maybe Mirali will feel comfortable attending," I added.

Savhoran shot a sharp glance at me. I couldn't see Pirian's face.

"We will have the ceremony after sunset, so that Ebonwatch may be present. Afterward, Savhoran and Amanda will make their cup-bonding vow."

I looked at Manda, whose cheeks were a little flushed. I wondered if it was too late to come up with some kind of gift for her. After all, I basically owed my connection with Lomen to her.

"And after the cup-bonding," Caeran said, "I propose we

formally admit Steven to Clan Greystone."

My heart gave a thump of surprise. Caeran was smiling at me, looking amused.

"Oh—ah, wow. I'm honored," I said.

"You have already contributed much to the clan."

I ought to be thrilled. Instead I felt hesitant. Lomen tilted his head, watching me. I took a swallow of wine and shielded.

I needed to think about it. It was a huge honor, yes—and I needed to be sure I felt right accepting it.

"I'm not exactly sure what that means," I said. "Are there duties that go along with being a clan member?"

"Keep the creed, be loyal to the clan," said Faranin.

"I don't even know the creed. I mean, I know a little about it, but not everything."

Len came in with a tea tray. She poured some for me, steam rising from the mug. I decided to let it cool a bit, and sipped some more wine.

"You make a good point," Madóran said. "Although the creed really applies to the ælven more than to humankind."

"There's no reason humans can't keep the creed," Len said. "I swore to do it when you brought me into the clan."

"But you had studied it, Len. Steven has not. Perhaps we should ask him to learn the creed, with the object of abiding by it."

"It that fair?" Lomen said. "It is asking him to promise in the future to abide by a rule he does not understand."

My hero. I gazed at Lomen, wishing I could hug him right then.

"We have no intention of making unreasonable demands," Caeran said.

"I do want to learn the creed," I said. "But I don't want to make an uninformed promise."

"No one asks that of you," Madóran said.

A thought was forming in my brain. I drank some more wine, swishing it around.

"The creed is the difference between the ælven and the

alben," I mused, half to myself.

"I would say, rather, that the creed is the difference between Clan Ebonwatch and the alben," Caeran said.

I looked at Savhoran, seated at the opposite corner to me. He sat erect, his hands folded around the base of his wine glass, which was still full. Easy to forget how hard his life was, and that it had only recently become so.

I suddenly understood what had been bothering me.

"I'm really honored to be invited," I said, looking at Caeran, "but I wonder if it might be more appropriate for me to join Clan Ebonwatch."

= 18 =

All the ælven looked shocked, except for Lomen, who turned a sudden chortle to a cough. His eyes glinted glee at me for an instant before he looked away.

Savhoran gazed at me in disbelief. "Why would you want to join Ebonwatch?"

"He cannot join Ebonwatch," said Faranin. "Ebonwatch's duty is to guard against the alben. He has not the strength to oppose them." He looked at me. "Forgive me, but it is so."

"That is Ebonwatch's traditional duty," said Madóran, "but this is a new embodiment of the clan. Guarding against the alben need not be its sole purpose."

I nodded; he seemed to understand where I was going. I took a pear from a bowl and rolled it around in my hands.

"See, I keep thinking about what we want to do—figure out this disease and cure it. That's what I signed on for, with Ebonwatch, the company. But that could apply to the clan, too. Ultimately, it's for Clan Ebonwatch that we want to beat this thing."

They were all silent. Either I'd said something profound, or something really stupid.

"And for all those who would otherwise be doomed to Ebonwatch's fate," said Bironan quietly.

Manda gave me a look of burning excitement, then stood and picked up her wine. "I want to join Ebonwatch, too."

She walked down the table to sit next to Savhoran. He looked at her, and even though he was facing away from me I could practically feel the love radiating from him.

"Well," Caeran said, "I see no reason why our mortal friends cannot join Ebonwatch if they wish. Savhoran, do you have any objection?"

Savhoran was beaming like a kid who'd been given a new toy. "None. They would be welcome." He tore his gaze away from

Manda and looked at me. "But Ebonwatch is strict in following the creed; we must be. If you are unwilling to commit to that..."

"I'm willing to commit to learning the creed, and to following what I understand of it so far. If I run into something I can't handle, I'll discuss it with you, and either we'll reach a compromise or I'll withdraw."

Savhoran nodded. "That is reasonable."

"Very well," Caeran said. "Then I propose a slight change. Before the cup-bonding, Amanda and Steven will be formally admitted to Clan Ebonwatch."

So that Mirali would see our support for those stricken with the curse. Subtle, Caeran.

Maybe it would make an impression on her. Even if it didn't, it was a statement I wanted to make. I was in this for all of the ælven, for their ultimate survival. Conquering koilohemia was the first step.

I felt Lomen's touch and looked at him. Gently, he took the pear from my hands and cut it in half with his knife, offering half to me. We shared it silently, and for some reason that made me incredibly horny. His eyes, dark green in the candlelight, were filled with a soft warmth.

Madóran looked at Len. "How is your translation of the creed progressing? Have you had time to work on it?"

"A little," she said. "I have questions about a couple of things."

She said something in ælven and they started discussing the subtleties of its meaning. Faranin put in his opinion. I stopped listening; I would read Len's work when it was done.

I finished my wine and sipped my tea. Savhoran and Manda slipped away together; the others were deep in discussion.

Caeran asked Lomen a question, drawing him in. Unable to contribute, I got up and went to the kiva fireplace in the far corner of the room.

The fire had burned down to just coals, glowing orange in the little cave-like space. I sat on the banco, took a small log of piñon from the bin and propped it over the coals, watching new flames sprout to lick at its edges.

So you would be my clan-brother.

I winced at the prickling that came with Pirian's thought-touch and the memory of horror it brought. Turning, I saw him just a couple of steps away. My skin crawled and my breathing shortened, but I kept myself together.

Why does your khi feel like that?

He grimaced.

The curse. It mars the khi. Did they not tell you that?

Not in so many words.

I suppressed a shudder. The prickling sensation was so much like the female alben's khi that I had trouble thinking straight.

A wry smile twisted Pirian's lips, and I sensed an echo of contempt. He must just love the idea of having humans as clan-kin. His opinion of us was perhaps slightly higher than Mirali's.

That was an improvement over what it had been when I'd first met him, I realized. I remembered the crack he'd made about my being a pet.

Pirian's eyes narrowed.

That was unkind of me. I apologize.

I gaped at him. Apologize? To me?

Madóran assures me that I owe you my life. I am grateful, however unpleasant you find my company.

Or you ours.

A flash of amusement crossed his face. *Indeed. I confess I am still mystified as to why Greystone is so interested in you humans. I must assume something—the promise of a cure for the curse, perhaps—has clouded their judgment.*

We will find a cure.

A shadow flicked through his eyes—doubt? Hope, quickly suppressed?

It's not just a game, Pirian. Len is devoting her life to this. She's brilliant, in case you hadn't noticed. She deserves your respect.

She has it. She, too, kept me alive.

Movement behind him caught my eye—Lomen, coming toward us. I looked back at Pirian.

Yes, we'll be clan-brothers. You're better off with Clan Ebonwatch.

Am I?

If you hadn't joined Ebonwatch, and you'd met those two alben on your own, would you have taken them up on their offer of entertainment?

His nostrils flared and his face went grim. Lomen took a step closer. I glanced at him and gave my head a tiny shake, then looked back at Pirian.

Amanda says you saved her life. Is that true?

It was inadvertent. I do not deserve credit for it.

What happened?

Kanna was holding her. Fool that I was, I sought Kanna out to reason with her. Our—discussion—gave Amanda the opportunity to escape.

I stared at him, absorbing that. Why had he declined to take the credit? I was seeing a side of him I hadn't glimpsed before.

Where did you find Poppy?

I braced myself for an answer I probably wouldn't like. Something softened in Pirian's face.

They had already chosen her when I joined them. I had no idea she was known to you.

Would that have mattered?

Probably not.

At least he was honest.

His head turned slightly and he glanced toward Lomen, then looked back at me. *Your friend awaits you.*

Pirian turned away, heading for the door to the north *portal.* The uncomfortable contact faded and I breathed a sigh of relief.

What was that about?

Lomen's touch was like cool water on a sunburn. I closed my eyes.

Just getting better acquainted.

I sensed his skepticism, but I was still a little freaked out. Felt like I'd been fencing for half an hour.

Lomen came and sat beside me by the fire. I basked in his khi, grateful for how wonderful it felt. I'd explain—or share—later.

Right now I just needed the comfort of his touch.

The ælven remaining at the table got up. Faranin and Bironan followed Pirian outside, and Len and Caeran came over to say good night.

I sat up straighter and looked at Caeran. "I hope you don't mind my turning down your offer. I really am honored by it."

"No, I think you have made a wise choice," he said, smiling. "Ebonwatch will be stronger for your presence."

"Well, I hope so."

They went out, leaving me and Lomen alone with Madóran. He joined us by the fire, sitting on the couch that faced the fireplace, and for a moment we sat together in silence. Madóran gazed at me, smiling.

Shall we try your experiment?

My mouth went dry with sudden desire. His khi and Lomen's both at once; it set me on fire.

What I wanted to try was how comfortable we might be on the couch, but I ignored that thought. Madóran was watching me, waiting.

Lomen, are you willing to try talking with us both?

Sure.

Are you talking with Lomen?

Yes. I looked from Madóran to Lomen. *Can you both hear me?*

Lomen nodded. Madóran looked at him, a slight frown of concentration on his brow.

I hear you, and I sense a connection...does Lomen hear me?

I looked at Lomen. *Anything?*

Is Madóran talking to you? I felt something, but did not hear.

I stifled a sigh. *I guess it doesn't work.*

No, there is definitely a connection. Madóran gazed intently at Lomen. *I believe it is something we could build upon.*

Madóran took Lomen's hand, which sent a zing of jealousy and desire through me. After a moment, he reached for my hand as well. I clasped his, and the desire intensified while the jealousy faded. Lomen took my other hand, closing the circle.

The air was tingling, and I thought I could actually feel khi flowing through our hands. So intense; I just sat there, awash in awareness of both of them.

This merits further practice. I believe you have given us a start, Steven.

He said something, didn't he? I could feel it.

Yes.

If we two could learn to speak together...

The hope in Madóran's thoughts was almost painfully intense. It surprised me; he was such a gentle soul. He wanted this so strongly.

Well, of course. To share the intimacy of mindspeech with another ælven; Lomen had said it was rare. If they could accomplish it, they'd have that special gift forever.

They'd have it after I was gone.

I put that thought aside, quite deliberately. No mooning over my mortality; that was useless. I'd treasure what I had, for as long as I had it. If I was lucky, I'd spend the rest of my life with the ælven.

Madóran turned to me, smiling with delight.

Thank you, Steven.

Entirely my pleasure.

His gaze shifted to Lomen. *Speaking of pleasure...*

A deep tingle went through me and settled in my groin. Oh, god.

Madóran released our hands, but the connection remained. We all stood. Abandoning the table mess for later, we went out to the *plazuela* and across it to Madóran's room.

It was a beautiful room, was my fleeting impression. The bed was large and comfortable, and I can't begin to describe what we did there, because it was so much more than physical. I think that night changed me forever.

I woke the next morning, alone in the bed but not lonely. Twin threads of awareness connected me with Lomen and Madóran. They were not nearby; out in the house somewhere.

I stretched, luxuriating, taking time to observe the room and the furnishings. All of it was lovely; most if not all was Madóran's work. There was plenty of carved and polished wood, both furniture and artwork. Lush fabrics of deep blue and green covered the windows and the bed. I was still lying there soaking in the atmosphere when the door opened.

Lomen came in, bringing me a mug of tea and a bowl of plain yogurt with sliced pears. Perfect.

Everyone spent that week preparing for Evennight. The ceremony might be simple—they all told me that it was—but the feast was apparently going to be elaborate. Madóran sent a written note to Mirali and her family, formally inviting them to supper followed by the ceremony. She sent back a note of acceptance, for which I quietly cheered.

The kitchen was the center of activity. I wandered in and out, chopping things when told to, generally trying to stay out of the way except when I was hungry. There was always something good to eat when I went looking.

When I wasn't helping with the food, I studied. Caught up on all the homework I could do outside of the lab. Read ahead in the textbooks, and got started reading the molecular biology book I'd checked out.

I found it fascinating. Whenever I read about what could be done on a molecular level to fight disease, a glow of excitement lit in me.

At Madóran's request, I spoke with him and with Lomen in mindspeech whenever possible. Part of his plan for building a connection between him and Lomen.

Lomen, Bironan, and Faranin decorated the *plazuela* for the ceremony. I didn't offer to help, because I suspected I'd just get in their way. They installed colored banners on tall poles at the four sides of the *plazuela*—yellow to the east, red to the south, blue to the west and green to the north—and strung wires of hanging lanterns between them. They moved the patio furniture to the *portal*, and on the afternoon of the feast day they poured dried herbs and flower petals in a big circle around the fountain.

I watched them through the kitchen window, open to let out the heat from all the cooking. I was at the small table chopping vegetables for a dish that was part of the feast. The smell of a turkey roasting in the oven was driving me crazy. Earlier, Madóran had baked bread, and I'd had a hard time keeping my hands off those golden loaves as they cooled.

I finished my chopping and carried the cutting board full of veggies to Madóran, who was at the stove. He frowned as I presented my work to him.

I think we'll need a few more carrots. Would you mind pulling some from the garden?

Glad to. Four? Eight?

Six. Thank you.

I went down the hall and out through the utility room. Didn't bother with the hat; I wouldn't be outside long.

It was mid-afternoon and the soil was warm from the day's sun; the rich smell of it rose to greet me. A cool breeze reminded me that it was fall. I knelt by the carrot bed and coaxed a half-dozen of them from the ground without breaking any of the tops.

I paused, closed my eyes, and just thought about how grateful I was to be there, in that beautiful place, with those amazing people. I'd never been religious, much to my parents' dismay, but at that moment I felt blessed.

I inhaled deeply, smelling the garden, the clear mountain air, the sun-warmed plants. Long, slow exhale, then I gathered the carrots and took them inside.

Manda looked up at me and smiled from the counter where she was mixing something. I washed the carrots in the sink, retrieved my cutting board, and sliced them up, saving the tops for compost. Madóran smiled as he slid them off the board into the pot.

Thank you, Steven.

Sure. What else can I help with?

He glanced toward the window.

I suppose it is time to start the salad.

I spent the next half-hour washing lettuce and slicing pears, which I then tossed with lemon juice to keep them from going brown. The pears were from Madóran's orchard and he had a couple of bushels of them in cold storage. Possibly enough for us to get sick of them, but that hadn't happened yet. The ones I sliced would go in the salad with fresh goat cheese from one of Madóran's neighbors, and toasted piñon nuts.

I nibbled on the cores before adding them to the compost bucket. I was trying to resist spoiling my appetite, but it wasn't easy.

Lomen and the others came in from the *plazuela*, looking for cool drinks. Manda told them to attack the iced tea in the fridge. Lomen poured himself a glass and came over to watch me.

Finished with the circle?

Yes, it is ready.

He looked at Madóran and I could tell he was trying to speak to him. Another part of the plan, less successful so far, but Madóran had said it would take time. Lomen sighed and took a big slug of tea.

Those banners are for the four directions?

Yes, and the guardian spirits of the elements associated with the directions.

Reminds me of the Indians, sort of. They have colors for the directions.

Manda put something in the microwave and started it. Whatever Lomen said in response to my comment was lost. It was really true that the thing disrupted khi. I wondered if it was actually scrambling our brain waves.

I glanced at it, then gave Lomen a shrug of apology. He nodded, waiting until the machine shut off before continuing.

I believe the Navajo use slightly different colors.

I nodded.

White is one of them, I think.

Do the Pueblos also use them?

I don't know. I would think they do.

Most cultures have some variation of these symbols.

Is that all they are? Symbols?

Symbols have power. Don't underestimate that.

I'd finished slicing the last pear. I tossed it into the bowl with the rest, added one more splash of lemon juice and gave them a stir, then cleaned up all the cores and washed my knife and the cutting board. Madóran looked at the pears and smiled approval.

Put them in the refrigerator, please.

That was easier said than done. The fridge was crammed with food. I covered the bowl and rearranged a couple of things to make room for it.

"We're going to have to start eating soon," I said. "There's no more room to store stuff in here."

Would you put these bowls of nuts on the dining table, Steven?

Sure thing.

There were four small bowls—beautifully carved with intricate knotwork designs and glazed in deep blue-green—filled with mixed nuts. I grabbed two of them and Lomen brought the other two. We crossed the entryway to the greatroom.

Someone had cleared away the remains of the previous night's dinner that we had so shamelessly abandoned. The table now had a green cloth over it, and was set for ten, with a wooden cradle at the west end. No chairs for Savhoran and Pirian; they would not join us until after the meal, for the ceremony.

The table was large for that number, so every place had plenty of elbow room. Multiple wine glasses stood at each setting, and little bowls of fresh wildflowers—blanketflowers and purple asters—sat between each pair of facing seats. Lomen and I set the nut bowls at intervals, spacing them around the three silver candelabra that I hadn't seen before. I picked one up and looked at it. Solid silver, looked like. I wondered how old it was.

I need to shower and change.

I turned to Lomen and smiled. *I won't distract you. This time.*

He made a disappointed face, but his eyes were laughing. He went out through the door to the *plazuela.*

Madóran came in with a handful of beeswax tapers. I helped him set them in the candelabra.

"Beautiful table," I said.

Thank you.

Going to be a wonderful gathering.

I hope so.

He sounded as if he had doubts.

Mirali's coming. That's good, it'll give her a chance to see that Savhoran and Pirian aren't a danger to her.

Hm. I suspect it will decide her, one way or the other.

I didn't like the trouble in his face. I wanted to lift his worries from him.

If she leaves, with her family, then we'll find others. For both Greystone and Ebonwatch.

He looked skeptical, and slightly amused. *How?*

Send a recruiting party to Europe, to reconnect with friends there. I've already mentioned the idea to Savhoran, and I think he would go.

This didn't erase the trouble from his face. If anything, it deepened.

I know you treasure your privacy. You won't lose it, Madóran. The compound Ebonwatch is building will have room. Caeran's buying a mess of land for it.

And I have a mess of land, as you say, here in Guadalupita. Others could build here without disturbing me, as Nathrin and Mirali have done.

As Ebonwatch gets bigger, it will probably keep more separate. They need to be near a larger population so they can hunt, so they'll want to stay close to Albuquerque.

That might comfort Mirali. I will mention it to her this evening, if I have the opportunity.

This will work.

He smiled. *You do not have to convince me, Steven.*

I want you to be OK with it.

He walked over to a window overlooking the front *portal*. I couldn't help wondering how often he had stood gazing out that way, over the centuries he had been here.

It does represent a change for me. I had given up hope. Now you have restored it, and that is painful.

He'd given up hope? Holy crap! A shiver went through me as I remembered what Manda had told me about the ælven and suicide. I buried that thought under a heap of white light.

I never want to cause you pain.

He turned to me with a soft smile. *I know.*

In that moment, he looked more weary than I'd ever seen him. It frightened me; I suddenly understood how the weight of years, of memory, could become such a burden that an ælven might choose to yield his immortality. I couldn't bear to think that might happen to Madóran.

I want to give you joy.

Joy might erase the pain, or at least ease the burden.

You do. He came over to me and kissed my forehead. *Now go and dress for the evening. Everything is ready.*

He left the room, unhurried. I followed him out to the *plazuela* and along the *portal*, but didn't try to catch up with him. Had a feeling he wanted to be alone.

When I got to my room I stopped and stood watching until Madóran disappeared into his own room. It occurred to me that Lomen and I would be leaving soon—we both needed to be in Albuquerque—so the mindspeech practice would be on hold until we saw Madóran again. I doubted he would be willing to relocate. It would take longer, then, for him to build a connection with Lomen.

I would miss him. I'd be just like Len and Manda, always wanting to drive up to Guadalupita. Laughing at myself, I went into my room to change.

Madóran had brought me a robe—that's what he called the caftans he liked to wear—but I'd decided I wanted to look like Ebonwatch. Savhoran always wore a plain, long-sleeved tunic and pants. I picked the most similar clothes I had with me, a white long-sleeved tee and faded jeans. Kind of casual for the fancy dinner, but I figured the ælven had different standards anyway. There weren't going to be any suits at the feast.

There was, it turned out, a long dress. Len was in the greatroom when I reached it, wearing floor-length dark blue velvet and a purple ribbon in her hair. She was sitting by the kiva fireplace, which had a fire laid ready.

"You look nice," I told her.

"Thanks. It was a gift from Caeran."

"It suits you." I joined her on the banco. "Shall we light the fire?"

"Caeran will do it. He's on his way, he just stopped for a word with Savhoran."

"We could light it, if there are matches."

"There aren't."

"What is it these guys have against matches? I can never find any."

"They don't need them."

I was about to say something sarcastic about rubbing sticks together, but Caeran came in and Len's attention was gone. She hopped up to meet him, running over for a hug.

Caeran was dressed in a robe, also blue, with violet embroidery around the neck and sleeves. I'd never seen him like that before. He seemed more ælven, if that was possible, and also older. The robe lent a grace to his movements, or rather accentuated his natural grace. I found myself bowing in response to his greeting.

"Could you light the fire?" Len said. "It's a little chilly."

Caeran gave her a look of slight surprise, but stepped to the fireplace. He held out his hand toward the wood, and flames started licking around the logs.

My stomach tried to drop out of my gut.

Len glanced sidelong at me and smiled. "Thanks," she said to Caeran.

What else could they do that I didn't know about? I shielded, hastily.

Holy crap.

Bironan and Faranin came in, followed shortly by Lomen. He came straight over to me.

What happened?

Uh—nothing. Tell you later.

Trouble?

No.

I could feel myself blushing. I walked over to the table and picked up a few nuts from one of the bowls. Lomen followed me. I looked him up and down.

You're not wearing a robe?

I am demonstrating my solidarity with you.

His tunic and pants were simple, but they were also a rich blue and I realized the fabric was finer than the cottons he and the others usually wore. The color made his skin glow and his hair look tinged with fire.

You look good. I'm sorry I don't have anything a little fancier.

You made a good choice.

A bell rang nearby, loud enough to startle me. Caeran hurried to the entranceway and I heard voices speaking in ælven. Mirali and family had arrived.

The next few minutes were spent bringing them into the great room, finding a seat for Mirali, and settling her and Nathrali comfortably, with accompanying praise for the baby and mother. About half of it was in ælven. Caeran and Lomen spoke exclusively in English, which was kind of them.

Len oohed and aahed over Nathrali and even said something short in ælven that made Mirali smile. I waited until most of the fuss was over to greet Mirali and tell her I was glad she had come. She gave me a polite smile, and I couldn't help thinking of duchesses.

Madóran came in and added his compliments to Mirali. She was gracious, and they chatted briefly, then Madóran gave a nod to Manda, who was waiting by the door. Manda disappeared toward the kitchen.

I decided I'd rather carry plates of food than listen to small-talk in ælven, so I followed her. Lomen came with me and paused in the entryway to bar the front door, dropping a heavy beam into brackets—fifteenth century technology. I raised my eyebrows as he joined me.

We are all inside. No one else is invited.

I wondered how often Madóran's neighbors dropped by. Not often, I suspected, but there was no harm in being cautious.

We presented ourselves to Manda, who told us which plates

and bowls to carry out first. Everything went onto a smaller table against the wall that served as a sideboard.

When I say smaller, I don't mean small. It was at least ten feet long and plenty wide, and by the time we'd brought out all the food, it was covered.

The others moved to the feast table, with Mirali at the west end and the baby settled in the cradle next to her, a little toy dangling overhead to amuse her. As we brought the last of the food out, Madóran stepped to the east end of the table and waved a hand toward the candlabra. The candles all lit, flickering briefly before settling into a steady glow.

"Welcome. May this Evennight be a celebration of gratitude and hope."

He filled his first glass with wine—a white, with a hint of sparkle—and passed the bottle along. It was a beautiful sight, the ælven all in their fine clothes around the sumptuous table. I wished I had a camera. I'd left my phone in my room.

The food followed the wine around the table. The meal was wonderful, but I kind of picked at my share. I was nervous about the ceremony, which surprised me. I kept thinking of Savhoran and Pirian, shut away in their rooms, waiting for sunset.

No feast for them. I wondered if they were hungry.

Manda, sitting to my left, nudged me. "What's the matter?"

"Nothing."

I applied myself to my turkey so as not to be obliged to talk. Despite my efforts to make sure everyone attended, I'd be glad when the evening was over.

The second wine was a red, and from the compliments directed to Madóran I deduced that he had made it. So he had a vineyard, too. I wondered how old the grapes were. Had he brought them from Spain?

It was good wine. I drank more.

I was glad to see Mirali loosening up. Maybe it was the wine, or maybe the company, but she started smiling more and looking relaxed.

So, good. If she was happy, maybe she'd stay.

Steven?

I looked up at Lomen.

Something is troubling you. Can I help?

It's not any one thing. It's a bunch of little things. I'm OK, really. Thanks.

He looked concerned. Madóran, too, gazed at me for a moment with his healer face on. Not wanting to worry them, I tried to think of something to add to the conversation.

"I got caught up on my homework, finally. How about you?" Inane, but it proved I wasn't completely withdrawn.

Lomen smiled. "I've read all my texts."

"All of them? Finished them?"

"Yes."

"Aw, he—heck. I thought I was ahead of you."

"Well, you're ahead of me," said Manda. "I just can't get into the French Lit class, and the instructor is a huge bore."

"Too late to switch. Can you put up with it enough to pull a decent grade?"

"Yeah, it just won't be fun." She stabbed a carrot. "How about you, Len?"

"I'm holding my own."

We drifted from school to talking about the new Ebonwatch complex. Caeran had a date to sign papers for the land purchase the following week. He was already looking for an architect.

Manda got up and fetched two platters from the sideboard, starting one at each end of the table. Dessert: cheese, fruit, nuts, tiny two-bite cakes perfectly decorated with buttercream aspen leaves, and crumbled dark chocolate. Madóran passed around a third wine, this one strong and sweet. I was full, but I nibbled a dried apricot and sipped some of the wine, which wasn't really to my taste.

Finally Madóran rose and invited everyone to adjourn to the *plazuela*. As I stood, I realized the light coming through the windows was twilight. The sun had set while we were feasting.

I helped clear dishes. Moving Mirali and Nathrali to the *plazuela* was again a production, but I left it to Nathrin and the other ælven who seemed happy to fuss over them. Me, I was glad we were moving on, though a small knot had formed in the pit of my stomach.

I told myself it would be fine, that Mirali was comfortable now and Savhoran and Pirian would be far away from her and everything would be fine.

If it wasn't fine, it would be a huge honking mess.

Mirali and family were settled at the west side of the circle, Mirali in a chair with the cradle beside her, Nathrin standing nearby. I glanced at the east side. No one there, yet. I supposed I could stand there until Savhoran and Pirian came out.

Manda and I finished tidying the kitchen. She was dressed in an ælven tunic and her jeans, also a nod to Ebonwatch, I assumed. Fashion-wise, Greystone had us beat hands down, but then we weren't about fashion.

"So, you're going to be my clan-sister."

She looked up at me, surprised. "Yeah, I guess so."

"Kinda nice. My real sister doesn't get me at all."

"Yeah?" She sidled up to me and slid an arm around my waist, leaning her head against me. "I get you, Steve."

"I know." I squeezed her shoulders. "I'm grateful."

"This is a big night for us."

"Yeah."

"I'm glad you decided to go with Ebonwatch. I wouldn't have thought of it, but it's exactly right."

I smiled, and the knot in my gut loosened a little. It *was* exactly right, and it would be all right.

Madóran was out in the courtyard. Manda and I went out to join the others. Bironan and Faranin stood flanking Mirali's group. Caeran and Len stood at the south side of the circle. Manda and I went to the east side.

That left the north for Madóran. Appropriate, since he lived north of the rest of us.

"Which element is north?" I whispered to Manda.

"Earth. Earth and winter."

The sky to the west glowed with twilight. Savhoran and

Pirian could come out now, though I knew that Pirian, at least, preferred full dark. I looked toward their rooms.

A touch on my arm made me jump. I turned to find Lomen grinning at me.

"Happy Evennight."

You snuck up on me!

His grin widened. "I made you a little gift."

He held out something blue. It was leather—butter soft in my hands—and had three oblong wooden beads along one edge.

"It's a bracelet. Shall I fasten it for you?"

I gave it back to him, pushed my sleeve up a bit, and held out my arm. "Sure, 'cause I bet I can't do it myself."

That's the point.

He slid the beads through buttonholes in the other edge. The bracelet fit me perfectly, a wide band of blue.

"Blue's a Greystone color, isn't it?"

"It's also an Ebonwatch color. Night blue."

"Night blue and what?" Manda asked.

Lomen plucked a pinch of my sleeve and smiled. "White."

I touched the bracelet, so soft. "Thank you." *I don't have a gift for you.*

No matter. Humans fret needlessly over equal exchanges. Everything evens out eventually.

He kissed my cheek and went off to the north side of the circle. He would stand with Madóran, then. Of course.

Madóran was talking with Caeran. He had a long, carved staff with ribbons floating from it. A little too fancy for a wizard, but that's what it made me think of, only Madóran was beautiful instead of craggy and old.

Maybe he was a wizard, though. He was probably the most powerful user of khi in the group. I mused on that, watching the fountain dancing in the evening shadows, its murmur a calming background.

Movement drew my gaze to the north *portal*: Savhoran. He came to join us, giving me a nod and bending to say something in Manda's ear. She gave a little girlish laugh, very unlike her.

Pirian had come out, too, and went to stand on Savhoran's other side. I looked at him, wondering if he was recovered now, but the dusk made it hard to read his face.

Madóran moved to the fountain and raised a hand. The lanterns hanging between the poles that marked the directions flickered to life, bathing the courtyard in warm firelight.

"Welcome, one and all, to the Evennight celebration of Clans Greystone and Ebonwatch. Today, day and night are equal. From now until Midwinter, nights shall grow longer. It is a time of harvest, a time of remembrance and gratitude, a time of preparing for winter."

He walked to the west side of the circle and stood before the pole there, raising his staff in the air. Mirali looked up at him, Nathrali in her arms.

"In the season of Autumn, we honor and thank the spirits of the West, guardians of Water, always precious in these lands."

Madóran moved clockwise around the circle, stopping at the north to greet the appropriate spirits. Lomen gazed at him, softly smiling. I listened, ready to be suspicious of anything that pushed my no-religion-thanks button, but Madóran's words weren't about worshipping anything or anyone.

A beeping started from the kitchen; some neglected timer going off. Manda's head turned; she was scowling.

"I'll get it," I whispered.

I hurried across the *portal*, waving away Len, who had turned to look. In the kitchen I tracked down the culprit and shut it off, then checked to make sure the oven was off.

I heard a soft sound, and realized what it was. The door to the garden, closing.

I flashed on Lomen barring the front door, but the side door wasn't locked. It had never been locked as far as I knew.

My heart started pounding so hard it hurt.

= 19 =

I had maybe a few seconds. No way to defend myself.

"Alben!" I shouted, the word tearing out of my throat.

Pelting steps—they were coming.

No weapons to hand. Knife block—too far and they'd just take it away from me.

Between me and the knives, the microwave.

I punched the cook button and hit start, then ducked back. Saw a shape in the doorway.

Pain slammed me, but didn't overwhelm me like before. I crouched by the counter, staying close to the microwave and its khi-disruptive field, praying it wouldn't turn off.

I heard shouting and scuffling from out in the courtyard. The pain stopped abruptly.

The figure in the doorway was gone. I straightened, trying to summon the courage to go out there.

A piercing shriek, feminine. Instinct took over and I ran out.

Khi was flying around, so much that the hair on my arms stood up. A clump of people on the ground at the south side of the circle: Len, lying still; Caeran and Lomen, grappling with a white-haired male.

Struggle to my right, too, but I ignored it. Terrified for Lomen, I threw myself against the alben male.

It broke up the fight momentarily. The male turned to face me, snarling. We were both on our knees, facing off like savage beasts.

I swear his eyes seemed to glow red, though I knew they were black. Maybe I sensed the blood that he craved, that drove him. Pain licked at the edge of my awareness and I cringed.

No!

Lomen's clasped fists bashed into the side of the alben's head.

Get away, Steven!

I staggered to my feet. The alben aimed a blow at Lomen but Caeran caught his arm.

This had to stop. Barely thinking, I grabbed a patio table from the *portal* and upended it.

Caeran still had hold of the alben's arm. The alben was trying to tear Caran's head off with his free hand, but Lomen was interfering, one hand on Caeran's shoulder and the other trying to peel the alben's fingers off Caeran's neck.

Holy gods! Memory of a lump of meat flashed through my mind.

"No!"

I brought the table down on the alben's head, not caring if I hit anything else. It stunned him enough to make him release Caeran.

I followed through, pushing the table top against his head, pushing him down to the ground. I knelt on the table. A stab of pain seared through my brain.

The next few seconds were lost to me, filled with agony. My brain was on fire.

All saw was red; all I knew was that I had to stay on the table. Easy, since I couldn't move.

It stopped abruptly. Gasping for breath, I blinked as my vision cleared.

Madóran had joined us. He, Lomen, and Caeran had the alben under control.

"The others?" I croaked. I didn't want to say Mirali's name.

"Safe," Madóran whispered

I got off the table and stood, shakily. To my right, Pirian and Savhoran were struggling with the female alben. I'd never seen her face but it didn't matter; I recognized her.

She let out a howl of rage that chilled me to the core of my gut. I wanted to run but instead I waded in.

My clan. My brothers.

Her attention was on them. I swept her feet out from under her with a kick, and nearly fell myself. She went to her knees with a startled yelp, falling against Savhoran.

I locked gazes with Savhoran over her head.

Use my khi.

His eyes widened, then I felt a pulling sensation. It didn't feel good; made me sick to my stomach. I dropped to my knees.

It was enough. The alben slumped in Savhoran's arms. Something glinted in the lamplight: a knife in her hand. Pirian took it from her.

"Drop her," he said.

Savhoran's gaze locked onto his. They stared off while my heart thumped three times, then Savhoran nodded and let the alben slide to the ground. He stepped back.

Pirian's eyes were cold black and a snarl curled his lip as he stood looking down at his tormentor. Lightning-quick he bent, pulled up her shirt, and made three strokes on her torso with the knife.

She screamed.

Madóran started toward them, but Caeran caught him. "No! The blood!"

Pirian's chin lifted, then he raised his arm and plunged the knife into the alben's heart. I shuddered, even though I hated her about as much as anyone could.

Anyone but Pirian.

She was still. Pirian straightened, leaving the knife embedded in its owner's chest.

The pulling sensation faded, leaving me shaking. The prickling had been there, too—not as strong as I'd felt it before, but definitely there. Savhoran turned his head to look at me, regret written on his face.

I heard Madóran's voice, sounding concerned. The only word that resolved was "Lenore."

Len!

I turned and saw her struggling to sit up, one hand against her temple. The other three were still piled on top of the alben male.

I got to my feet, not without some struggle of my own, and went to help Len up. Got her away from the alben, into a chair on the *portal*. I sat next to her, still feeling nauseated.

"You OK, Len?"

"Uh..."

"I'll get you some water."

"No, stay." She caught my arm.

I put my arm around her. She started to sob.

Manda came out from behind a bush and stepped up to Savhoran. He turned when she spoke to him, then nodded. I didn't hear what she said.

She went to the entryway door. Pirian stooped, caught the female alben's hair in one hand and yanked. It was vicious, but it didn't matter; she was dead.

Savhoran picked up her feet and they carried her out of the house, Manda opening the doors. I could hear her unbolting the front door.

I closed my eyes. If only I had locked the side door. I should have thought of it, when I saw Lomen bar the front.

Useless shoulds. I squeezed Len's shoulders and looked back at the other alben.

Bironan and Faranin had come out and added their khi to the pile-on. Five ælven against one alben: that ought to take care of him.

Firelight gleamed on Madóran's face. He was weeping, I realized.

Faranin said something in ælven. The three on the ground adjusted their positions, making room for Faranin to join them.

He knelt, took the alben male's head in both of his hands, and jerked it sharply to one side. The snap made me jump.

Len gave a little gasp.

"It's over," I said.

Faranin stood, looking down at the alben as if he didn't quite believe what he'd done. Len took charge even as Caeran was getting to his feet. She got up from her chair and returned to the courtyard.

"Go to Mirali and stay with her. All of you. We'll let you know when we've finished cleaning up."

Madóran raised heartbroken eyes to mine.

Go on. We'll be all right. Go tell Mirali they're dead.

He closed his eyes briefly, looking pained, then nodded and headed toward the west *portal* with the others.

It took us a while to clean up the blood, from the puddle at the edge of the circle out through the entryway and the front door.. Savhoran and Pirian came back and got the alben male's body, then left again. Avoiding the work, I thought sourly, but it turned out they were working, too.

I was in the laundry room rinsing out rags when Savhoran came in smelling of smoke. In response to my querying look, he nodded.

"We have built a pyre."

Pirian stalked past me without a word. I watched him cross the courtyard, then looked at Savhoran.

"What did he—carve? On her stomach?"

"Nyah. It means 'no'."

Oh.

"Thank you for coming to our aid. Your help was crucial."

I met Savhoran's gaze, and saw grief in his eyes. Like Madóran, he regretted the loss of the alben, even though they were beyond rehabilitation. I wondered what atonement he would choose. Whether he'd be able to get Pirian to atone at all.

I cleared my throat. "You two should shower up. I'll come collect your clothes and wash them."

Savhoran nodded and started after Pirian.

I got some bleach and scrubbed down every place that had been touched by alben blood, then washed all the rags and Pirian and Savhoran's clothes, also with bleach. Finally, I was the dirtiest thing still around. I got the robe Madóran had brought for me, threw my clothes in the washer with more bleach, then showered and scrubbed, and scrubbed some more.

The shower gave me time to think. I would rather not have remembered all that had happened, but my hindbrain was yelling at me that there was something important I needed to acknowledge.

I thought through everything I knew. There were some gaps, like what had happened to Len, but the answer to that seemed fairly obvious.

By the time I emerged, the ælven had gathered in the great room. I felt a little self-conscious in the robe, but no one seemed to notice.

Mirali and Nathrin were there with Nathrali, looking frightened but gamely remaining. Faranin sat talking to them in ælven.

Len had made tea, and brought me a steaming mug as I came in. "You're the hero of the evening, in case you didn't know."

I shook my head. I hadn't done much.

"You OK? I gather the alben attacked you first."

She took a deep breath. "Yeah. I'm OK. Not like it hasn't happened before." I could imagine what she was remembering.

Caeran joined us. "We could not have subdued him without your help. Thank you."

He held out his hand.

I brought mine up, and he clasped my forearm. I returned the grasp, then left go. Simple gesture, but I knew it meant a lot. The ælven weren't a touchy bunch.

Manda and Savhoran came over. It reminded me to look for Pirian, but he wasn't in the room.

"How did you keep the female away?" Len asked me. "The male attacked me alone. If it hadn't been for that—"

"Uh, it wasn't intentional. She came after me because I shouted, I guess."

"She knocked you down?"

"No, I—"

That was it. My heart skipped a beat as I realized the significance of what had happened.

"I turned on the microwave. It kept her from getting complete control of me."

Len's eyes widened. "Steve!"

"I know. We've got to add that to our plan."

"Add what?" Caeran asked, frowning in confusion.

"A khi-disrupting microwave field. Preferably portable. It will give us squishy mortals some defense."

"Wow!" Manda said. She threw her arms around my neck. "Our idea man! You are so brilliantly awesome!"

We talked about how to engineer such a gizmo, and I felt a thrill of excitement. It would work. We'd *make* it work. I'd have to learn more about brain waves.

Lomen came up beside me. "I could change my course of study to engineering, in order to pursue this."

"You wouldn't mind?"

"I like tinkering."

He slid his hand into mine. *Thank you for acting quickly.*

I pulled him away from the others, toward a chair where Madóran sat staring numbly into space. The two of us knelt to either side of him. He stirred, and looked at us.

Madóran. It's over.

He smiled faintly, though his brow was creased with sadness.

Will you finish the ceremony?

I don't think Mirali will be willing to go back out there.

Not out there. In here. It will give everyone some closure.

It took a little coaxing, but he agreed. Lomen and I went outside to fetch his staff.

The courtyard was chilly, despite the heat from the abandoned lanterns. Their light interfered with the starlight, but I could still see the Milky Way overhead. The *plazuela* was peaceful again, with no indication of the violence that had happened there.

We would never forget it, though.

Lomen picked up the staff and came to me.

This was a good idea.

I hope so.

I know it. I think you are also a healer, in your way.

He leaned forward to kiss me. I nearly melted into a puddle, but he knew exactly when to stop.

You can be a puddle later. Madóran needs us.

I nodded, and we went inside. Lomen handed the staff to Madóran, who seemed to gain strength just from touching it.

We all stood, sorting ourselves to the same directions where we had been at the start of the ceremony. It was a much smaller circle now, with all of us closer together. Madóran stepped to the west side and nodded to Mirali, who stood there holding her child. Then he walked to the north, picking up where he'd left off.

Lomen's hand tightened on mine as we watched and listened to the celebration of Evennight. It didn't take long; Madóran merely greeted the spirits of the directions, then said a few words about gratitude for the harvest and for our safety and well-being,

Mirali stayed for the formal induction of me and Manda into Clan Ebonwatch, which was nice of her. Savhoran looked very serious as he asked us to swear that we would uphold the parts of the Ælven Creed that we understood and learn about the parts we didn't. I hadn't sworn very many oaths in my life, and I felt kind of nervous, but at least my voice didn't waver.

Len gave the two of us copies of her translation of the Creed, as far as she had completed it, beautifully calligraphed on parchment and tied with blue and white ribbons. She must have planned that ahead of time. I was touched.

Madóran brought a silver goblet, old-looking, over from the table. He filled it with wine and walked over to our side of the circle.

"Savhoran and Amanda, do you wish to cup-bond before these witnesses?"

They looked at each other, and I could feel the warmth between them.

"Yes." Savhoran took the goblet, raised it to Manda, and said in a husky voice, "I am yours and yours alone, for a year and a day."

He sipped, then offered the wine to Manda. She put her hands over his, and they both raised the goblet for her to drink. She repeated the vow, Savhoran sipped again, with both of them still holding the goblet. Madóran held his hands out toward them, smiling.

"May the spirits who guard you bless your partnership."

That was it. Simple, but it raised emotions in me that were

hard to evaluate. Lomen slid his hand into mine and I looked at him. He was smiling softly, a warmth in his eyes that filled me with quiet joy.

That was the end of the ceremonial stuff, but the room fell quiet as Savhoran approached Mirali. He stopped two paces away from her and bowed.

"Thank you, Mirali, for honoring us with your presence. Clan Ebonwatch is at your service."

I saw her swallow, but she nodded graciously and said something in ælven. Savhoran replied briefly, then withdrew, coming back to the Ebonwatch side of the circle. He and Manda sipped the wine in the silver goblet, and I knew that they were silently conversing.

Mirali and family left not long after that. I didn't know what time it was but it felt late. The clean-up had taken a while, and the whole chaotic evening had been pretty exhausting.

Gradually the others drifted away, though Madóran stood talking with Len and Caeran by the door to the *plazuela*. Lomen and I retreated to the fireplace and sat gazing at the flames.

Oh, I need your help...

I took the bracelet Lomen had given me out of my pocket and held it out to him. He laughed softly as he fastened it on my arm again.

This is my atonement, for giving you such a gift. I am doomed to this duty.

Yes. For the rest of my life.

Our gazes met, and our palms came together. He squeezed my hand.

Madóran came over to join us. Caeran and Len had slipped out.

Bear me company tonight? I would rather not be alone.

I turned to him, still holding Lomen's hand.

Whenever you wish.

I glanced at Lomen, wondering if he had heard or at least sensed Madóran's request. He smiled. Whether he had heard it or not, he understood.

About the Author

Pati Nagle was born and raised in the mountains of northern New Mexico. An avid student of music, history, and humans in general, she loves the outdoors but hides from the sun.

She writes in a variety of genres, but is most often drawn to fantasy, historical fiction (as P.G. Nagle), and mystery (as Patrice Greenwood). Her stories have appeared in *Asimov's Science Fiction*, *The Magazine of Fantasy & Science Fiction*, and in various other magazines and anthologies, including *Elf Magic*, which featured "Kind Hunter," the story that sparked the ælven world.

Her Blood of the Kindred series includes *The Betrayal*, *Heart of the Exiled*, and *Swords Over Fireshore*. The Immortal Saga, a contemporary series featuring the ælven, began with *Immortal* and *Eternal* and continues with *Forever*.

Pati Nagle still lives in the mountains in New Mexico, with her husband, two feline muses, and lots of wildlife. She loves to walk in the woods and look up at the stars.

www.patinagle.com
www.pgnagle.com
www.patricegreenwood.com

Books by Pati Nagle

Immortal Series

Immortal
Eternal
Forever

Blood of the Kindred Series

The Betrayal
Heart of the Exiled
Swords Over Fireshore

Other Titles

Many Paths: Stories of the Ælven
Coyote Ugly and Other Tales
Pet Noir
Dead Man's Hand
Kokopelli and the Virgin

patinagle.com

About Book View Café

Book View Café Publishing Cooperative (BVC) is a an author-owned cooperative of over fifty professional writers, publishing in a variety of genres including fantasy, romance, mystery, and science fiction.

In 2008, BVC launched a website, bookviewcafe.com, initially offering free fiction and gradually moving to selling ebooks of members' backlist titles, then original titles. BVC's ebooks are DRM-free and are distributed around the world. BVC returns 95% of the profit on each book directly to the author. The cooperative has gained a reputation for producing high-quality ebooks, and is now moving into print editions.

BVC authors include New York Times and USA Today bestsellers; Nebula, Hugo, and Philip K. Dick Award winners; World Fantasy and Rita Award nominees; and winners and nominees of many other publishing awards.

bookviewcafe.com